WHISKEY PRINCE

WHISKEY PRINCE
A Taking Risks Novel

TONI ALEO

Copyright © 2014 by Toni Aleo Books LLC

This book is a work of fiction. Any names, characters, places, and incidents are products of the author's imagination or used fictitiously. Any resemblance to actual events or persons, living or dead, is entirely coincidental.

All rights reserved. Except as permitted under the U.S. Copyright Act of 1976, no part of this publication may be reproduced, distributed, or transmitted in any form or by any means, or stored in a database or retrieval system, without the prior written permission of the author.

Interior designed and formatted by E.M. Tippetts Book Designs

What's life without a little risk?
-Sirius Black

one
Amberlyn

I'm an orphan.

When I lost my father, I remember feeling like I would never breathe again. I was Daddy's little girl. He made me feel like a princess, he loved me the way a father should, and he spoiled me in every way possible. He was a very handsome man, with dark brown hair, light green eyes, and dark stubble that he left a little longer than he should because it gave my mother a reason to fuss at him. He loved when she fussed at him; he said it meant she loved him. He had a low, tenor voice, one that could be used to do the commentary for movies or documentaries. He used to sing to me, an old song from his homeland. Even now, when I am nervous, I sing it. It helps. Somehow, it helps dull the pain of not having him.

I was twelve when we lost him to a drunk driver.

Somehow, my mother and I survived losing him, though. We learned to go on with him still deep in our hearts and souls. We helped each other to cope with the pain of losing him. She was not only the most amazing mother, but she was a great father too. Some days were hard. I'd wake up and say I was having a bad Dad day, and she would reply that she was, too. We would just cry, for hours, but then she would hug me tightly, tell me that the sun was shining and so shall we, and we did until the day she found out she had throat cancer.

My favorite thing about my mother was her smile, but she soon stopped smiling and so did I. The day I found her at the table with tears dripping from her eyes, I asked if she was having a bad Dad day, and she shook her head and just kept apologizing. I didn't understand, and when she told me what was going on, I didn't want to believe it. It couldn't be happening. I had already lost my dad and now my mom, too? It wasn't fair.

When you were eighteen, you were supposed to be excited for prom, boyfriends, going off to college, and starting a new, refreshing life. But not me. All that came to a halting stop. My dreams of learning the written word, and maybe meeting a boy to spend time with, went up in flames. Instead, I became a caregiver for my mother. I stayed home and studied online as I waited hand and foot on her. I watched for two years as my mother slowly died before my eyes, and to be honest, I don't think I'd have it any other way. At least I know she went, knowing I loved her more than life itself, when she cupped my face and slowly took her last breath before joining my father in heaven.

When the hospice nurses came after I tucked my mother in bed and had a good, long cry, they were surprised how strong I was and commended me on it. I said it was because of her, and how she raised me to be strong. They knew she begged me to put her in a home, but I'd be damned. She was my best friend. She cared for me my whole life, and I was going to care for her. Plus, I knew she felt more comfortable with me than some nurses she didn't know. It wasn't as if her parents could come and help. They had long passed before I was even born. All she had was her brother who lived in New York, and he couldn't be bothered with her.

Even now, as I watch him from across my mother's casket, which is covered in beautiful, white roses, I can't help but wonder why he came. He isn't even crying. He is just standing there, with the same blue eyes as my mother, looking as if he'd rather be playing golf than acting as if he is mourning her. I choke back the tears as I look around at all the people who have come to pay their respects—neighbors, family friends, and coworkers. Even some of my old high school teachers are here, and I feel nothing. I want to jump into that casket with her and go to heaven too. I don't want or know how to go on without her. Who is going to help me mourn her?

Wiping away the tears rolling down my cheeks, I take in a deep breath as I softly start to sing my father's song. In my head, I hear only my parents and not myself as they softly sing Liam Clancy's, "The Parting Glass" to me. My mother couldn't sing for anything, but none of us cared. We would all sing, and most of all, we were all happy. But now, my throat feels tight, my limbs are numb, and I just feel empty.

When the song I am singing plays over the speakers, that's when I squeeze my eyes tight because I know they are lowering her into the ground. I don't want to see it. I hate knowing it is happening. Soon, it is over and everyone is hugging me, gently squeezing my hands, wishing me well, and saying that they are there for me if I need them. When my uncle is the last to come up to me, I want to scream at him, *Why did you come*? I hate that he wasn't there for her because I know if I had a sibling, I would always be there for them. Especially someone like my mom—she was so sweet, so caring, so loving—and he couldn't even be there at the end for her. Couldn't be there for me. His only niece.

I can tell he is uncomfortable, and I'm glad he is. As he runs his hands through his dark red hair, he lets out a breath before saying, "Amberlyn, I'm sorry for your loss."

"It's your loss, too," I say, crossing my arms over my chest. The dress I'm wearing scratches my ribs, and I want to pull at it, but I don't. Instead, I hold his gaze as he slowly nods.

"You're right, our loss, and I want you to know that I am here if you need anything."

"I won't."

He looks away. "Yeah, I know you won't, but in case you do."

I don't say anything, even knowing he is waiting for me to. What does he want me to say? Thank you? Hell no.

"Anyway, here," he says, opening his suit jacket to pull out an envelope. "Ciara wanted me to give this to you."

I take it quickly because I see my name in my mom's handwriting on the front. "What is it?"

"I don't know," he answers. "She sent it to me in a letter and said to give it to you on the day of her funeral. She also told me to tell you to call me once you've read it, and I'll tell you what we will do next."

I'm confused. I look up with my brows pulled together as I say, "What? Do what next? I am going to pick up the pieces and figure out how to live without her. How the hell are you going to help me with that?"

He runs his hands through his unruly hair, and I see something I haven't seen all day—pain. He is in pain, and it completely boggles my mind. He didn't care about her or me—why is he in pain?

"Just read the letter, Amberlyn. When you are done, call me, and we will go from there. Again, I'm sorry and I wish that things had played out differently. I cared more about work than I did my family, and now I have to live with that for the rest of my life."

With that, he turns and starts to walk away. I watch his retreating back and without thinking, I say, "Yeah, you did."

I follow behind him to where my beat-up, red Honda is waiting for me. Jumping into it, I numbly drive home to the house I grew up in. A beautiful, ranch-style home is one of six that surround a large lake. There is a dock out back that I would sit on for hours and read until my eyes hurt. There wasn't a summer day that my mom or dad didn't find me out there almost sunburned, claiming I only needed to read one more chapter.

I love this house and I love this neighborhood, but I just don't know if I can live here anymore. The thought of leaving has my stomach in knots though. I know there is money coming in, and I could sell the house and start over, but where? How? How am I supposed to live without her? Without him?

Shaking my head before I start to sob, I push my key into the lock, unlock the door, and then enter the house. Parts of my mother and father are everywhere, along with parts of me. My dad's guitars still sit in the corner, untouched for the last eight years. My mother's knitting things are still overflowing in a basket by her favorite chair, along with all her law books, which I used to read to her to calm her at night when the pain was unbearable. And then everywhere I look is a notebook or a novel of my own. The house looks exactly the same, and I feel it shouldn't. I feel that it should look different or changed, the way I feel I have.

Forcing my feet to move, I head to my mother's room, ignoring her hospital bed, and falling into the one she shared with my father. Taking in a deep breath, her flowery scent intoxicates me. I close my eyes to imagine her beside me, her eyes a bright blue, not the dull color they were before she passed, and her bright red hair falling in heaps of curls around her face as she softly ran her slender fingers through my dark, brownish red hair.

When tears start leaking from my closed eyes, I take in a shuddering breath before I open them and stare up at the ceiling. Her letter is burning in my fingers, and a part of me doesn't even want to read it right now. I want to ignore it all—act like the last couple days didn't happen, but I know I can't. Not only is my uncle expecting my call, but I am also curious why.

So I open the letter. When a check for ten thousand dollars and what looks like a plane ticket falls onto my chest, I ignore them. Through tear-filled eyes, I read my mother's letter.

> *My dear, sweet Amberlyn,*
>
> *I'm so terribly sorry. I don't think I can apologize enough for not being there for you as you start your adult life. I hate that your life has been so hard, and I wish that there were a way I could change it all, but I can't. I feel though, that instead of letting this hold you back, you should grow. I believe I have given you all the tools to make your life the best it can be. You are smart, beautiful, and unbelievably talented. And more than anything, I want you to live your dreams.*
>
> *I know you are probably lying in my bed, wrapped up in a little ball, and bawling your eyes out. Baby, that is fine. Cry. Cry it all out. Then remember that the sun is shining, and you have to as well. As much as I wish I were there with my arms around you, I can't be, but I am in your heart, along with your father, and baby, we love you. So much.*
>
> *I know that your uncle Felix said for you to call him after*

reading this, and you are probably wondering why, so let me explain. I don't want you to live in the past, and I have a feeling you will. I think that you won't have a reason to get out of bed if you stay in the home that we built. You've never really made friends, never really dated, and I want you to do those things, but will you if you are living in our home? I don't think so. So here is what I propose: Your father's sister has offered to take you in at her bed and breakfast. Back home, in Ireland.

I think our biggest mistake was moving to the States, but your father was convinced that he was going to be a singer. I believed in him, so we left. As you know, it didn't work out, but we made a life here and never went back. I wish we had, and I'm sorry we didn't, but now you have the chance. This is the opportunity of a lifetime for you. Something I know your father would have wanted you to do.

So go for a year, work for your aunt, go to school, and live, my sweetheart. There is so much history in Ireland, and I think you'll not only enjoy the beautiful world but the people as well. I know this seems drastic and that I am asking a lot of you, but my sweet darling, I am worried you'll get stuck, and I don't want that for you. I want you to live all your dreams, and I think Ireland is the best place to do that.

So go. Your aunt, Shelia, is expecting a call to let her know you are coming. She also holds the next letter that I have written for you so, if anything, you should go for that. It has my wishes for you. After a year, if you haven't made Ireland your home, then come back and everything will be here for you. Uncle Felix will keep the house going until you decide what you want.

I want you to try for me, but I also want you to stay there for you. I miss you. I love you. Please don't let us hold you back from living the most amazing life possible. We are so proud of you and love you so much.

Go start a new life.

Love you to the moon and back,
Mom

I let the letter fall to my chest as the tears gush down my face. I don't know what to think or even do, for that matter. How do I leave everything I know behind and start over in a place I have no clue about? How do I go and live with someone whom I have never met? She is asking way too much of me, but I know she is right.

So with a heavy sigh, I roll over to my side. My gaze falls on a picture of my father and mother in a tight embrace, both smiling as they look into each other's eyes. Reaching out, I take the frame in my hand, bringing it in close to my chest against the letter, the money, and the ticket to my new life. As sobs pour out of me, I whisper, "Why did you guys have to leave me?"

two
Declan

I want to stab myself in the eye with one of the many forks that lay before me.

"You're twenty-two, Declan. It's time."

I roll my eyes as I lean back in my chair, picking at the greens on my plate. I know that it can be said that twenty-two isn't old at all, and that may be right, but to my da, I'm ancient. He was married to my mother by nineteen, my grandda married my grandma by eighteen, and so on and so on. I'm the oldest out of my family who is not married; even my sister, at only seventeen, has the prospects of a husband once she turns eighteen. This may very well be the twentieth century, but to the O'Callaghan family, you get married, you run the whiskey distillery, and you have kids. I'm not against any of this. Not at all, but if I'm to get married, I want it to be because I'm mad about her. Not for the reason my da wants.

Letting out a long breath, I say, "I know, but what will you have me do? Marry the first girl who gives me the eye?"

My da sits up in his chair as he shakes his head. He has aged a lot in the last couple of years. My ma says I favor him. If that is what I will look like when I'm older, please someone do me off. He just looks so angry. Wrinkles line his face, and his brow is set in such an apoplectic way. We may have the same blue eyes and blond hair, but that's it. I don't even think I act like him, but my sister informs me that sometimes I do, which I need to change. "That is not what I'm saying."

"Yes it is," I admonish him. "You want me to pick the first lady I see and not worry a bit if I actually fancy her. The thing is, Da, that I want to be mad about her if I'm going to marry her."

"That's what we want for you, Declan, but you haven't even dated," my ma says, which is not entirely true at all. I've been with my fair share of women, but none of them has given me what I need or want. They are just there, wanting me for my money.

I let my head fall back as my kid sister, Lena, giggles beside me. She favors my ma, long, blond hair, shining blue eyes, always the center of attention when it comes to other blokes. She got into some trouble a couple years back, and it basically ruined the family. Slowly but surely, we are coming back from it. We are close, but not as close as we should be. When she quickly stops laughing, it's probably because my da has set her with a look. The same look he is probably glaring at me with, not that I care. "I have dated, Ma, just nothing worth my time."

"Keeva was delightful, a real gem," Ma informs me, but I disagree.

Making a face of pure disgust, I say, "She was a bucket of snots, inside and out. She only wanted me for my money."

"Everyone will want you for your money, lad. That's what we are, what you are—deal with it."

I shake my head. "I will not. I want a girl who loves me for me, not because I am the Whiskey Prince of Ireland."

"But you are," Da stresses, and while he is right, I don't care. "And with that title comes responsibilities, and you know what they are. Get married and own the business. I know you want that."

"Of course I do, but I'm not going to settle for anything less than I deserve. How could you want me to anyway?"

Da shakes his head as his mouth sets in a straight line. "I'm done with this conversation. You are an O'Callaghan, Declan, act like one. Get married. You have only six months to do so before you are skipped in line, and we give it to Lena's soon-to-be husband."

That gets my blood boiling as my sister gasps besides me. No way in fucking hell is her boyfriend, who couldn't even tell a pot still from a whiskey barrel, going to own my business. I look to my ma, but she is as stone-faced as he is. Fuck! She agrees. "Da! That is insane! I can run the business and not be married."

"No, you can't. Dear, you have to be married. Not only have your grandda and father decided on this since apparently an O'Callaghan man has always been married before his twenties, but because it's been that way since your great-great-great-great-great-grandda started the distillery. He believed that a man in love had the compassion to run a great company, and because of that, only a married man can own the family company." Ma says that like I haven't heard this a billion times since I was old enough to be interested in owning the distillery. I know the expectations of my family. I may not agree with them, and I may think that they are downright stupid, but I know them nonetheless. I just wish I had some leeway here and maybe even some more time. Six months? Before they pass it to my sister's soon-to-be husband? I can't even keep a girl more than a night because I get bored with her or because she's out for my money. I want more than that. I want to have it all. I want what my parents have, what every O'Callaghan man has had.

I throw my hands up in frustration. "Yes, in love! I have to love them for that to be true! Don't you see that I want it to happen, I just haven't found her yet?"

Da stands quickly, his seat falling behind him as his fist comes down on the table, making my ma and sister jump in surprise. I don't even flinch. He doesn't scare me. Nothing does. "So fall in love! Do what I say, Declan, or you will not own the business."

Pushing my seat back, I stand, mirroring my da in height at nearly 6'2 as I hold his vexed gaze. I want him to see in my eyes that I want these things, that I don't want to lose my chance to make our whiskey better than before, but I know all he sees is that I'm not what he was at my age. My ma stands too, her hands out in a pleading way as she says, "Enough. Sit down. Let's finish our dinner."

"I'm not hungry," I say before turning and walking away, despite them calling my name, demanding that I come back. Ignoring them, I walk through the many halls of the O'Callaghan estate. With over sixty rooms, one would think I would get lost, but I've had the same room my whole life. I was born in this room, which is bigger than most suites in a five-star hotel. It's the room that I'll bring my bride to, and more than likely, my child will be born in here too. That's the way the O'Callaghans do things.

As much as I would like to say that I don't want these things, that I want to do something completely different, I don't. I want the same traditions, this way of life. I want my children to grow the way I have and then their children to do the same. I love what my family stands for. I love our brand, our whiskey, and I will do anything for the things I love.

But do I give up my need to have what I desire, what I've dreamed about, to have the traditions and life that have been mapped in the stars before my birth? Or do I stand strong and look for what I want? What I deserve? Looking around my empty room, which is filled with furniture older than my grandfather, I decide that I am not going to find any answers here, so I turn and head for the front of the house.

On my way, I pass by our housekeepers, and unlike my sister, I do not say a thing, only give a curt nod as I head to the place that brings me peace. When the fresh air hits my face once I am outside, I let out a breath and then take in a deep one, filling my chest with the air of my homeland. Ignoring my car, I make my way to the stables to where my Irish Draught, Cathmor, awaits me. When I enter, my stable hand, Mitch, is putting the saddle on my friend as I run my hand along his white chest, which is speckled with black. He snorts loudly, greeting me with his furry lips on my face.

"Howya, Cathmor, good lad?"

He snorts again as Mitch says, "He's ready. Good day, sir."

"Thanks, Mitch," I reply before mounting Cathmor. When Mitch backs away, I kick Cathmor to go, and like a bullet, he is off. I always love to ride to the distillery rather than drive. There is something about the air hitting me in the face and the speed of the beast beneath me that pulls all the stress from my body. It's relaxing and soothing as he runs through the fields of my home. The trees are in full bloom, the grass so green, and the sky blue. I can feel the lake on my skin from the wind, and I can't wait to get down there to fish or take my boat on the water. Summer is my favorite time because of the beauty my land provides me with. Well, my da's land. In six months' time, I could have nothing.

Depressing, I know.

Kicking Cathmor's side so he will go faster, I leave that thought in the dust as he takes a sharp turn around the lake that separates our land from that of the Maclasters' Bed and Breakfast. I've never been there, but my best friend, Kane, enjoys going to the pub that is a part of their establishment. He tries to get off with the owner's daughter, Fiona Maclaster. I haven't seen her yet, but from what Kane says, she is easy on the eyes.

When the large, stone building that holds my family's dynasty comes into view, I kick into Cathmor again to get there. Not only would being around the smoky and spicy aroma of the whiskey calm me, but I could use a glass too. Stopping before another worker, I dismount Cathmor and run my hand down his beautiful mane, saying, "Good ride, lad, thank you."

To the worker, I say, "Please give him plenty of water. He ran the whole way." The worker, whose name I notice is Cal from his name tag, nods as I hand him the reins and make my way inside.

As soon as the aroma of whiskey hits me, I take in a deep breath, savoring it as I look around the room. With large windows letting in the sun, the room is like its outside, stone, with a dark, dungeon feel. Some people may fear the O'Callaghan distillery, but I love it. Have loved it since I was a little boy. Heading to the back distilling room, I shut the door behind me to give myself privacy before heading to where my bottle of whiskey is hidden. Passing by the pot stills, I run my fingers along the copper base, lightly, making sure not to burn my fingers. My great-great-great-great-great-grandda learned how to make whiskey from a Scottish pal, and because of this, we use pot stills to this day. I've always loved the look of them and enjoy this room the best because it reminds me of my history.

My dynasty.

Reaching for my bottle, I sit on a stool as I pour only a little in the bottom of a glass. Bringing it to my nose, I take in a deep inhale, the smells of vanilla and caramel overloading my senses before I take a small sip, moving it around in my mouth, savoring the smooth flavor before swallowing it. It has a kick, but it's one I enjoy. This is my bottle, the one I plan to name *Cathmor* once I have my chance to own the name. My da isn't adventurous with his whiskey, keeps it to the books. But me, I like mixing and trying new flavors, and I feel that *Cathmor* will blow people away. It has taken me five years to find the right flavor, and I want my chance to share it with the world, which means one thing…

I need a wife.

When the door opens suddenly, I pause with my glass at my lips as my best friend walks in and shuts the door. With a grin on his face, Kane says, "Saw you sneak in here, thought I'd join you."

I nod as I place my glass down, picking up one for him before filling and passing it off. Taking it, he holds it against mine before saying, "*Sláinte.*" We both take a good sip, savoring the flavor as we sit in silence.

"It's not good to drink alone, Dec."

"Da pissed me off."

"When does he not?" Kane scoffs. "What did he do this time?"

I take another sip before shaking my head slowly. "Pressuring me into marrying off."

"Again?" Kane asks, even though we both know that Da won't stop pressuring me until I do what he wants.

"Yes. I told him I want to marry for love, and he said fall in love then! Says I have six months to get it done, or I lose my chance at the name."

A shocked look comes over my mate's face as he exclaims, "Well, you best do it!"

"Come off it! I'm trying."

"You do no such thing. You don't go out and meet anyone."

"I do too," I insist. "I go to the pub and meet women all the time."

"Fucking shite, ya do! You go to the pub that your da's mates drink at—not somewhere that would produce a wife."

I let out a sigh; Kane is delusional. "I've met plenty of women there."

"Sure, but have they stuck? No, they are slappers, out for your money. You need to meet a good woman, someone who will stick. Someone to be mad about."

He's right, but I won't give him the satisfaction of knowing that. "Fine, what do you suggest then?"

"Come out with me. We'll find you someone."

That gives me the shakes. The places that he goes make me nervous. The kind of places that are full of people I don't know, but they know who I am because of the news or magazines. Because of that, they treat me differently than they do Kane. Then again, Kane is easy to get to know. He is fun and charming. Me, I'm off, as he says. I don't know how to act normal when people I don't know stare at me or talk to me. My shyness, as Kane has so nicely informed me, is probably the only thing that makes me not like my name, the title I have. It isn't easy being the Whiskey Prince. Not only does it draw attention to me, but it seems like everyone wants something from me. Sometimes I come off a little abrasive because of it. Even being my best mate, I can't tell this to Kane. He wouldn't understand. His life is easy, ladies flock to him, and no one wants anything but his company. With me, it's different, and I hate the way it makes me feel.

"Fine. Soon, I'll go."

He lets out a long breath. "Fucking hell, lying like that to your best pal? I can see it in your eyes, your mannerisms. Leaving the O'Callaghan land gives you the willies, but I'm telling ya, it's for the best. You don't want to lose your precious land, do ya?"

I shake my head as he says, "I know you don't, so come on, let's find you a wife."

"Fine, I'm going to have to be ossified," I say as I take a hearty sip of my whiskey, needing the liquid courage.

Kane lets out a long laugh as he shakes his head. "Not tonight, my friend. You need time to adjust to the idea, savor it, but when you're ready, I am."

I nod because I know that Kane would do just about anything for me, as I would for him. That's what twenty years of friendship gives you, and I'm thankful for that. But the question is—when will I be ready? As I look around the place that I know I can't live without, I figure I need to get ready pretty quickly.

Because I can't lose this.

Amberlyn

three

One would think that after a month of living and working in a very busy pub in Ireland that I would at least know what people are saying when they talk to me.

But I don't.

"I plan on being pissy drunk," one of my patrons informs me with a slight slur, or maybe that's his brogue, not sure, but he seems excited.

I look back at my cousin Fiona, confused, and she shakes her head, a smile playing on her pouty lips. "He plans on getting really drunk tonight," she says in her just-as-thick Irish accent. It has been Americanized though, thankfully, from having an American for a father.

I look back, meeting the gaze of my elderly patron as I pass him his pint of beer, and smile. His green eyes are shining, and he is wearing an intoxicating grin with a long, scruffy beard. I have to admit, I don't know him, but I know he is going to make my night. People like this make me love my job. I love meeting the people, talking to them, despite not knowing what they are talking about half the time. I love working at the high pace that the pub requires, and I love working with my cousin. I never would have thought this a month ago, but I love being a bartender!

"Sounds like a plan!"

He takes a long pull of his beer and wipes his mouth with the back of his hand before pointing his finger at me. "American, yes?"

I nod. "Guilty as charged. Only been here a month."

And what a month it has been. Of course, my Aunt Shelia and Uncle Michael have been unbelievably accommodating and have given me a lovely home. It isn't the home I had with my mom and dad, but they love me as if I were theirs. Shelia is excited to have me, and always talks about how much she loved my dad and mom. It's refreshing. I think she expected to get some heartbroken girl, and while, yes, I am heartbroken and I miss them more than ever, I had time to accept that my mother was leaving me. So while I may still have my moments of complete heartbreak, where I sob until I can't breathe because I miss her, I am able to go on with my life and do as she asked.

Live each day as if I were dying.

When I got here, though, I was scared. Shit, I'm still scared, but her letter that my aunt had waiting for me was so comforting. I knew that I had to do everything that the letter said. I also memorized it, remembering everything about it, because I never wanted to forget my mother's words, her handwriting, or how the letter smelled like soft roses. Just like her favorite perfume that my dad had given her. While she told me repeatedly that she loved me and that she was sorry she had to leave me, she also gave me three things she wanted me to do this year.

Take a risk.
Do something drastic.
Fall in love.

While each one scares me to the core, I haven't had a chance to do anything yet since I have been settling in and adjusting to life here. I don't even know what I'm going to do though! Take a risk? Yeah, no clue. Do something drastic? Um, a tattoo is drastic, right? Yeah, I can do that as soon as I get over my fear of needles. And fall in love? Is she crazy? All I've ever done with a boy is kiss one, and she wants me to fall in love? Jesus, that involves sex, doesn't it? Since no one has ever been in my pants, that could pose a problem. A huge one! I'm pretty sure I'm the only virgin in Cong, County Mayo, and that is just downright sad. My mom is asking for a lot, but I can't help but love her more for each word she wrote. She wants me to start over, she wants me to be happy, and I have every intention of doing that.

I miss my home, but I believe in what my mom is doing here. Plus, Uncle Felix has everything under control. Surprising, I know. We stay in contact weekly. He is living in my home, packing up my parents' things, and moving his in because he is starting a new life in Tennessee. If I come back after the year, then he'll move out and find his own place, but if I don't, he plans to buy the house from me.

I never expected him to be so helpful. This transition has been great, and I think that's because of my mom's hard work. She knew what she was doing. I have to trust her, and I know I have to leave all caution in the wind. Something I've never done. I've always been the one to be ahead on things, caring for my mother, paying all the bills on time or even days before. I have never just lived, and this is my chance. My chance to be me—Amberlyn Reilly.

Not sure who that is, but I am excited to get to know her.

The other great thing about this transition has been that my cousin and I have become instant best friends. Completely awesome, right? I totally love her. She is the sister I never had and simply breathtaking. Fiona is a year older than I am, with sweet, bluish-green eyes and long, brownish-golden hair with high cheekbones covered in light freckles, and pouty lips. She is stunning, slim, but thick in all the right places. The boys go gaga for her in the pub, but she ignores them all. She is my lifesaver, especially when the older customers with the thick brogues come in. I have no clue what they are saying to me, but she's run the pub for so long that she has no problem getting them what they need while I stand there like a fish out of water.

I don't let it derail me though. I am on a mission to make a new life. Hopefully, while I'm at it, I'll catch on to this language.

"*Céad Míle Fáilte!*"

That's the name of the bed and breakfast, but that doesn't mean I know what it means. I glance over to a smiling Fiona, and she says, "He is saying 'Welcome,' like a hundred thousand welcomes."

"Oh, awesome, thanks! It's wonderful to meet you!" I gush as I go to the next patron and the next. My night is busy, but that's what I've come to expect from the Céad Míle Fáilte. It's the best, and the busiest, pub slash B&B in all of Mayo, as numerous people have told me every night.

"He's here," Fiona says as she passes by me. I glance up from the pint I'm filling to look at her as she lays down a plate of food for one of my customers. Her face is flush, a grin pulling at her lips.

I smile as I ask, "Who?"

"Kane Levy," she says out of the side of her mouth. "Over at the end of the bar."

I look over my shoulder, but before I can focus on anything, she smacks me in the arm.

"Don't look!" she scolds, and I laugh as I pass a pint to a college guy. He smiles his thanks and throws five euros in my tip jar.

"Thank you," I say before turning to Fiona. Before I can say anything, the college guy says, "You're quare good-looking. Will ya be my missus?"

Without my even having to look at her, Fiona says, "He wants to marry you."

Now see, this is one of those moments I could take a risk, or do something drastic, maybe even have the potential to fall in love, but the thought of doing any of that with this extremely cute guy has me wanting to hide under the bar.

He is obviously drunk and supercute with big, brown eyes, but he's not my type. Call me picky but I want someone who is going to make me shiver with need, and I'm not shivering. So with a smile, I say, "Not today."

He goes to say something more, but Fiona puts her hand up. "Brian, we'll be having none of that. Go on now. She's not interested."

He doesn't say anything. His face falls with rejection as he turns with his beer and heads to the table where his friends are waiting. Fiona watches him, and when he sits, she turns back to me. "Be on the lookout for that one. He is quick to want to marry someone. Asks me like every month."

"Oh, I'm glad to see he isn't selective."

She laughs as she nods. "Total eejit. Don't pay him a bit of heed, but as I was saying, he's here."

"I know, but you won't let me look!" I laugh, but I can't help but be as giddy as she is. She is grinning ear-to-ear, eyes bright as she watches him from over my shoulder.

"He is so yummy. Look at those eyes."

I roll mine as I remind her, "I can't! You won't let me."

"Fine, go reach for that um, jug and look," she allows. I shake my head as I turn, reaching for the jug she pointed at before looking down at where a sinfully hot man sits. Oh, goodness. No wonder she is all giddy. Dark-as-night hair, deep brown eyes, high cheekbones, and squared jaw that is covered in dark stubble. When his eyes meet mine, I turn quickly, breathless as I look into Fiona's eyes. "Fucking hell! He is beautiful!"

"I know! He comes in every other night, and I haven't had the balls to say anything."

"You need to. He is smoking hot!"

Fiona pauses her gaze on him, and then looks down at me. "You go chance your arm with him. He gives me the chills, and I feel stupid when I try to talk to him, but he's checking out your arse. Go on."

I shake my head quickly. My heart speeds in my chest as my hands quickly cover my ass. Don't ask me why I do that—I have no clue. "No way. He is way too much man for me."

Her head falls to the side, her eyes boring into mine. "What does that mean?"

I wave her off with a nervous laugh. "Don't worry about it. He's obviously someone you want to talk to, and we all know the young guys come in for you."

"They do not! They come for both of us."

I roll my eyes as I wave her off. "Go."

"Okay, I'm going to."

"Good!"

She pumps her arms as if she is getting ready to go for a run and then passes by me, sauntering toward him in a way that only a confident woman could pull off. I watch as his mouth spreads into a huge grin as she leans against the bar and starts to talk to him. I want to eavesdrop, but that's rude, so I go back to work, hating myself for being so inexperienced.

Later that night, Fiona and I work quickly to close everything up so we can go to bed. I'm beat and my feet are killing me, but Fiona doesn't look the least bit tired. She is smiling, hard, and I know it's because she spent most the night flirting with Kane.

"He is so perfect," she gushes as she loads the dishwasher up.

I smile as I listen to her go on and on about how perfect he is. It's cute. I ask her, "You ignore everyone else who hits on you—have you crushed on him long?"

She nods sheepishly. "Oh yes, and I don't even know what I'll do if he asks me out! I'll probably freak."

She screams, and I can't help but scream too. I've never had this, the female bonding over a guy. I didn't have a sibling growing up and not many friends. I was kind of a nerd, with my nose deep in a book. I don't hate that about myself. I pride myself in my knowledge of the written word, but doing this, gushing with Fiona about Kane, makes me wish that I didn't wait until I was almost twenty-one to experience this. This is something a teenager does, but while most girls gushed over boy bands, I was swooning over Mr. Darcy and Edward Ferrars. Some may call it odd that I was in love with heroes from my favorite romance novels, and maybe they have raised my expectations of men, but it's what I did. It's why I want to be an English teacher, just so I can share these amazing men with the youth today. So they can see that a man with manners is way better than a man with swag.

"He has me acting a fool. It's insane! I know!"

I smile at her exclamation as she runs her hands through her hair. "I'm glad. You are beautiful when you smile like that."

She grins, but then her brows come together as she says, "Can I ask you something?"

I nod. "Absolutely."

"You said earlier that he is more man than you could handle? What did you mean? It's been bothering me."

I shrug, not going to answer, but she reaches out and takes my wrist with her hand. "You can tell me anything, you know that. I wasn't trying to offend you. I just wanted to give you a chance with the first guy you fancied."

I shake my head, placing my hand over hers. "Not at all. I'm not offended, and I wouldn't say I fancy Kane. He's a good-looking guy, but he isn't for me. Plus, you like him."

"Okay, but plenty of guys come in here looking a lot like Kane, and you brush them off—why?"

I shrug again, nervous as my heart pounds against my ribs. Looking up into her eyes, I smile sheepishly. "It's just that I'm not experienced with guys like you. I've never really dated or anything. My only kiss was with my neighbor. I'm kind of a weirdo."

"Sorry? Do you mean you've never got off with a fella?"

I pause as I look into her aquamarine eyes. Did I really want to admit that right now? To my surprise, I'm slowly nodding my head, and then I say, "Yeah."

She can only blink as she holds my gaze. "I'm sorry, but I have no clue what to say. You're gorgeous, Amberlyn! What are you waiting for?"

I grin shyly as I shrug my shoulders. "I never had time. Too busy with my mom and school and stuff."

Her eyes fill with sympathy before she wraps me up tightly in her arms. I smile against her shoulder as I hug her back. I really love Fiona, and I feel my mom knew that I would, hence the reason she sent me here. I mean, don't get me wrong. I instantly loved my aunt and uncle when I met them, but with Fiona, she just gets me. She understands and loves me, even when I admit horribly embarrassing things. She doesn't make me feel like crap for it. In a way, she gives me hope with her sparkling, bluish-green eyes.

"Well, that is going to change. I promise you that!"

I laugh as she pulls away and says, "Maybe Kane has a friend?"

I shrug. "Maybe, but I'm not looking for a quick lay. I want a relationship. I want to be wooed."

"Wooed?" she asked, obviously confused.

"Yeah, like romanced," I supply.

"Oh! Sure, sure! Kane is good at *wooing*," she says with a wink.

"I don't doubt that. He looks like it."

"He is and no worries. We will find you a fella who will knock you on your arse with his wooing!"

"I can't wait."

"Me neither, I'm excited! For us!" she yells before her eyes get all glassy and dreamy-looking. She then starts to spins in place before stopping and holding her hands to her chest, a euphoric look on her beautiful face. In that moment, I want what she is experiencing. I want to know what it feels like to be completely taken by a guy. Even though I was scared at first at the thought of falling in love, now I think it is something I might need to try.

four
Declan

"I talked to that girl from the pub last night."

I glance up from where I am checking shipping forms. I hate this part of my job. It's so boring, so tedious. I'd rather be malting than doing this shite. "Oh really?"

A smile pulls at Kane's lips as he looks down at his own stack of paperwork. He has been working for my da since we were both fifteen. His dad is a malter for the company, and his ma is my ma's lady's maid. That's why we've been so close our whole life; he's always been there. He usually works in sales, but today he is helping me with shipping since we are a wee bit behind.

"Yeah, she is something, Dec, honestly."

"Fine, okay, what's her name again?"

"Fiona Maclaster, her parents own the pub and B&B."

"Sure, I know who you are talking about. I haven't met them yet though. Heard good things about them."

When I look up, Kane sets me with a look and I ask, "What?"

He lets out a breath as his hands come out before him in obvious frustration. "Because you don't feckin' leave! You said you'd go out with me. Have you? No."

"I don't have time."

"You have plenty of time. Ya just don't have the balls to step out of the gates of your home to meet someone. It's like you're Rapunzel up in your tower. Jump out, Declan, and get your feet wet."

I roll my eyes. "You act as if I'm a hermit. That is not the case—not by a long shot."

"Yes, it is. You stay locked up in this damn castle and don't do anything that would potentially make ya happy."

I throw my hands up. "Fuck off, Kane! I do all types of things that make me happy. I read, I write, I ride, I take the boat out—I'm happy."

Kane looks at me, stone-faced, as he asks, "How do you say that with a straight face? That is the stupidest shite you've ever said. You are not happy. You are content, and believe me, that's nowhere near happy. I also like how ya didn't deny that ya don't leave the castle. We both know you don't. Everywhere ya go is on the grounds, and if you need something, you have it brought in."

I let out a breath as I look back down at my paperwork. "I don't have time for this right now."

Kane scoffs. "You never do."

"Leave it alone, Kane," I warn. I'm not in the mood. My dad has been on me about these shipments, about my part in the company, and then of course, about my mission to find a wife. I don't need to be lectured by my friend too. So what if I don't go anywhere or do anything? I am busy. I am trying to own a fucking company here.

"Fine, when you lose it all, it's on you."

As if I really needed that reminder.

"You're right, it will be, so leave it be," I snap before letting out a long breath and running my hands down my face. An awkward silence falls between us, and I hate that. He roughly moves through the paper and I do the same, both of us mad but neither of us wanting to admit that the whole argument is stupid. That he is right. He's always right. I don't want to come out of what I know. It scares me to go out where people know me and I don't know them. To try to meet someone and know they probably only want me for one thing. I know it'll never happen if I don't try, but a part of me just wants to wait it out, hope she falls into my lap, and that I never had to leave what I know. The unknown scares me.

Looking across the desk at my best friend, I shake my head. I know he is only looking out for me. He's always been that way. He's always played the big brother role with me, and I've let him because it always helped me out. When we were younger, I was the gimp while he hit his growth spurt early and had a mustache by the first year of secondary school. When anyone picked on me on the pitch, Kane was there, ready to kill anyone who had anything to say about me. I tried to be tough like him, but guys could sneeze, and it would brush me to the side. Then I hit my growth spurt, but I was still weak. Kane suggested that I work out more to tone up, so I did. Soon, I was as big as he was, and no one messed with us after that.

Back then, I had no cares. I didn't think that a girl wanted to date me because of my money. They wanted me because I was good-looking, buff, and the best on the pitch. That all went to shite after Keeva though. She showed me what some women could be like. I won't say I loved her because I don't think I did. Love is soul-deep, like life-consuming, and while I loved getting it on with Keeva, I never saw her as a wife. No matter how hard she tried to convince me she could be. Her dad was a politician and good friends with mine. They thought it would be great for our families to unite. I didn't agree. She was great in bed, but she annoyed the shite out of me.

So I went with the flow, enjoyed her company, ignored her reasons on why we should get married. But when she asked me to buy her things, and then get mad when I said no, I started to pull away. While I didn't mind it before, dinner here, a beer there, and maybe some knickers for me to tear off, I did mind when she asked me to buy her a car. I said no, of course, because that was just crazy to me. She wasn't my fiancée or my wife, so why would I? She then accused me of not loving her, which I didn't, and when I said that, she said some really awful things, one being the only reason she stayed with me for so long was for a new car.

I know, a bitch, right?

But losing her and learning from her only made me keep the people who matter close to heart, and it also made my wall when it comes to outsiders extra thick. With Kane though, I am pretty much an open book. I could never shut him out, nor would I. I glance up at him to find him chewing on a pen, his brow together as he types something into the computer.

"So, she's good looking?"

He doesn't look up, but I do see his mouth pull up at the side. He was really taken with this girl, and I am actually looking forward to meeting her. "Yeah, she's a looker, that's for sure."

"Maybe I'll go up to the pub with you, check her out."

That makes him look up, and I can tell that he doesn't believe me. I smile as I shrug. "I'm nervous."

He lets out a breath as he pulls the pen out of his mouth, pointing at me with it. "Don't be. You act like you're gonna walk in, and everyone is going to attack you! No one cares if you are out and about."

"You know that is not true. There are blogs about me, and I'm in the paper if I do anything around here. Kane, people care. Don't downplay us to make me feel better. I know where I come from."

He waves me off. "Ah, who cares, put a hat on. Let's go get a few scoops down at the pub and have a bit of craic for a change. Be young and wild! You deserve it. No one can hate you or judge you for that."

I shake my head. "I'm young but not wild, you know that. It's easy for you. You don't have this pressure on you to do what is expected. I do. It's been that way since I was born."

"I know and I get it, Dec, I do, but stop living for everyone else. Be one of the lads. Have a bit of fun!"

I laugh at that, and he smiles as he leans toward me. "Do something for you, Declan. Leave all these worries, the things that Keeva did, behind ya, and find someone who makes you happy. You can't hide behind these gates, because if you do, you'll not only lose everything, you'll regret it too. I don't want that for my best friend."

I let out a long breath. "I already do."

"Then let's change it. Let's go out, even if it is only once a week. At least you're getting out."

My heart speeds up, banging against my chest as I take in a lungful of air. "Where though? The pub?"

"The pub, a GAA match, go into town, a party, anything. You've got to do things off this flippin' land. I don't even remember the last time we left together."

I look away because I can't remember either. I think it might be when my dad moved from the distillery to the office. "Yeah, I know."

"Well, what do you say?" he asks with a wide grin.

I swallow loudly as I drum my fingers against the desk. Looking up at him, I shrug as I say, "I'll think about it, okay?"

That doesn't please him, and I can tell. He shakes his head as he leans back in his chair. "No, don't think, just say yes. To start, let's go to lunch off the property tomorrow. We can go to the pub and my future girl."

I scratch my head, my fingers getting tangled in my curls. As much as I want to meet Fiona and try what he suggests, I can't seem to make myself agree. "Ugh, I don't know."

He laughs. "Yes, ya do. You don't want to, but you know ya will. Ah, go on!"

"Fine, fine, yeah, I'll go, but enough about that. Let's get this done. I want to go fishing this afternoon, and since you're making me go to the pub, I'm making you go fishing."

He groans, but then he must realize that he won because a grin replaces his sullen look as he says, "Fine, I'll bring the beer."

Placing the boat on the water, I get in after pushing it off the bank. My little boat isn't anything to be impressed with. I made it myself when Kane and I were ten. He isn't much of a fisherman. He'd rather use the boat to bring ladies out, but me, I like to just be on the water. I may fish, read, or just lie at the bottom and let the sun warm my face. You know, maybe Kane is right, what man likes to do that for fun? Lie in the sun? What am I—a woman? For fuck's sake.

"What's wrong with you?"

I look up from where I'm baiting my line. "I think you're right. I'm turning into a fucking girl."

Kane laughs. "No, I wouldn't let that happen."

"I like to lie in this boat, alone, and let the sun warm my face."

"Jaysus, what color are your lace knickers?"

"Fuck off!" I say, but he just laughs. "I feel like a fucking gobshite."

"Don't worry, you are, but everyone still loves you."

I set him with a look that he just laughs off before throwing my line out and leaning back in the boat. As I wait for a bite, I glance over to find Kane holding his pole between his legs while he plays on his phone. I sort of hope that a fish bites and takes the pole, or maybe even him, into the water. That would be a show for sure. Knowing that he is bored, I ask, "Are you going to ask her out?"

He nods. "Soon enough, have to feel her out. Right now, I'm hot for her, but I don't want to rush it, ya know?"

That has me chuckling. "When have you ever been worried about rushing it with a girl? You're usually rushing straight into her bed or yours."

Kane smiles as he nods. "Yeah, but it's different with her. She has a smile that stuns me, and a body that makes my mouth water. I want to get to know her."

I smile as I turn the reel, bringing my empty hook back. I don't say anything as I rebait; I'm too lost with my thoughts. Kane isn't the type of guy to want to get to know anyone. He wants what he wants and goes on, so this Fiona must be something. It also makes me realize how much what he has been saying is true. I have locked myself up from the world, but who can blame me? When I leave the gates, it's like I'm the freak show of the circus. Everyone stares, and I don't know why. They do the same to my ma, da, and Lena, but they don't care. They live as if they aren't there. For me, it is different. It makes me nervous and makes me feel like every move I make could be the wrong one. I need to let this go, though, because my friend could get married and have kids while I lie in my boat, watching the clouds pass by. Alone. And I don't want that. Not at all.

"Will she be there tomorrow?"

He nods. "She's always there. Even though, there is a new girl, I think she said her cousin, working there now. She's a Yank and very pretty. I can't remember her name for the life of me. You'd fancy her though. She's got those sweet eyes and freckles you like."

I laugh. "How do you know I fancy sweet eyes and freckles?"

Kane shoots me a grin. "Because I know you."

It's true and he's right, but that smug look on his face doesn't have me admitting that. I shake my head as I reel in again. There is a fucking fish that is taking my bait and when I catch him, I'm gonna fry the fucker.

"Speak of the devil."

I glance up. "What?"

"There she is, and damn, she's got one hell of a body!"

"Who?" I say, looking across the lake at where he is pointing. When I see her, my tongue falls out of my mouth. Literally. Putting it back in, I ask, "Fucking hell, who is that?"

An angel is the only thing that comes to mind.

Her hair is reddish brown and long, down the middle of her back. She has big, black sunglasses covering her eyes, and I can tell from where I am that she has lush, plump lips that are glossed and shiny. She is wearing a bikini, dark green that makes her porcelain skin shine. Kane said she has freckles, and while I can't see them on her face, they dust her chest and arms. Her breasts are large, her ass round, and thankfully, I get to admire it as she lays a blanket on the grass before dropping to her knees to lie down on it. I watch as she puts a baseball hat on her head before reaching in her bag to pull out a book that she lays to the side. Her body shines in the sun, probably from the oil she has pulled from her bag and is currently lathering her legs up with. I can't take my eyes off her. She is magnificent, beautiful, and I wish like hell I knew what color her eyes are.

"That's not Fiona, is it?" I ask, basically pleading that it isn't.

"Hell no, Fiona is thicker. That's the cousin, the Yank."

I refuse to let my eyes leave her breathtaking body as I ask, "And you don't know her name?"

"No."

"But she works at the pub?"

"Yeah, you know, a lot of our beautiful town is full of women like that."

I tear my eyes away from her, look back at a grinning Kane, and say, "I don't care about them. I care about her."

"She is hot."

I shake my head. "No, she's glorious."

I watch her for another minute as Kane chuckles beside me. I have the urge to know her. To learn what her favorite movie is. What book she is reading. I want to know why she is here and not back in America. I want to know everything, but most of all, I want to find out what color her eyes are and get lost in them. I want to learn her name and then whisper it before dropping my lips to hers. I want—no, I *need*—to know her.

- Turning to my best friend, I ask, "What time did you want to go to lunch tomorrow?"

I am answered with a knowing laugh, but I don't care because I just saw an angel I am going to make mine.

five
Amberlyn

The sun warms me all the way to the core, and I've decided that I found the honey hole of the Maclaster land. I need this. Last night, hearing stories of my mother and father in their younger years from my aunt and uncle had me biting back my tears. God, it was horrible. I almost lost it plenty of times, but I held them back until I was in the privacy of my own room. Then I spent the night bawling my eyes out, holding myself as the hot water of my shower hit me. The shower is my favorite place to cry. No one can hear me, and I usually have an hour to myself before Fiona or anyone comes to find me. I hate that I still cry so much, I mean, I knew she was leaving me. I had counseling, I met with my youth group leader, I knew what to expect, I knew what pain was coming, but I don't think it prepared me for how much I would miss her. Them. I miss my dad just as much, and it just hurts. They left a hole in my heart, and I try so hard every day to do what she asked me to do, but it just seems so hard.

I want to break down. I want to quit life, ball up in the fetal position, and beg her to come back to me, but I know she can't. I know that she is watching me and rooting for me. So for her, I wake up each day, put on makeup, get dressed, and I fucking smile as I try to live the life she wants for me. I try to leave my sadness, my heartbreak, and my shyness all behind me to try different things. I want to be the Amberlyn Reilly that my mom and dad would be proud of, and that girl is happy.

So since last night was shitty for me, I decided to do something that would make me happy and that was to get lost in a good book on a beautiful summer day. When I asked Fiona where I could go to read, she rolled her eyes before pointing out toward this majestic lake behind the B&B. For some reason, everything in Ireland just seems so much brighter and more vivid to me. I've lain near the lake that sat behind my house year after year, and it had never been as nice as it is lying here now.

After lathering my body up with tanning lotion, I wipe my hands on my blanket before picking up my book. It's an oldie but a goodie, and I'm excited to get lost in the world of Elizabeth Bennet and Mr. Darcy. Something about this country makes me want to catch up on all my favorite Jane Austen books. Maybe it's the land or the history, but I just love it here. I'm so glad that I took the chance to come here. I love that I am learning who I am and finding my own way. I just wish my mom and dad were here physically to see me do it.

I lie back with my book on my forearms as the sun kisses my body. I'm hoping for a tan, but let's be honest, I'll probably just burn. Can't blame me for trying though. Fiona is so beautifully tanned. It's fake, but those damn tanning beds scare the shit out of me. When I tried to express this fear with her, she waved me off, muttered something that sounded very close to eejit, and walked away. So here I am, hoping for a natural tan.

But to my surprise, Mr. Darcy isn't keeping my attention. There is a boat on the lake with two very handsome guys inside. I am pretty sure one is Kane. He looks just like the guy who Fiona has been gushing over, and I'm almost confident it is him. I have no clue who the other guy is. One thing is for sure, he won't stop staring at me. I guess he thinks I don't know since he can't see my eyes. I see him running his gaze all over me, and I can't say that I mind.

I pride myself in the fact that I have 20/20 vision, and from my spot on the bank of the lake, I can see him perfectly. I can't see the bottom of him, but the top is impressive. He is thin but toned, with large arms that I find incredibly sexy. He has a round face with a square jaw and a wide nose that I think brings character to his face. His lips are thin, but what I love most is his hair. It's curly from what I can see, but it's covered in a beanie. I don't completely understand why, since it is in the nineties today, but whatever, he's cute and he can pull it off. A smile pulls at my lips as I tear my gaze off him.

Maybe I'll get lucky, and he'll come into the pub.

Maybe he could be my risk or my something drastic.

LATER AT dinner, I settle into my seat beside Fiona as my aunt serves us. Like I knew I would, my body aches from where the sun has caused havoc on my skin. I should have never stayed as long as I did, but I couldn't stop watching Kane and his friend on the boat. I'm almost positive Kane's friend was waiting for me to leave because when I got up to go, he started to row the boat back to the bank. I may be flattering myself, but it made me smile nonetheless. I've had a grin on my face that won't go away, even after rubbing aloe all over my burning body.

As Shelia loads my plate up with sliced pork and potatoes, I look over at Fiona to say, "I saw Kane today."

She glances over at me as Shelia asks, "Who's that?"

"Ma, just a second," Fiona says, turning to me. "Where? What was he doing? He wasn't with someone, was he?"

I roll my eyes. "He was out on a boat, and yes, with some guy. I've never seen him before."

Her brows came together. "The lake? Outside?"

"Yeah, that's usually where lakes are."

She smacks me playfully as my uncle laughs from across the table, and my aunt asks once more, "Who this is Kane fella?"

"Some guy, Ma, I fancy him a bit," Fiona says quickly before looking back at me. "What was he doing on the lake in a boat?"

"Fishing."

She is confused, that is obvious, as she turns to her father. "Da, why would Kane Levy be on the O'Callaghan Lake?"

Michael shrugs his shoulders. "Hell, I don't know, darlin'. I don't even know who Kane Levy is."

"Who? Alice and Paul Levy's Kane?"

We all look up at Shelia as Fiona says, "Yeah, ya know them?"

"Of course I do. Kane is over there because he works there. He's been friends with the young O'Callaghan lad since they were wee bit babies. It was probably him who Amberlyn saw."

Fiona smacks her hands together as she nods. "That's right, I knew that. Yeah, it was probably him. They are best pals, but I can't believe you saw him. No one sees Declan."

I don't touch my food when it is placed before me. Instead, I ask, "Why?"

"I don't know. He just disappeared a couple years ago. Rumor is he has locked himself away for his bride who is coming in another couple of years."

So he is engaged? That's depressing, but I am also confused. "Locked himself away?"

"Yeah, up in that big 'ol castle of his."

"Castle?"

Fiona laughs as she covers her mouth. "Yeah, he's the Whiskey Prince."

"He's a prince!" I exclaim. "That's so cool!"

Michael chuckles before saying, "No, Amberlyn, he isn't like real royalty. That's just what he is called around here. The O'Callaghans are basically our royalty. They are kind of like your Kennedys. I don't know why only Declan is called the whiskey anything. It isn't as if we are calling his parents the king and queen or even the daughter a princess. It's weird really, but that's the Irish folk for ya," he says playfully, but he gets a smack by my aunt anyway.

"I don't know why we've done that either; we just have," Shelia says as she sits down. "I think his grandda said it once when he was born, and it stuck."

I'm extremely interested in this because I was attracted to him, but also because it is interesting and I want to know more. "Is his dad the president or something similar?"

He shakes his head. "Senior O'Callaghan was in politics for a bit, but the reason they're a big deal is because they are very, very rich. Whiskey is a good business to go into. Everyone loves to drink. Because they are so rich and they do so much for the town, they are worshiped."

"There was a festival when Declan and his younger sister, Lena, were born," Shelia adds. "The whole town shut down just to get a glimpse of the next heir to the business, and then they did it for Lena because Noreen O'Callaghan wanted to show off her beautiful baby girl."

"And everyone talks about them. They are a big deal around here," Fiona says as she tears apart a piece of bread.

"If that's true, then why haven't I heard anything about them in the last month?" I ask, surprised by it all. He seemed so normal, hanging out on the lake, fishing.

"That's 'cause he doesn't come out. The rest of his family does, but Declan keeps to himself, only stays on the grounds. It's like its own world over there. No one is allowed on unless invited," Fiona says as Michael nods his head.

I'm interested and disappointed at the same time. Disappointed because my chance of ever seeing him in the pub has died, but interested because I want to know why, and more than anything, I want to know him. Deciding that I have thought way too much about a person who has no connection to me and probably never will, I reach for my fork and dig in to the amazing food that my aunt cooked.

But soon my thoughts drift back to the guy on the lake.

The Whiskey Prince.

It's busy, like uncommonly busy this afternoon, and I blame it on Shelia for serving her famous cottage pie. I don't like it much, but apparently, the whole town does. Every table is full of men and women, loud and boisterous as they eat and drink. I made the joke that I couldn't believe people drink in the middle of the day when I first started at the pub, but I soon learned there really isn't a time when a person doesn't drink in this country.

As Fiona takes orders quickly, I fill them just as fast, passing out the dishes before filling pints and basically looking like a chicken with my head cut off. When everyone is served, Fiona and I lean against the bar and take in deep breaths. I reach for my cup of water and drain it as she drains a beer before flashing me a grin.

"I need a drink after that. Curse ma for making her pie today—people are here from three towns over! I wouldn't be surprised if some came from Dublin!"

I nod in agreement. "You're probably right."

She laughs as she fills her beer a little from the tap, draining it and standing up. "Okay, I am going to go get plates. You refill drinks?"

"Sounds like a plan," I say as I put my cup down and start with the bar patrons. I like the way we work together. We have a system, and it works for us. She always says that it is easy now, but when we both start school again, it's going to be tough since we'll be tired all the time. I'm not looking forward to it. I thought about saying I didn't want to work, but I would feel like an ass not working for my keep. So, I decided I would try it out, see what happens. I still have most of the money my mom had out for me, plus her life insurance. I don't like to touch it, though. I worry about my school and paying for that, so I mainly live off my tips.

I make my rounds, picking up pints and cups, refilling them and talking to my patrons the best I can. Everyone is just so happy, and in return, it makes me happy. I joke with everyone as they tease me for being a Yank, and I even flirt some with some of my older regulars. It's innocent and doesn't make me nervous the way it does with the younger guys. They don't care, they only want the entertainment, but younger guys actually want attention and that freaks me out. I've been getting better though. The night before, I actually talked to a college fella who stayed until close to flirt with me. He was sweet, promised to be in tonight, but I doubt he will. Fiona says he has a girlfriend, and I scolded her for not telling me earlier. She claimed it was because she wanted me to practice, but I wish she hadn't. I don't like flirting with guys who have girlfriends. I wouldn't want someone doing that to my guy.

When I round the bar to refill a pint, the pub falls silent. Looking up to see what is wrong, I see that everyone is staring at Kane. And then I see him. Declan O'Callaghan. He is visibly uncomfortable, but that isn't what has me staring at him like the rest of the bar. No, it's his eyes. This close, I can tell they are ice blue, and they are breathlessly beautiful. Unlike the roll-out-of-bed style that Kane is sporting, Declan is more polished up. In khaki pants with a dark brown belt and a light blue, button-up shirt with a brown tie hanging loosely from his neck, I can't help but feel tingles as I watch him. When I notice the brown beanie on his head, I want to laugh. What the hell? It's hot out! I'm grinning at the silliness of it, but when my eyes fall to his face to find his lips are set in a straight line, my grin falls. If I weren't attracted to him, I would think he was an asshole with how angry he looks. I want to know why he looks that way.

No one is talking, and poor Fiona looks like she's seen a ghost as Kane and Declan take a seat at the bar. Kane removes his baseball cap, laying it on the bar, and I fully expect Declan to remove his hat, but he doesn't. My grin returns as I place the pint on the bar and head to where they sit. I am excited, giddy almost, to get the chance to talk to him. Silly I know, but I am.

"Welcome, guys. What can I get you to drink?"

"A pint for me. Dec?" Kane says, glancing over at him. I do the same, and his eyes are intense on me. Gosh, his eyes are so blue. Almost sparkling, but his brows are squished together, along with his lips, in a straight line. He looks like he's in pain.

I laugh as I reach out, poking the middle of his head, causing his eyes to widen in surprise. I swear I hear people gasp, but I ignore them as I say, "I'm just asking what you'd like. No reason to look at me like that! Are you suffering from ARF?"

He blinks a few times as Kane laughs from beside him. "ARF?"

I really don't know what has gotten into me. Is it the nerves of being around him? I don't know, but I can't stop smiling as I say, "Asshole Resting Face. You look so mad. It's a beautiful day, the birds are singing, and you are in the best pub in Mayo. What do you have to be angry about? Plus, we are serving cottage pie, a delicacy that people come from all over for. My aunt Shelia is the best cook ever, and I promise it will wipe that frown right off that beautiful face of yours. So let's try this again, what can I get you to drink?"

He looks down, a smile playing on his lips, before looking back up at me, "Are you calling me an arsehole?"

I shake my head, a playful smile resting on my lips. There is something about him that keeps me from looking away. He is beautiful, interesting, and I like the way his face warms with color when I gaze into his eyes. Leaning on the bar, my face resting in my hands, I say, "No, not at all. I just don't understand the look. You don't even know my name, and you are glaring at me. What did I do to you?"

He leans toward me, and God, he smells delicious—something woodsy and spicy. This close, I can see that his square jaw has a tad bit of stubble, not much, but enough to make me want to reach out and touch it. With his eyes locked on mine, he says, "You're right. What is your name?"

In a low voice, I say, "Amberlyn Reilly. Shh, don't tell, but I'm a Yank."

He smiles and winks. "I'll take it to me grave."

I have always been intrigued by the accent here in Ireland, but Declan makes it positively sexy. With redness warming my cheeks, I lean back, holding on to the bar as I ask, "Great, so since you don't look like you want to stab me any longer, what can I get you?"

Kane laughs, but he doesn't. He just watches me. He's so serious, and that just makes me more curious. "A pint of beer please, and also some of that cottage pie."

Kane says, "I'll have the same."

"Coming right up, fellas," I say before turning to go get them a beer. Before I can, Fiona is dragging me to the back, despite my protest. "What the hell?" I scold.

"What the hell? Amberlyn! You just poked the Whiskey Prince in the head and called him an arsehole! Are you crazy?"

"What? He thought it was funny because obviously I was joking!"

"He's the Whiskey Prince!"

"So? He seems just as normal as us."

Exasperated, she says, "Jaysus! Amberlyn, he is a big deal, okay? Wait…" She pauses, taking a large breath before setting me with a look. "Who is the most famous person ever that you love?"

I don't even think before saying, "Justin Timberlake."

She goes to say something but pauses before saying, "Oh good Lord, that's a fine one. He is so good looking."

"I know, beautiful," I gush with a dreamy smile, but then I am taken aback when she waves her hands widely in my face.

"Focus! Imagine that Declan is Justin Timberlake. That is how big he is here. Maybe even bigger."

I want to ask why because it seems silly to me that a whiskey maker is so famous. Before I do though, I say, "He does kind of have Justin's hair from NSYNC."

"He does, doesn't he?"

We both look around the corner at where Kane and Declan are talking. He looks so good, leaning against the bar carelessly, but I can see the tension in his shoulders. He is nervous, and I want to ease that. I don't like that everyone is still staring at him either. He is a normal guy wanting some beer and pie. Can't he eat his damn pie? I look back over at her. "He is so dreamy."

"I know, but he is engaged and totally off-limits to us mere mortals. I don't even know why he is here. It's weird. I mean, look at the way everyone is just staring. It's odd, you know?"

I don't have to look, I know they are, but what I hate more than that is she just reminded me he is engaged. I forgot that part and now all my hopeful thoughts come to a crashing halt as my gaze falls back on him. He really is a gorgeous man, but like she said, completely out of my grasp.

"I'm not going to treat him any differently. He is just a normal guy to me."

She shakes her hand. "I'm telling you that you have to, Amberlyn. He isn't normal."

"Why though?" I ask before she walks away.

"Because he is the Whiskey Prince."

six
Declan

My nerves are all over the place.

Since the moment we walked in and everyone's gaze fell on me, my heart has been beating out of control. Then I sat down, she looked into my eyes, and everything disappeared. It was only us.

Amberlyn.

Fuck, she is beautiful. I thought she was something yesterday, but today, all glossed-up, wearing a sweet green dress with her hair tied up on top of her head, I can't form a coherent thought. Kane was right when he said she had sweet eyes and freckles. Fuck, what a sight they are. They shine bright, her eyes, an unbelievable aquamarine that I've never seen before in person. They have specks of gold in them and shine even when she is looking at me all perplexed. Her freckles dust along her nose and cheeks, also in various spots all over her body. Her skin is red, and I figure that was from sitting out in the sun too long yesterday. The back of my neck is burnt, but having all the time I did to stare at her was completely worth it.

Even with her running around the pub working, I can't help but watch her and know where she is every second. Everyone loves her. They all talk and have a laugh with her, and when she laughs, I swear the world comes to a stop. I want to make her laugh.

Problem is—I'm not sure how to do that.

"You should ask her out."

I look over at Kane, who is stuffing his gob with the fabulous cottage pie. Amberlyn was right. It was the best—not that I'd admit that to my ma or grandma. "Fuck off," I scowl, shooting him a look as she comes up to us.

"Need anything, guys?"

Say something. Say anything. Tell her yes, that you need her number! Say something, you eejit! I scream to myself in my head.

"No, we are fine. Thank you."

For fuck's sake, I'm a gobshite. Pure and simple.

She sends me a quick grin before rushing off to fill pints for Fiona, who, by the way, is just a good-looking as Kane claimed. I wish I would have said more, but I feel something between us. She keeps glancing at me, holding my gaze as she fills things from the tap or makes drinks. The air is sizzling, and surely, I'm not the only one who feels it.

"Kane Levy, I'm not happy with you!"

I look up to find Fiona glaring at Kane. I glance over to see my best friend with a smirk on his face as he leans toward her.

"Is that right?" he asks.

"Yes, you didn't call me and tell me you were coming in. I would have at least made sure my hair was done!"

He laughs as he shakes his head, reaching out to take her hand in his. She glances down at their entangled fingers before looking back up at him. Her face is warming with color, her eyes bright as she leans into the bar, closer to him.

"You're undeniably the most gorgeous woman in the world. Bad hair and all."

She giggles as he reaches out with his other hand, tucking a piece of hair behind her ear. I can see their chemistry; it's blinding. I like her for him too and can see why he's so taken with her. I'm also jealous—I want what they have. I want Amberlyn to come over and get lost in my eyes. I want to touch her, feel her against me. Oh, I have it bad.

"When ya gonna ask me out?" she asks, bringing my attention back to them.

He chuckles, letting go of her hand and picking up his fork. "When I feel like it."

"When's that?" She's biting her lip, looking extremely sexy, and I'm surprised Kane isn't drooling over her. She's a sight, that's for sure.

"Not sure yet."

"You'd better hurry, I have plenty of offers," she says. He laughs.

"Then by God, off you go. They won't last a second. You're mine."

I scoff at that, but Fiona's face reddens. She is about to say something, but Amberlyn calls her, "Fiona, come help me."

"We will finish this later."

Before she can walk away, Kane takes a hold of her wrist and says, "Yeah, over a drink tonight? Maybe go see a movie when you get off?"

She bites into her lip again, and I have to applaud him for his way with the ladies. She is his, she may not know it and might not want to admit it, but her body language says it all. With a nod, she says, "Yeah, I'll get off early. I'm sure Amberlyn won't mind."

"Sounds good, text me."

"I will," she promises, and then she is off. I glance over to see Kane grinning, licking his fingers before draining the rest of his pint.

"She's mad about you."

"And I'm the same about her," Kane admits as he looks away. "She's a great girl."

I take the last bit of my pie before pushing my plate away and say sullenly, "We need to get back."

"Yeah, I know," he says as he stands, throwing some bills on the bar. "Fiona, I'm off. See you tonight?"

"Yeah, see ya," she calls from where she and Amberlyn stand, stacking dishes. Amberlyn looks at me and smiles. I want to say something, anything, but all I do is look away like a gombeen. Once outside, I let out a long breath as Kane clasps his hand on my shoulder.

"So, Dec, how ya feeling?"

I nod. "Okay, actually."

"Been telling ya that for years. It's good for ya to get out."

"Sure, and she's extremely good-looking."

"Fiona? Oh, I know."

"No, Amberlyn," I correct, and he grins as he squeezes my shoulder.

"Yeah, she is. You should ask her out."

I nod. "I want to. Give me a few."

"Want me to ask Fiona to get you together?"

I shake my head quickly. "No, promise me, Kane, that you won't say a word. I want to do this myself."

He stops, holding his hands up. "OK! Sure! I promise. Take it easy, Dec. I'm just trying to help."

I must have said that sharper than I intended, but I know Kane. I know he wants to help, but I can't let him. I want her to want me for me, not because her cousin asks her to. I feel something between us and I'm sure she feels it too, but I want to be sure before I ask. Before I put my heart out there, because she could be one to fall for. It's sudden, I know, but I just feel it. Soul-deep. And I've never felt like this before, so that has to count for something.

Now all I have to do is get my head out of my arse and do something about it.

I'VE BEEN sitting in my car outside of the pub for an hour now.

I can't bring myself to go in. I drove here all on my own, didn't even tell Kane I was coming, but for some reason, I can't get out of the fucking car. My hands are shaking and my heart is pounding, but I know I have to ignore that. Letting out a breath, I sit up in my seat, shaking out my hands before pushing the door open and getting out. Shutting the door, I lean into my car and take in a lungful of air.

I can do this. I can. Sure. No big deal.

Forcing myself to walk, I head to the door and pause, my hand hovering over the handle as I take in deep breaths. This is not a big deal. I am freaking out for fuckin' nothing. Pushing in, I am prepared for the stares, but I find the place empty.

"Welcome to the… hey!"

I look up to find Amberlyn behind the bar, a rag in her hand and a smile on her beautiful face. "It's you."

I nod. "It's me."

"Come on in, you have your fair share of seats to choose from since the place is empty. You've missed the rush. I hope you're not hungry 'cause I'm the only one here, and I can't promise that you'll get something edible," she says with a laugh. Her laughter surrounds me, willing me to walk in and sit down in front of her just for the chance to hear more of it. "Pint?"

I nod. Hopefully, it will calm my nerves. "Please."

"Sure!" she says as she fills the pint. "Now, please don't tell me you want food."

A smile plays on my lips. "Actually, yes, I came for lunch."

She lays her head down on the bar, looking up at me through her long eyelashes. She is so pretty, so sweet, and I love the playful way about her. "Ugh, you're killing me, Declan. Okay, what do you want?"

"I can go somewhere else," I say, even though that is the last thing I want.

She straightens up quickly, shaking her head. "No, please, I'm sorry! I'm just a horrible cook, and I don't want to keep you from coming back to the pub!"

That won't ever happen.

"I doubt you're that bad."

"You're right—I'm horrible," she says, smiling at me. "But nonetheless, what can I get ya?"

I glance at the menu real fast and decide on, "Bacon and cabbage?"

"Oh, thank God, all I have to do is warm that!"

I smile as she rushes off to fill my order. I take the time to drain my pint, praying it calms my nerves and gives me the courage I need to talk to this beautiful woman. When she comes back, she smiles as she lays my plate before me. "Here ya go."

"Thanks," I say as I start to dig in and she refills my pint. Putting it beside my plate, she leans against the bar as she watches me eat. I know it should bother me, but it doesn't.

"Good?"

"Sure, real good."

"Thank goodness," she says with a big grin. It brightens her whole face, and suddenly I've forgotten how to chew my food as I get lost in her eyes. But then she looks away and asks, "So, about yesterday…"

I pause as I watch her. She is nervous, maybe even a little embarrassed. I don't know why she would be though. Yesterday was grand, but today has the chance to be better.

"Apparently, I offended you."

"You did?"

"Yeah, I'm not allowed to touch you or joke around with you, so I'm sorry, and I won't do it again."

My brow furrows as I watch her. "Why not?"

"'Cause you're the *Whiskey Prince*. I mean, I don't get it, you're just a regular guy to me, but apparently, to my family, you are the Michael Jackson of Ireland. So, I apologize."

I laugh. "The Michael Jackson?"

She smiles. "From what I've been told."

I shake my head, and when her gaze meets mine, I smile. "You didn't offend me yesterday, Amberlyn. I like that you think I'm a regular guy. It's grand, and it's how I want it to be."

She bites into her lip, and it hits me in my core. She's stunning. Her eyes are shining, her lips glossed, and I love the color pink on her. More than I do the green from yesterday. But unlike yesterday, her hair is down and falling in her face. I want to be like Kane and reach forward to tuck it behind her ear, but I can't bring myself to do it.

"I'm glad. I didn't want to offend you. I was just being myself."

"Good, keep being you. I don't want anything less than that."

She smiles, backing away slowly as she promises, "Believe me, I won't."

We share a smile. She looks away as she busies herself with wiping the counter, but I'm not done talking to her. "You know that secret I'm taking to me grave?"

She nods as her grin grows. "You're still keeping that, right?"

I laugh. "Yeah, but can I ask what brought you to this great country of mine?"

Her smile falters a tad before she looks away. "My mom passed away two months ago."

Her visible pain stabs me in the chest. "I'm so sorry."

She tries to smile, but it doesn't reach her eyes. "Thank you. But that's the reason I'm here. Never in a billion years did I think I'd come here without them, my parents, I mean. My dad passed away when I was twelve."

Fuck, that's unthinkable! This poor woman. Both her parents? How is she standing, smiling, and living a life? I would be lost. I love my parents. Yes, they are always on me, but we are a loving family. We need each other. I don't understand it. Most of all, I'm impressed by her. She is strong. That's easy to see, and it amazes me. "Wow, I'm sorry again."

"Thanks, but she wanted me to start a new life. My parents grew up here. My aunt Shelia is my dad's sister. My mom had this whole plan about me coming here and trying something new. She was afraid I'd get stuck if I stayed in the States. I'm pretty confident she was right."

"That's amazing. Fair fucks to ya for taking the risk. That's a lot to take when you are hurting, I'd think."

"Yeah, it sucks. I miss them, so much, but I'm happy with my choice of coming here."

I am too, I want to say, but instead I just nod before taking a bite of my bacon. When I look back up at her, she is watching me, her eyes boring into mine. "Can I ask you something?"

"Sure, yeah, go ahead."

I fully expect her to ask me why they call me the Whiskey Prince, but to my surprise, she asks, "What's up with the beanie? It's hot out!"

I laugh as I look down, shaking my head. My cheeks are warm and my heart is pounding, but I feel so alive. Looking up, I say, "I don't like my hair."

"Why? It's so cute!"

"That's why—people think it's cute. Cute is not a manly word," I say, deadpan, but she just laughs before reaching out and pulling it off my head. I go to reach for it, but she puts it on her head, a grin on her face that is nothing less than intoxicating.

"Stop, you don't need this. I like your hair, and I'm sure the rest of the world will too."

I want to reach for it off her head, but I have to admit, she looks pretty fuckin' cute with it on. So I return to eating. "I don't care if they like me. Sometimes, I wish they'd stop staring."

"Oh goodness, me too! I don't get it. Why are you such a big deal to them?" she asks, but then, before I can answer, she says, "Sorry if that came off rude!"

I shake my head, my mouth forming in a grin. I've never smiled this much. It's weird but exhilarating all at the same time. I like the way she makes me feel. I like the way her eyes stay locked with mine. I like her. Placing my fork down, I say, "It's always been this way. My great-great-great-great-great-grandda started it. He wanted to be admired for what he did around here, and people flocked to him. They made a big deal when he got married, when he had kids, and then it just carried on and carried on. When I was born, my grandda called me his little Whiskey Prince and it stuck. I don't like it, but it is what it is, I guess."

"Wow, that's neat."

I shrug. "I don't think so. I think it's weird."

She smiles. "Well, I hope you know I'm not like everyone else, and I don't plan to treat you any differently."

"It's 'cause you're a Yank," I say with a wink, and she grins.

"Yup, but remember—take that to your grave," she says, returning the wink.

"Will do."

"Good. Well, I hate to say this, but I have to get some stuff done before my family gets back for dinner rush, so I'm going to actually work while you eat, okay?"

"Sure. I'm almost done, and then I'll be out of your hair."

She reaches for a bucket but looks back at me to say, "But maybe you can come back?"

Breathlessly, I say, "Sure, that'd be grand."

She sends me a wide grin before turning to start cleaning. I want to say more, maybe ask her to dinner, or anything really, just to see her, but I don't. Instead, I finish my food and my pint as I watch her. She has a great ass, round and full in her fitted blue jeans. I also love the way her hair falls down her back. Knowing if I don't leave now I never will, I lay some money on the bar before standing up. She is over by the window, wiping down tables, and she looks up at me when I push the stool back under the bar.

"You outta here?"

"Yeah, I have to get back to work."

Walking toward her, I stop in front of her as she smiles up at me. "I didn't know you work. What do you do?"

"I push paper mainly, but I help run the whiskey business."

"That's cool. I bet it's awesome."

"It really is," I say. Silence falls between us as we stare into each other's eyes.

"All right, well, until next time."

It would be sooner than she thought, but I didn't want to sound like an eejit, so I just ask, "Can I get my hat back?"

She laughs as she pulls it off her head. "Totally forgot I had it. Here ya go, but I promise you don't need it."

"I'll keep that in mind," I say as I put it back on, tucking my hands in my pockets afterward. I rock back on my heels, not wanting to leave, but knowing I need too. She has work to do, and I do too. I've been hiding out for too long as it is, and Kane is probably blowing my phone up. "Okay, so I'll go."

"It was good seeing ya again, Declan."

"Yeah, you too, Amberlyn. Have a good day."

"You too," she says as I reach for the door and push out of it.

Once outside, a grin is on my face and I know that I can't wait to see her again.

seven
Amberlyn

*D*eclan has been in almost every day for the last two weeks. He usually comes during my dead hour when Fiona is out doing errands, and I love sharing that time with him. We don't say much, usually just small talk while he eats and I clean, but it's fun. He's quiet, and because of that, I find him intriguing. I want to pick his brain, find out what makes him tick, but every time I go to do just that, I feel like an asshole because what is that going to do for me? It's not like I can date him. He has a fiancée, even though he has never mentioned her. You would think he would have by now, but he hasn't, which makes me wonder why, though I can't bring myself to ask. So I have to keep this completely innocent, but it's hard because I want more.

Like today, he looks positively provocative. He is wearing a thin, black T-shirt with a pair of khakis and a black beanie. He walked in with aviators on, and I don't know why, but they made him hotter. Especially when he pushed them up on his head, and my eyes met his. I mean, honestly, my heart kicked into overdrive and my panties got damp. I'm so attracted to him. It scares me the way I feel about him, especially with the fact that he is off-limits to me. I guess the phrase, *you want what you can't have,* is completely true because I want Declan O'Callaghan, and it seems like whenever I say how cute or hot he is, Fiona is there reminding me about his relationship status. It's annoying.

But most of all, I'm annoyed by how much I like him, especially when he smiles. His smiles are breathtaking. Hell, everything about him makes me breathless. Like now, I'm all the way across the pub, but I can feel him watching me when I move, and I don't know why he does that. Doesn't he know that it makes me giddy inside? That it makes me warm all over? I turn, catching his gaze, and he smiles as he holds up his pint.

"Can I have some more beer?"

"Sure!" I say as I head around the bar. "Holler at me next time."

"You're busy."

"Yes, but I'm here to serve you!" I say, and I swear his eyes darken. I don't know why, but suddenly it is extremely hot in here. I look away, filling his glass with beer before looking back up and handing it to him. He nods his thanks as he takes a long pull. The air is crackling around us or maybe me. Hell, I don't know, but I have to say something before I come out of my skin. "Do you have to go to work after this?"

Not even close to what I wanted to say.

"Yes, I have to go give a tour to a new buyer. He's an arse. I don't want to deal with him at all."

I laugh. "Sounds like a blast."

He doesn't smile. "Loads."

I can't help but laugh again. I don't want to stop talking, so with a wide smile, I say, "Guess what I'm doing tonight."

His eyes are shining as he looks up at me. "What's that?"

"I'm getting my first tattoo!"

"Really?" he asks, a smirk growing on his face.

"Yup! I'm pretty excited and scared shitless, but it's gonna be awesome."

"Sure, what are you getting?"

"My mom and dad's names in a sparrow on my ribs," I say, trying to ignore my jumpy nerves. I am scared, but Fiona guaranteed me it won't be that bad. I don't believe her, though. I'm still trying to adjust to the idea. The whole thing wasn't even supposed to happen, but Fiona found me crying last night as I held my mom's letter in my arms. I couldn't tell her what was wrong, but thankfully, she didn't ask. She just held me. Then when I was able to speak, I told her that I just missed my mom, and I was so upset with myself because I hadn't done anything from her letter yet. So she read it and decided that she wanted to help me honor my mom's wishes. It was sweet, and I think that moment brought us closer. When I said that I was thinking about a tattoo for the something drastic part, she was all about it. So we are doing it. A tattoo. Yay!

I wish I were as badass as I just sounded there.

"That's really exciting, Amberlyn. I can't wait to see it."

His eyes run over my body to the spot where my hand lays over where I plan to get the tattoo. I can feel his gaze on me, running over my breast to the spot, which makes me gasp for breath. Letting out a long breath, I look up at him and smile as I say, "Yeah, I'm nervous but I'm excited. Do you have any tattoos?"

He nods. "Sure."

"Show me!"

A smile plays on his lips as he stands up, slowly pulling his shirt up and over his head, which causes my tongue to promptly fall out of my mouth. I've seen men shirtless, I have. I mean, there are the Internet and movies, but what is standing in front of me is God's gift to women. All I see are ripples of muscles, abs for days, and toned arms. I can't believe it because, when I looked at him, I didn't see him having this kind of body. But hell, he does. Maybe spending all that time locked up in his castle did a body good because holy crow, he is hot! And of course his pants are hanging low on his hips, and for goodness' sake, he has the V! Swallowing loudly, I remember I am supposed to be looking at his tattoos, so I shift my gaze from his mouthwatering muscles and take in the awesome piece on his shoulder. Leaning over the bar for a closer look, I'm amazed at the detail. It looks as if the skin on his shoulder has been ripped away and underneath is armor with a Celtic symbol on the arm. It has amazing detail, blood and stitching in spots so it looks like the skin is trying to be held together. It's mind-blowing.

"That is fabulous."

He smiles. "Yeah, I figured if I'm the *prince,* I need to have armor for battle. I'm really into our history here, and I love the whole aspect of royalty and stuff."

First, I am so turned on that he loves history, that's hot, and second, I love the way he says prince. He says it all slow and sexy like. Looking up in his eyes, I smile. "That's so cool! I am, too. I love reading about the Knights of the Round Table and cool shit like that. Best book ever is *Lord of the Rings.*"

"Fuck yeah, I love it, and *Beowulf* is another good one."

"Heck yeah! I love that kind of stuff. I'm reading *Pride and Prejudice* right now."

He scoffs. "Such a chick book, but it's good."

"Yeah, it's awesome," I say, and then I realize how close I am to him. I look up from his arm into his eyes, and my breath hitches. God, he has beautiful lips, and I swear his eyes are darker than normal again. Is he coming closer to me? Holy shit! He isn't going to kiss me, is he?

"Um, Amberlyn, why is Declan O'Callaghan standing without a shirt on in my pub?"

At the sound of my aunt's voice, I fall back off the bar, almost tripping over the pipe that we use to stand on, and turn quickly to find her staring at us. My heart is pounding in my chest, my throat tight, and my face flushed. I look back at Declan, and his face is burning with color as he puts his shirt back on. Guilt floods me as I realize what just happened, what this looks like. It's only Aunt Shelia, but what if it gets back to his fiancée? Quickly, I tell the truth. "He was showing me his tattoo."

She sets me with a disapproving look before sending a warm smile over to

Declan.

"Oh, well, that was a sight to see!" she says with a laugh. "For a show of masculine greatness like that, my lad, your lunch is on the house."

Declan's face is still bright with color, but he shakes his head. "No, ma'am. I'll pay for what I ordered."

"You will do no such thing. Don't take his money, Amberlyn," she warns before disappearing around back. I glance back at Declan and I can't help it, I burst out laughing. I don't know if it is because I want to ease his guilt, trying to play it off as not a big deal, but soon he is laughing nervously, too.

When I finally calm down, I say, "Jeez, that was awkward."

"Sure was," he said before standing and pulling his wallet out.

"Oh no, you don't. I'm not getting in trouble for you!"

A smile pulls at his mouth as he concedes. "Fine, I'm just leaving a tip."

"No way, I don't want it. I know she is still watching, so just promise you'll come to lunch tomorrow. Wednesdays are horribly slow, and I'll be completely bored during this time."

I don't know why I said that. I need to draw back a little, and I hate how much it pleases me when he doesn't even blink, he just quickly says, "Yeah, I'll be here."

"Awesome. Have a great tour," I say as he heads for the door.

"Will do, have fun getting your tattoo. I can't wait to see it," he says with a wink. He sends me one last grin before he's gone, and as the door slams shut and silence fills the pub, I can't stand how alone I feel.

Or how my heart is still beating out of control.

I HAVE no clue why we are busy tonight. It makes no damn sense! It's a Tuesday and we were supposed to get off early so I can go get my damn tattoo, but it's looking like it's not going to happen.

"This is insane!" I complain as I pass out the pints of beers to everyone.

"It really is. Hopefully, it will die down soon."

When the door opens and a group of guys comes falling in, I send her a look. "I don't think so."

"Ugh! I got them. Keep the bar happy."

"I will," I say as she heads toward the group. Working quickly, I pass out pints, and when I'm asked for a whiskey on the rocks, I smile as I reach for the O'Callaghan Black. Every time my hand touches this bottle, I think of him, but then I curse myself because that is just dumb. Blah. But I can't help it; all I see are his gorgeous, thin lips coming toward mine. A part of me wishes that my aunt hadn't had interrupted us. Then I remember that he is not single, and I shouldn't be kissing him. That causes me to get mad because he almost kissed me, and he is engaged! Damn it, this is so stupid, and I need to just stop it with the Whiskey Prince. He is bound to get me in trouble just like his potent whiskey would. But, like an addict, I don't know if I can.

Ignoring my depressing feelings, I hurry to fill orders.

"Amberlyn, I need a pint, please."

I glance up to see Kane leaning against the bar with his brows pulled together, and I know that something wrong. "Everything okay?" I ask as I quickly fill him a pint and pass it his way.

"Tough day," he says with a shake of his head. "Had to deal with this arse of a gobshite."

I smile. "Yeah, Declan told me he had a tour today."

"Yeah, it fucking sucked," he says before taking a long pull of his beer. Wiping his mouth with his hand, he looks back at me as he asks, "I thought ya were getting a tattoo tonight?"

"Do you see the pub? We aren't going anywhere."

"It'll slow down," he said with a shrug. "No worries."

"Says the guy who gets to drink beer and not have to serve anyone."

He toasts his pint to me as he laughs. "Touché"

I send him a smirk before rushing to the end of the bar to serve the sandwich my aunt has laid out for me. Taking the cash from the patron, I turn to put it in the register when my gaze meets his.

Holy shit.

"So I heard that the Whiskey Prince has been coming in here, and I can see why. Where did you come from, beautiful? Must have been heaven because you are simply an angel."

Wow, corny much? But even so, I can only blink as I look into the sharp blue eyes of this beautiful stranger. He is something, that's for sure. Thick, blond hair that is in disarray under the ball cap he wears, shoulders thick and broad, his waist trim, and a smile that is unstoppable. Good Lord, he is mighty fine.

"Nope, America."

He smiles as he pushes up on the bar, his eyes boring into mine, but I am looking at his arms, full of tattoos, even his neck has them. They are amazing designs, and I want to get closer to see what they are. I want to know him. I don't know why because he is obviously not my type, but I'm attracted to him for some reason.

"Ah, the Yank, sure, I've heard of you, but no one told me you were better looking than Fiona."

I don't know how to answer, so I just smile as I try to remember what I'm doing. Oh yes, serving people. "What can I get you?"

"Your number, and if the Whiskey Prince is here, point me in his direction."

"He isn't here, Casey. What's it to ya, anyway?"

We both look over to where Kane is looking at Casey with a look that could kill. I've never seen Kane look so mad, and I wonder what is going on because his scary look doesn't seem to scare Casey. He is just laughing.

"He doesn't come out for years, and he used to be my pal. I'd like to say hi," Casey says before winking over at me, but the tension in the air makes me feel like there is more to the story than that.

"He is no friend of yours. I don't want to hear you mention him again, or we can take this outside," Kane threatens. Before I can say anything, Fiona is there.

"What's going on? Everyone good?"

Kane is holding Casey's gaze, but while Kane looks like he is about to break a beer bottle on the bar and stab Casey in the neck, Casey is grinning, with no cares in the world.

"Nothing at all," Kane says, snaking an arm around Fiona's waist. She looks back at me and shrugs her shoulders. I don't know what to do or say, so I look back at Casey and say again, "Can I get you something?"

"Sure, a whiskey straight up, and don't think I have forgotten that you're going to give me your number."

I laugh as I reach for the whiskey, pouring him a glass before sliding it to him. "Never said I would."

"Not yet, but you will," he says with the kind of smile that could knock me on my ass. There is something about him. He is a complete bad boy, and I like that. "How ya liking Ireland? Loving it?"

I nod. "Yes, very much so."

"Yeah, it was okay, but now that I know you are here, I feel like the sun will be shining bright tomorrow."

I bite into my lip, trying to hold my laughter in. "Wow, laying it on thick aren't you?"

"Is it working?"

"Maybe," I say with a wink before going down the bar to refill some pints. I can feel his hot gaze on me. I know he is checking me out, and I like how it makes me feel. I'm glad that I wore a pair of short shorts and a yellow tank that shows off my breasts. I don't know why I want to look good to him, but I do, and I'm glad that my sunburn has lightened up into a small tan. When I glance over my shoulder at him, he is smiling at me, moving his thumb along his bottom lip, causing my nipples to harden against my tank. Jesus, he is fine, and it surprises me how hot I am for him.

He is the first guy since Declan that I am actually attracted to, and I feel like the forces beyond are trying to push me away from Declan—for good reason, of course. Maybe my mom brought Casey to me to distract me from my feelings. I can't do anything to risk Declan's relationship with whomever he is with, and because of that, I feel like I need to act on this attraction. Moving toward him,

I say, "I like your tattoos."

His eyes don't leave mine as he says, "Thanks, I did some of them, but it's hard to tattoo yourself."

"Oh cool, so you're a tattoo artist?"

"Yup, the best in town."

I smile as I lean into the bar. "Wow! I'm going to go get my first one tonight."

"I know. You are coming to my shop. That's why I'm here. I came to pick ya up."

His eyes are dancing with mischief, and I can't help but love being under his gaze. He makes me feel tingly all over, and I like him—he is intoxicating. "You lie."

"Never! I wouldn't do such a thing. Not to such a looker of a lady."

I eye him, a grin playing on my lips, as I say, "You're a total flirt."

"Oh sure, I am, and you like it. You do; I can tell."

I shrug. "Maybe."

"No maybe about it. I know you do. By the end of the night, I'll have your number and my artwork will be on your skin."

I love his confidence, and I especially love the way he is looking deep in my eyes as he grins. I like the color of his eyes too. They aren't your normal light blue. No, they are dark, almost purplish, and they have me gasping as I get lost in the depths of them. I can't help but feel drawn to him, and I know he is bound to be a fun time.

"Sure, why not."

"Atta girl!" he yells as he stands up, clapping his hands together. He leans against the bar, taking my face in his hands before laying a loud, smacking kiss on my lips. It happens so fast that when he pulls away, his eyes boring into mine, I don't know what to do, but I do know that my lips are tingling from the quick feel of his. His eyes are darker, his smile beaming, and I have to smile back, instead of hitting him upside his head, as I would have done to any other guy that would kiss me without even taking me to dinner first.

"By the way, the name's Casey Burke."

"Amberlyn Reilly."

His grin grows as his gaze drops to my lips. My heart bangs against my ribs, and I swear he is going to kiss me again, but instead, he says, "A beautiful name for a beautiful girl."

Oh, he is good. Butterflies are fluttering in my stomach as he holds my gaze. I thought tonight I was going to only mark off the *do something drastic* by getting my tattoo, but I am beginning to think that I might be able to mark off *take a risk* too.

Because Casey Burke is a walking risk.

One I want to take.

eight
Declan

There's a party at the Carney.

I look down at my phone and laugh. So what if there is a party? Why would Kane tell me that? I won't go. I haven't been to a party at the Carney since I was eighteen, and I have no desire to go to one now. No fucking way.

Amberlyn is going.

Okay, maybe I will go.

Sitting up out of my chair, I put down the book I'm reading, *The Hobbit*, since Amberlyn had mention loving the *Lord of the Rings*. I hadn't read it in a while and decided that tomorrow we could discuss it, if I can keep myself from trying to kiss her again. Man, that was close and so wrong of me. I haven't even told her I like her or even run the idea of going out with me across her, and I was about to kiss the hell out of her. I mean, really devour her beautiful, pouty lips. I don't know what came over me. Usually, I have more control of my actions, but with her, my control is shot. She constantly has my head spinning and my heart racing. It's crazy, and I think that it's about time for me to do something about it.

Not sure what that will be, but we've been doing this dance of getting to know each other too long. I know there is a chance she will say no because she is still recovering from the loss of her mother, but I feel like I could help her with that. I could kiss away each tear. It would be an honor, and I know I can be the man who her parents would want for her. Rounding the corner of the hall, I halt when I come face-to-face with my ma. I reach out, taking my mother by the back of the arm to steady her. She smiles as she brings me in for a tight hug.

As we part, she asks, "Declan? Where are you off to?"

"I'm going out."

She cups my face. "Good, I've noticed you've been out a lot. The media are going nuts about it."

I know, and it makes no sense. How do they catch me without me knowing? It drives me insane. "Sure, I've seen it."

"They say you've been at the Céad Míle Fáilte. Someone there worth your time?"

She is meddling, but I don't expect anything less from her. I'm surprised that Lena hasn't been asking me questions either. Of course, I want to tell her about Amberlyn, but I want to wait until things are where I want them. I don't want to bring her up, and Ma immediately starts planning our wedding. I know for sure that would scare Amberlyn off, and plus, I don't even know if I want that with her. Yes, I am attracted and I like her a lot, but I don't know how we work as a couple. I need that before I start screaming from the rooftop that Amberlyn Reilly is my gal.

"Yeah, the best damn beer in town."

She scolds me with her eyes before playfully smacking me. "Fine, don't tell me, but be careful, okay?"

I nod. "Sure, Ma."

"Grand. Well, have fun tonight."

"Will do," I say before placing a kiss to her cheek and then walking toward the door. Our butler opens the door for me and follows me out to open the door of my car. I smile my thanks before getting in and driving off. My nerves are fried, and my heart hasn't stilled since Kane said Amberlyn would be at the Carney. I really don't want to go, but I will deal with it as long as I get to see Amberlyn out of the pub. Not that I don't love seeing her there because I do, but I want to see what it is like between us outside of it. Does she only like me because I'm a paying customer, or does she like me for me? I hope that she does since I'm almost positive she wanted to kiss me this afternoon. It may have been all in my head, but then again, her breathing hitched and I saw her eyes start to drift shut.

It was the hottest thing I had ever seen.

Letting my foot push the pedal harder, I drive with ease down the winding roads to the Carney. When I see the rows of cars and then the lights, I know I have reached it. It hasn't changed much in the last couple of years, and like before, couples are in every place, getting a feel as drunks move around them like they aren't there. Cups and bottles litter the ground, and people are everywhere. This is what the Carney is known for—beer, sex, and drugs—all outside. Smashing time, right? Yeah, it used to be my scene, not so much anymore.

Weaving through the crowds as the music pulsates around me, I keep an eye out for Kane. He messaged me that they were by the bonfire where the DJ is. When I come up to that spot, I see Amberlyn first. She is dancing with Fiona, a wide smile on her face as they hold hands, dancing to the techno beat. Her hair is moving, her breasts bouncing, and fuck, I'm getting hard just watching her. I blame it on the shirt; it shows way more of her delectable breasts than usual, and it doesn't help that the shorts are shorter than normal either. She looks so carefree, so happy, that a wide smile comes over my lips.

When a hand comes down on my shoulder, I look over to find Kane. He is grinning like an eejit, handing me a beer as his eyes redirect to where the girls are dancing.

"Glad you came," he yells over the music.

"Couldn't miss seein' her."

As she bends over, shaking her ass in Fiona's pelvic area, I know that this was the best idea ever. God bless Kane, such a great friend for inviting me. I don't even care that we are in a cesspool of vermin. Nope, all I care about is that gorgeous girl dancing with no cares in the world.

"Reminds me," he says and I look over, but before he can say anything, someone clasps my wrist. Looking back, Amberlyn is grinning up at me.

"You're here!"

I nod. "Yeah, came for the party."

"That's so cool! I'm drunk; can you tell?"

I laugh because I can. Her eyes are glassy, and she is sort of wobbling. "Just a tad."

She laughs as she leans into me. I can smell her flowery smell, and it clouds my senses as she says, "I got my tattoo!"

"Let me see then," I yell over the music.

She grins as she pulls her shirt up too far, not only giving me a great view of her black lace bra but also, the very fresh tattoo. Being a gentleman, I do my best to ignore that I can see her rosy bud through the lace of her bra and focus solely on the tattoo. It's an intricate design, the names Ciara and Tomas intertwined with the lines of the sparrow. It is beautiful.

"Breathtaking," I say.

"I love it so much," she whispers. I can barely hear her, but I can see the tears welling up in her sweet eyes. She is strumming my heartstrings. I want nothing more than to wrap her up in my arms and never let go. Shaking her head, she grins up at me and yells, "Catch up with me! Drink! Then let's dance!"

I'm not much of a dancer, but I'd give it a go just for the excuse to touch her. Before I can say that though, she says, "Oh wait! No, we can't do that."

"We can't?" I ask as Fiona laughs loudly, wrapping her arms around Amberlyn.

"Come on, let's go dance!" she says, pulling Amberlyn away before I can ask again why we can't dance together. I watch them for a moment before turning to Kane.

"What was that about?"

Kane looks nervous, a little off-put as he shrugs. "Listen, I didn't know he was coming."

"He? Who the fuck is he?"

Kane nods toward the girls again, and when I turn, I see Amberlyn in the arms of someone else. Someone I hate. Someone I'd love nothing more than to kill. My nails bite into my palms as my heart pounds so loudly that it's the only thing I hear. I see nothing but red as Casey Burke's hands run all over Amberlyn's body. The body I want to touch and cherish.

"What the fuck?"

"I don't fuckin' know, Dec, I come into the pub for a beer, and next thing I know, he's in there, hitting on her and shit. I thought you had her locked down?"

I shake my head slowly as I run my hands through my hair, knocking my hat off. Leaning down, I pick it up before putting it back on my head. "Not yet. Fuck me."

Kane shook his head. "She seems to fancy him, but I know she fancies ya more! You should have danced with her."

"I didn't have a chance to say yes. Fuck," I say again, kicking the ground and throwing my beer to the side as I watch that piece of shit rub on the first girl I've had feelings for in a long while. "What do I do?"

"Tell her how ya feel! She'll forget all about him."

My body shakes with anger and maybe nerves as I watch them. Amberlyn looks beautiful, carefree, as she moves against him while holding Fiona's hands. They are having a grand time while I'm sitting here, fucking pissed. Damn it. "Now? Do I tell her now?"

He shakes his head, his eyes out on where Fiona is watching him as she dances. "No, they are drunk. Wait till tomorrow."

"Sure, yeah, okay. I'm getting out of here. Should've told me he was here."

Kane nods. "I was hoping that you'd ignore him and stay."

"Sorry, pal. Gotta go."

"Sure, see ya tomorrow."

I glance back at Amberlyn. "You make sure she gets home, okay?"

He nods, a smile playing on his lips. "Yeah, I'm driving."

"Great, see ya tomorrow."

"Night," he says as I start to walk away, but first I look back at where Amberlyn is swaying to the music, her eyes closed as she gets lost in the music. When Casey's lips come along her jaw, I want nothing more than to go over there and knock his teeth out, but I can't. What happened is over. Nothing I can do to change what the outcome was. I just have to live with it and do everything in my power to make sure that Casey Burke never hurts anyone else I care for again.

Especially Amberlyn.

Sleep wasn't an option the night before until Kane texted me to say they got home okay and that Amberlyn was safe and sound. I wish I wouldn't have left, but to protect my reputation, I knew I had to. Casey brought out the worst in me, and I couldn't risk embarrassing myself in front of Amberlyn. I know I would have, so I trusted that Kane would take care of the situation, and from my understanding, he did.

"Yeah, I dropped them off. Fiona came out after getting Amberlyn in bed. We made out a bit, and then she went back in."

I reach for the car door. "Was Casey all over her still?"

Kane looks away as he tucks his hands into his pockets. "Yeah, they look pretty homey."

"What the fuck, man. Should I even go?"

Kane shakes his head. "Man, I don't know, but if ya want her, go get her, or shut the hell up. I'm tired of it."

What a wanker! "For fuck's sake, I'm just asking what you think!"

"Why does it matter what I think? You don't do it anyway."

"I do, too! I go out now, I do things, and I'm about to go tell Amberlyn I'd fancy a chance to take her to lunch or dinner."

Kane rocks back on his heels as he lets out a long breath. "You're right. It's just that I'm worried this is going to go bad, and then you'll go back to the way you were. I'm just nervous for ya."

"Well thanks, now I'm really confident about this."

Kane shrugs his shoulders, and I can see the worry all over his face. Expelling a long breath, he says, "Be true to her, Dec. Tell her the truth. If it doesn't work out then… I don't know, man. Just promise me you won't go back to the hermit."

My body is shaking with nervousness, but I promise. "I won't."

"Good, off with you then. Go get your woman."

I send him a wave before getting into my car and driving off. I have ten minutes before I get there. As I drive, my heart is pounding against my chest. I try to play the words that I want to say in my head, but I don't know them. I don't know how to sell myself to a girl because I've never had to. They've always come to me. Now the girl I want could be off the market and out of my hands. It irritates me, and within seconds, the whites of my knuckles are showing as I grip the steering wheel too hard. Soon doubt fills me as I pull into the pub, and I don't want to get out of the car.

We've been talking for weeks now. Every day I come here, and we chat while I eat. It's been the best times of my day. If I go in there and she doesn't feel the same for me, then everything will be ruined. Will I still come here? Would I keep my promise to Kane? I don't know but before I can talk myself out of going inside, I jump out, locking the door as I head in. When the door shuts behind me, I look up to see Amberlyn with her head on the bar, her arms outstretched before her, hanging over the edge.

"Don't mind me, first full-blown Irish hangover."

I chuckle as I head toward the bar, pulling out a stool beside her and sitting down as she says, "Where did you go last night? You disappeared."

So she noticed. That's a good sign. I don't want to tell the truth, so I say, "I had to go back home to give my ma some milk."

She looks over at me, and my heart drops for her. Her eyes are glassy, her face flushed, and her hair is a mess. She looks like roadkill, but she is still so beautiful to me. "Don't you have servants to do that?"

I chuckle. "I do."

"So why did you do it?"

I shrug. "I needed an excuse for why I went home."

She sits up, looking deep into my eyes. "You don't need an excuse with me, Declan. Just tell me the truth."

"I didn't want to watch that tool all over you."

She only blinks, and then her brows come crashing together. "Why does it matter to you who's all over me? Plus, he wasn't all over me. We were dancing."

I looked away and then say, "Because it does. I don't like it."

I look up to find her still watching me. The place is dead, but it's silent too. She doesn't have music playing like usual. I feel myself breaking out in a sweat, and it's rolling down the middle of my back. She makes me nervous.

"Sorry if this comes off rude, but you don't have any right not to like it. I shouldn't matter to you."

I lean back in my seat as I scoff. "Is that so?"

She nods. "Declan, you are engaged. You're not entitled to have a say in what I do, especially when you already have someone, and we aren't dating, for that matter."

I lean in toward her because surely I've heard her wrong. "Come again?"

She looks confused as she asks, "What didn't you understand?"

"The 'I have someone' part. I'm not engaged."

Her beautiful face scrunches up as she says, "What? Yes, you are!"

I shake my head quickly. "No, I'm not. I've never been engaged."

Looking away, she lets out a breath before grabbing a pint and filling it. I want to tell her I'm not thirsty, but then I realize she isn't pouring it for me. She drains the pint before setting it down and shaking her head again. Looking up at me, she points and asks, "You're not engaged?"

"No."

"Well, fuck me," she says, and I smile.

"Well, if you're offering, I'd like to take you to dinner first. Maybe get to know you a little better before."

Her mouth turns up at the side, but then it falls just as fast as it comes. She shakes her head slowly. "I wish I would have known you were single before because I'm sort of seeing someone right now."

I feel like she is stabbing me with each word she says after *because,* but I can't let her see that. So holding her gaze, I say, "So stop, let me take you to dinner tonight."

"He's taking me," she whispers, looking sad as she says it. I hate the words. Hate them with everything inside me. I want to beg her to say no and go with me, but that would make me look desperate. "I'd feel weird dating both of you at the same time. It isn't fair to either of you."

I nod as my fingers bite into my thighs. "I guess I should have acted sooner. I lost my chance."

She looks down at the bar, playing with the edge of it as she whispers, "Don't say that."

"Why?"

"Because I don't want to believe it. I know that we don't know each other well, but I like you a lot, Declan. I would love the chance to get to know you better."

I want to run and hide. But at the same time, I never want to leave, afraid that I'll never see her like this again. In here, just us, life is great. Outside of these walls, life is shit, and it irritates the living hell out of me. My heart is out of control in my chest, and blood is rushing to my head. I want to say that to her. Knowing she has the same feelings has me holding on to the stool so I don't fall off. I don't know what to say next. When she looks up, looking at me through her long, dark lashes, I'm breathless.

"I like you, too."

Did I just say that?

She slowly lets out a long breath. "I don't know what will happen between Casey and me. It could be nothing, but I've said yes, so I need to honor that," she says as she folds her hands nervously.

I nod my head, looking down at the bar. "I respect that."

"I'm sorry."

"Don't be."

"I feel like I'm ruining everything between us," she says, unsure of herself, so I reach out, my hand shaking as I take hers in mine. Her hand is small, warm, and so soft. It calms me but at the same time, it excites me at the possibility of her body feeling just like this.

When she looks up at me, I smile. "Never. I won't say that my pride isn't dented or that I'll wait for you, but I hope that I get the chance to show you who I am."

"Me too."

I'm taking this better than I thought I would. Maybe because I know Casey can't carry a candle compared to me. He is the slime of the universe, and the thought of her going out with him scares me.

Taking in a deep breath, I say, "Promise me something though, Amberlyn."

"Anything."

"Be careful," I stress, my eyes locked on hers. "Call me whenever, don't worry about the hour, and always text Fiona to let her know where you are."

She looks confused, but she agrees. "Okay."

When the door opens and we both look back to find the man of the hour walking in, our hands part, slowly sliding away from each other, and even though I don't want to, I decide that it's time for me to go.

nine
Amberlyn

*D*id that just happen?

My head is pounding and I feel like I'm going to puke, but I'm not sure if it is the hangover or what just happened with Declan. I want to cry, but at the same time, I want to cut Fiona. But then again, I should have freaking asked! Instead, I sat back and allowed myself to fall for a guy I thought I couldn't have, when in all reality, I could. I mean, fuck! That's not fair. Life isn't fair! I mean seriously, the last couple of months have been hard, and then this? Really?

I guess I could cancel my date with Casey, but that is so incredibly rude. And I know if I make up an excuse, he'll figure out another way to ask me. I've only spent a little bit of time with him, but I feel like I've known him for years. He is so open, very persistent, and I do like him. He is nice, hot, and funny, but he isn't Declan. I've had a thing for Declan since the moment I saw him, and now he's sitting here, telling me he has feelings for me, and I have to turn him down. How is that fair?

And to top it all off, now Casey is here, and Declan is pulling his hand from mine.

I mean, really, if someone would have told me I was going to be in this moment months ago, I would have laughed at them. I went from being the most unavailable person to having not only one guy wanting me but also the fucking royalty of Mayo. Seriously? How does this happen? I am having a hard time believing it, and to make sure this isn't a drunken dream, I pinch myself. When pain shoots up my arm, I groan. Fucking hell.

I didn't even know Casey was coming, and by the looks of it, Declan is not happy to see him. I have no clue what is going on between these two, but I have every intention on finding out. Casey, on the other hand, doesn't seem to care one way or another. His eyes are on me, a grin on his face, and a single daisy in his hand. He looks great today, too. His blond hair is a mess, and it looks like he just rolled out of bed, but I find it sexy. As he comes around the bar, gathering me in his arms and hugging me tightly, I find myself breathless. He smells good, spicy and sexy. When I look up into his face, I find myself smiling, even though I feel like shit. His eyes are bright as he leans down and brushes his lips on my cheek.

I try to back away some because I don't want Declan seeing this. I feel like an ass just hugging Casey, but he is grinning and he has a daisy. I can't exactly just wave.

"You look like hell today," he says, and I laugh.

"Wow, thanks." I pull myself from his arms and glance over to the bar to find that Declan isn't there. When I look out the window, I catch his car speeding out of the parking lot and my heart drops. Damn it, I might have just fucked that all up.

"Doesn't mean you don't look hot, too," he whispers in my ear.

I laugh as I push him away, but he isn't letting me go. He pulls me back into his arms and looks deep in my eyes. I look up, surprised, because I have never been handled like this before and it's weird. I don't like being pulled around, but it seems like Casey does that a lot. I've only known him for a day, and he's kissed me more in one night than I've been kissed my whole life. It makes me nervous, but at the same time, I wonder if this is how a relationship is.

"Ugh, no making out in the pub. Take that shite outside," Fiona says, causing me to jump in surprise. I wiggle out of Casey's arms and grab a rag to act as if I am wiping the counter. He laughs as he comes around the bar, going on a stool and setting Fiona with a look.

"Don't act like you have never done it."

Fiona flips him the middle finger before going to the back, leaving me alone with him. I want to ask her to come back out. I don't know why it is weird today with him. I was so comfortable with him yesterday. Was it the alcohol? Or is it the fact that I now know Declan is single? How shitty is that? Casey has done nothing but be nice to me. Yeah, we may need to set some ground rules on the whole touching me thing, but he's a nice guy. He brought me a daisy. But then again, something is off. I don't know. I just feel weird.

"What brings you in?"

He smiles. "You. I thought we'd make plans for tonight."

I smile back at him. "Of course, what would you like to do?"

"Anything you want. We can go driving, we can go to dinner, go back to my place, whatever you like."

The only thing that appeals to me is dinner. "Dinner would be great. I'm not working tonight."

"Great. So I'll pick you up at six?"

I nod. "That would be fine."

"Awesome," he says. Getting up, he leans over the bar toward me. I'm pretty sure he is going to kiss me, so I ask, "How do you know Declan O'Callaghan?"

He pauses, his strong forearms on the bar as he looks at me. "Went to school together."

"Do you two get along?"

He shrugs. "Sure, why?"

"Just asking."

"Do you talk?"

I nod. "Yeah, he comes in to eat almost every day."

He eyes me suspiciously, and I have no clue what that is about. "Yeah, like I said, we went to school together, used to be friends, but not so much anymore. He doesn't really come out and mingle with the common folk anymore. He let the money go to his head like the rest of the O'Callaghans do."

I don't believe that for a second, but I smile anyway. "Oh, he seems nice to me when he comes by, but I guess I don't know him that well."

"Yeah, he's a shithead. Watch out for that one," he says before hopping off the stool. "I'll see ya tonight."

"All right, bye."

He sends me one last grin before shutting the door behind him. I lean against the bar, resting my chin in my hand as I replay our conversation. Why was that weird? Forced even? And why can't I stop thinking about the way Declan held my hand?

"Thank God, he's gone."

I jump once more and send Fiona a disgruntled look. "You scared the living shit out of me."

She laughs. "My bad."

"No worries," I say as she passes by me, her arms full with the plastic tray from the dishwasher. "You don't like Casey?"

She looks up at me as she loads the glasses in the cabinets. "He's annoying. I went to school with him, dated him for a while too. He's okay but not really my favorite person. I'm surprised you fancy him, actually. He's an eejit. You should ignore him."

"Why's that? And when did y'all date? Is it okay that I'm dating him?

Fiona throws her hands up, palms facing me, as she sets me with a look. "Whoa! You're dating him?"

"Yeah, he asked me to dinner."

She lays the tray on the bar and wipes her hands on her apron. "Okay, first, we dated when I was like fifteen. It was mainly just sex."

"You had sex with him?" I gasp. "That is not cool! I can't date him when you slept with him."

"That's not the reason you can't date him."

I'm confused. "Huh? This doesn't make sense. You're my cousin, my best friend… Why would he go after me if he's slept with you?"

Fiona only looks at me, her eyes holding mine for so long that I don't know if I should say something. She looks as if she is deep in thought, and I'm not sure what to think of it. "Listen, Casey has some history. He may think you don't know his history and that you'll give him a fair chance. Most of the ladies in this town already know, but I'm not letting this happen. Like you said, you are my cousin, my best friend, so no way."

My heart speeds up as she continues to hold my gaze. "What? What history?"

Fiona lets out a breath. "Don't get mad, okay? I didn't think you'd actually go out with him. I thought we were just having fun last night, and he is the best tattoo artist in town. Now I see he is blinding you, and there is no way I can let you go out with him. I mean, it's your choice, but I strongly advise that you don't."

"What are you talking about? What's going on?"

"He was accused of raping someone."

My heart drops. Surely not. Casey? "Excuse me?"

"It wasn't proven. It is only rumored, but yeah. Mostly everyone believes it."

My heart is pounding, my throat dry, and I feel dirty. "I let him touch me. Why didn't you say anything last night?"

"Kane was there, I was there, nothing was going to happen, and like I said, I didn't think you really fancied him, Amberlyn. I understand that he is hot, but I thought you were only havin' a bit of craic."

I'm shaking my head before she finishes talking. "I was, but I liked him. I thought he was nice."

Fiona shrugs her shoulders. "He's charming. He never treated me badly. That's why I find it hard to believe, but people who know the girl claim it to be true."

"The girl?"

"Lena O'Callaghan."

Declan's sister. "Oh, fuck."

Fiona nods. "Yeah, it wasn't pretty, but a lot of it was covered up because Lena was out with an eighteen-year-old, drinking at fifteen. He apparently left her outside the gate, drunk and passed out. She was found by the guards, and when her ma was getting her to bed, she noticed bruises and scratches all over Lena's thighs. They took her to the clinic, and they said she had been raped, but since her mom gave her a bath, there was no evidence to get, ya know? Everyone saw her with Casey though, but he still claims it wasn't him. I don't think anyone believed him. Lena doesn't remember what happened, so they couldn't really press charges. Old Man O'Callaghan has been trying to get him out of town for years. Last I heard, he offered to pay him to leave. He won't, though."

While I want to know why, my head is spinning, and I feel like I might throw up again. That is insane. The guy who touched me, gave me a tattoo, and kissed me had apparently raped a girl? Left her outside a gate, drunk? And I was about to go out with said guy? Shaking my head, I lean against the bar, before crying out and standing back up. I leaned right up against where my new tattoo is. Rubbing my tender skin, I look over at Fiona. "I can't go out with him."

"No, you can't. Ma and Da will have a fit. Ma doesn't even like him in the bar."

"Wow. I wish you'd never let me go anywhere near him."

"I honestly didn't think anything of it. I mean, you like Declan. They are completely opposite."

She was right. "Yeah, I guess. No wonder Declan hates him."

"Oh yeah, so does Kane. They all used to play on the same hurling team together in school. That's how Casey met Lena. He claimed he loved her and all kinds of other stuff before this happened, but her da wasn't having any of it. He said that Casey wasn't good enough for Lena. So they saw each other in secret. Lena claimed they never had sex, so did Casey, but he could have gotten in trouble if they had. So no one really knows, but it was quite the scandal."

I am flabbergasted by all this. I know that these kinds of things happen in the world all the time, but I've never been face-to-face with it. It has me trembling, and I can't believe it. Plus, what the hell do I say to him? I mean, this is insane. Do I tell him the truth that yes, there could be a chance that this is all hoopla, but I can't risk the chance that it's not? I mean, how is that fair to him? He has been nice to me, and I am going to write him off from one rumor. At the same time, what if Aunt Shelia forbids it? I know I am a grown woman, but I respect her. Oh for goodness' sake, why am I even entertaining this? I may not know if it is true, but I know I won't be able to look at Casey Burke the same. He has been ruined for me.

"This is nuts."

Fiona nods as she wipes up the water on the floor from the plastic tray. "Yeah, the town talked about it for a good year before rumors of Declan's engagement came to surface."

"Which, by the way, isn't true."

She glances up at me. "What?"

"He isn't engaged."

"Yes, he is," she insists.

"No, he told me he isn't. He asked me out."

Her eyes go wide as she slowly stands. "The Whiskey Prince, Declan O'fucking-Callaghan, asked you out?"

I nod, my eyes wide, as I say, "Yeah."

"What the hell did you say?" she screeches.

"I said no. I was going out with Casey! I thought I would be a slut if I dated both of them!"

Fiona's hands shoot up in the air. "Are you kidding me? You don't say no to the Whiskey Prince! Are you crazy? And how does that make you a slut? I've dated multiple guys at once. You got to weed out the bad ones."

I roll my eyes. "I'm new to this, remember?"

"Oh yeah, but still, I can't believe you said no."

"Yeah, I can't either," I say as I let out a breath. "I'm pretty sure I've ruined everything with him too. Casey came in when he was here."

"Ack, and he didn't hit him? They don't usually coexist in the same place."

I shake my head, my mind still going a mile a minute from all of this. "Nope, he just left. He didn't even say bye to me."

And I feel so…so…lost. I don't know what to do about Casey, or Declan, for that matter. Of course, I'm going to call off the date with Casey, but do I call Declan? Do I tell him that I decided I don't want to date Casey and that I want to date him? Will he even want to see me?

"You look so sad, Amberlyn. I hate that. I'm sorry. You have to understand why I told you."

I nod, looking over at my cousin. She is working her lip, and I can tell she is worried about me too. "No, I know, and I think that Casey had no chance. Not when I really want Declan."

She comes over and wraps her arms around me. I lean into her, needing the comfort and love. I rest my head on her shoulder as I say, "I just hope he still wants me."

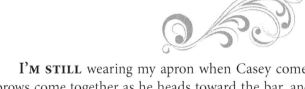

I'M STILL wearing my apron when Casey comes in later that night. His brows come together as he heads toward the bar, and my stomach drops. He cleaned up, his hair brushed, and his clothes neatly ironed. He really had tried, and I'm about to cancel our plans, but it wasn't fair to him or me. I can't believe I actually thought Casey had a chance. The more I thought about it, the more I know I was stupid to think that. I also really need to work on my judgment of character. The first time he kissed me should have been a warning sign, but no, I thought my mom sent him to me. Blah, I'm so naïve.

Leaning against the bar, he reaches for me, but I sidestep out of the way. I'm not sure if he notices, but still, with a grin, he says, "You ready?"

"Hey, sorry, can we go outside real fast?"

"To leave?" he asks as I go around the bar. I don't answer him as I walk past him, heading out the side door. He follows behind me, and when I shut it, he is practically towering over me. I take a step back, crossing my arms as he asks, "What's going on?"

"I am sorry, but I can't go out with you tonight, or any night for that matter," I say softly, watching his face as it slowly turns from confusion to annoyance.

"No?"

"No, Casey. It was unfair of me to make a commitment to you. While I am attracted to you and I like you as a person, I've been sort of seeing someone else."

"Sort of seeing?"

"Yeah, I didn't know if he felt the same, but today he informed me he did, and because I care for him, I don't think it would be fair to try to start something with you when I have no desire to."

He scoffs. "That's a load of bullshite, and you know it. Fiona told you about us, and then probably told you about Lena. It isn't true, you know. I didn't touch her."

"I understand that, but you did sleep with my cousin, and that's just weird for me."

"It was centuries ago!" he complains. "I don't even fancy her at all. I want you."

"I don't feel the same. I'm sorry."

"Why are you lying?" he asked incredulously, and my heart picks up in speed.

His shoulders are taut, his eyes are blazing with anger, and I hate to say it, but I'm a little scared. I shouldn't have come out here with him. Looking toward the door, I beg Fiona to come out. Glancing back at Casey, I say, "I'm not. I'm sorry that I have upset you and I wish you the best, but nothing can happen between us."

"I know you want me."

I shake my head. "I'm sorry, I don't. I think I was trying to distract myself with you to keep myself from feeling something for the other person. I feel like shit about it, but nothing will ever happen between us."

"I feel something between us. I know you want it."

"No, I actually don't—"

Before I can finish my sentence, my face is in his hands and his lips are moving against mine. My protest is lost against his lips. I try to push him away, but he is passionately, with tongue, kissing me. His grip on my face is ironclad. My heart is pounding so hard that it hurts. My eyes sting with tears as I slam my fist against his chest, but he isn't letting up. His hands tighten on my face, his nails digging into my skin, and I cry out. He takes advantage of that, pushing his tongue farther into my mouth. I want to vomit from the stale taste of cigarettes, but instead, I do the only logical thing.

I knee him in the groin.

Grunting, Casey rips his mouth from mine, pushing me away. I lose my balance, landing on my ass with a yelp, but I quickly move away from him as he yells, "You fuckin' bitch!"

My heart is in my throat, my eyes blurry with tears, and my face is throbbing with pain.

"Is everything okay?"

I jump as I look to the left to find a figure walking toward us as Casey yells, "Fuck off."

But the person keeps coming toward us until he is in the light. When I see that it is Kane, I thank the heavens above.

"Amberlyn, are you okay?"

"Yeah, fine," I say as I get up slowly.

"Mind your own, Kane," Casey warns, but Kane ignores him, looking me over.

"Are you sure?"

"I'm fine," I reassure him, but he must have seen the marks on my face because he whips around to set Casey with a look. Casey's hands come up, but before he can even say anything, Kane's fist connects with his face. I screech in surprise as he falls to the ground, holding his face.

"Get the fuck out of here, Casey, and don't come back. Don't you ever look at her again. Don't you even mutter her fuckin' name. I will hurt you if you do, you fuckin' wanker."

Casey shuffles to his feet before giving me a look. I think he is going to say something or hit Kane, but honestly, he'd be stupid to. Kane takes a step toward him, making Casey back away, and says, "Fuck off."

And then, Casey is gone.

Turning to me, Kane cups my face. "Are you sure you're okay?"

Fiona is so lucky. Kane is amazing, and I will always be indebted to him for being there for me. I nod as I say, "I am. I promise."

"He didn't touch you anywhere else, did he?"

I shake my head. "No, he kissed me, I kneed him in the balls, and then you showed up."

Kane laughs. "Attagirl!"

I smile as I cup my burning hot cheeks. "I'm glad you came when you did."

"Yeah, me too."

When my lip starts to wobble, Kane takes a step toward me, his hands on my arms as he looks at me with his coffee-brown eyes. "What is it?"

"I can't believe this happened. Why was I so stupid?"

His eyes soften as he wraps his arms around me. "No, you weren't stupid at all. Don't worry about it. Tomorrow is a new day, and Casey won't ever touch you again. If he does, I'll kill him."

I smile, but then I shake my head slowly. "Why did I come out here with him alone?"

Kane wraps his arms around me gently, pressing his lips tenderly to my temple. "Shhh, it's okay. It's over."

Yeah, it is over, but I just can't believe I was so stupid. I should have never agreed to go anywhere with him. I should have told him inside, but instead, I took a chance. Now my face hurts, and I feel violated. On top of all that, I can't help but think about Declan. How he would never do this to me. How I'm positive he'd treat me like I was his princess, unlike how Casey treated me. How did I let this happen? Looking up at Kane through tear-filled eyes, I say, "It's not only that. I fucked things up with Declan, too."

A smile pulls at his lips as he shakes his head. "I'm sure you can fix that. He's mad about you, Amberlyn."

Hopeful, I ask, "You think?"

"I know, so don't worry about that. Let's go in, get your face cleaned up, and then you can restart tomorrow. The sun will shine tomorrow, and so should you."

I jerk to a pause and look up at him quickly, completely shocked at the words he just muttered. My chest is heaving, my heart banging against my chest, and I almost don't believe what I just heard.

"My mom always said that."

His mouth curves into a warm grin as he says, "So does mine. Great moms think alike."

He wraps his arm around my shoulder, and as we walk toward the front entrance, my whole body is tingling. I am still reeling over the words he muttered. My mother's words. I know some don't believe in spirits and ghosts, but I do, and I can't help but think that my mom whispered in Kane's ear. In return, relief washes over me, and I know that tomorrow will be better.

Because she is looking out for me.

ten
Declan

I'm not sure why I'm here, but I am.

It's become a habit for me. I work through my scheduled lunch, make sure that all my workers are working, do whatever stupid paperwork is sent my way, and then I get in my car to head to the Céad Míle Fáilte. I've become a creature of habit, or maybe I'm just a glutton for punishment. I'm not sure, but before I know it, I'm walking up the cobblestones to the door and pushing it open.

And there she is.

She looks as hot as ever in a pair of worn jeans that hug every single inch of her and a green tank that I know would show off a nice view of her breasts if she were to turn to look at me. Her hair is down, reaching all the way to the middle of her back, and as she reaches up to put a bottle on the shelf, I get a glimpse of skin from where her shirt rises.

For fuck's sake, this was a bad idea.

Of course, my heart kicks into speed, my dick gets harder than a slab of marble, and I feel breathless. When she turns, a smile is on her face to greet me, but then surprise floods her face as her eyes meet mine. Slowly, the smile falls and she quickly gets off the ladder she is on to come toward the bar as I do the same.

"Hey."

I sit on the stool and say, "Howya," before reaching for the menu that sits before me. The tension is thick. I can feel her within reach and I want to touch her, but I know I can't. Through my lashes, I watch as she tucks her hands into her pockets before rocking back on her heels.

"Didn't think you'd be in today."

I glance up, and when I do, I wish I hadn't. Her face is flushed, her eyes shining, and Christ, her breasts are practically falling out of her shirt. She's stunning. It hurts but even more so when my eye is caught by the vase of daisies that sits behind her. I assume they are from that fucking gobshite and quickly look away as I say, "I have to eat."

I know that comes out a little harsher than I intended it to, so I look up, meeting her sad gaze, and add, "And it doesn't hurt that I like spending time with you."

A smile pulls at her lips, making me notice there are marks on her cheeks. Cuts, maybe. "What happened to your face?"

She looks away as she reaches for her pad of paper. Without looking at me, which isn't like her, she says, "Oh, nothing. I'm glad you came in. We have cottage pie today—your favorite. Would you like some? With a beer, maybe?"

"Sure, that's fine," I answer. She works quickly to fill my order, never meeting my gaze or even talking to me. I glance back at the daisies and roll my eyes at the mere sight of them. I want to ask how her date went, hoping she'd say they didn't go because a car hit Casey on the way to get her, but I don't want to know the answer if it isn't that one. Instead, I say, "Nice flowers."

She looks back at them and nods. "Yeah."

Yeah? That's all I'm going to get from her? I'm not sure what is going on, but I don't like it one bit. "Amberlyn."

"Yeah?" she says as she wipes the bar, still not looking at me.

"Can ya look at me real fast?"

Her hand stops on the bar before looking up at me. "What's up?"

I hold her gaze, and I know something is wrong. "Everything okay?"

"Yeah," she says before going back to wiping the bar.

"Are you sure? You're actin' weird."

She nods her head. "Yeah, just trying to get some work done. Sorry, I'm tired."

Yeah, from having a blast with that sheep-shaggin' fucker. My blood starts to boil as I stab at my pie, throwing it in my mouth, not really tasting it as I eat. Nothing is said as I finish and she meticulously cleans the bar, making sure not to miss a single germ. It's annoying, and I want to scream out from the mere stupidity of it all. So she is dating someone else when I had my heart set on dating her... Does it mean we can't be fucking friends? Laying my fork down, I sit up straight and set her with a look, intending to say just that, but before I can, Fiona flutters in.

"Howya, Declan!"

I nod before picking my fork back up. "Howya."

I look down to start eating, but before I can get a bit of pie to my mouth, Fiona exclaims, "Ugh! Amberlyn, why haven't you thrown these away yet?"

I glance up just in time to see Amberlyn shaking her head. What the hell is that about? Fiona glances at me and then slowly looks back at Amberlyn, her eyes wide.

"Okay," she draws out as she bends down, I guess to pick up something, but then I notice that Amberlyn bends down at the same time. This is just a fucking gas! Standing up, I look over the bar to find them whispering like little schoolgirls.

"Secrets don't make friends, ladies."

They both look up at me, surprised, before scrambling to their feet. Amberlyn looks over at me as Fiona rambles, "She was helping me tie my shoes."

I glance down to see her bright pink toes. "You're wearing flip-flops."

Amberlyn bites down on her lip as Fiona lets out a loud laugh. "Aye, you got us. You just look so hot today, Declan. You have us blushing!"

While it would do nothing but please me immensely to think Amberlyn thinks that, I know Fiona is lying. "Come off it, Fiona. I don't care. I can leave so ye can have your private talk."

"No, finish your lunch. I'm gonna go lie down. I'm supertired."

"Okay, I got this," Fiona says as she refills my pint. I watch as Amberlyn throws the rag in the sink before turning to look back at me. "Will you be in tomorrow?"

"Sure."

She gives me a small smile before saying, "Okay, see you tomorrow."

"Have a nice nap."

Her smile grows as her cheeks dust with color. "Thanks."

I grin as she turns around, watching as she walks away, but then she stops, grabbing the vase and tossing it in the can. She doesn't look back, leaving me to try to figure out why she did that.

"What's the matter with her?"

Fiona shrugs as she moves to the fridge before she starts to restock it with the beer Amberlyn carried in. "Tired, I guess. We worked late last night."

Huh? "I thought she went out with Casey."

Fiona pauses, only for a second, but I caught it. I know she is lying when she says, "Yeah."

I wait for her to say more, but it is obvious she isn't going to. "So she worked and went out?"

She nods without looking at me. "Sure."

"Are you lyin' to me?"

She looks up guiltily. "Yup, are ya done with this?"

She reaches for my plate, disappearing to the back before I can say anything. I don't know what her game is, but I don't like it. Doesn't she realize that I care for Amberlyn? That I would love to be able to take her out, get to know her outside of this fuckin' pub? When she comes back out, I'm still waiting, and I think she thought I wouldn't be.

"Yeah, I'm still here."

She smiles, shaking her head. "I don't know what you want, Declan. I can't say anything."

"Why?"

She shrugs, not looking at me again. She reminds me a lot of Amberlyn. They act more like sisters than cousins. They favor each other. "I have no clue."

I eye her. "Are you lying again?"

She nods with a grin playing on her lush lips. "Sure am."

Deciding that she is hopeless, I lay some money on the bar and then turn to leave.

"Did you give up on her?"

I pause, looking over my shoulder at her. "What do you mean?"

"On Amberlyn, did you give up because of Casey?"

"It's only been a day, Fiona. I just hope it doesn't work out."

"And then you'll ask her out?"

I nod, my face warming with color. "That's my plan."

She shoots me a wide grin, one that lights up her whole face, as she leans on the bar. "It's a good plan."

My mouth pulls up at the side, and I look down at the floor. Somehow, I feel as if she is telling me that things with Casey aren't going to last, and that alone has me practically skipping out the door to my car.

BACK AT the distillery, I'm catching up on work when my mother flutters in. I am surprised to see her but even more so when my sister comes in behind her. Lena is almost as tall as I am, skin and bones, with long, blond hair and ice-blue eyes. She has sharp angles to her face, but lush, pink lips that men gawk at. She looks like an ice princess, and I used to call her that, until Casey happened. I've always felt like what happened was my fault. I was the one who brought Casey around; I was the one who gave him her number when he asked for it. I thought it was innocent. He said he needed help with school. Casey was really bad off in history. He had failed before and had to repeat it, putting him in her class. Lena was a straight A student. I soon learned it was all a lie. He was looking to get in with my sister, to be set for life.

He comes from a poor family. His da ran out on them when he was born, and his ma has always been very sick, rendering him to care for her and work two jobs through school. However, he never let that interfere with his life. He always wore a bright smile; he was happy and carefree. He was a great pal, fun to play with out on the pitch, but that all came to a crashing halt when he came in, hands locked with Lena's, saying he wanted to marry her. She was so young, so innocent, and over the moon in love with the fucker. To this day, I still get so angry that my heart feels as if it will come out of my chest. I sometimes feel that he's another reason why I withdrew myself from everyone. How can someone claim to be your friend, but pursue your baby sister behind your back, and then rape her? It's horrifying, and I still can't believe it happened to her. She is such a beautiful person, inside and out, and despite what happened, she still smiles.

She reminds me a lot of Amberlyn.

Leaning back in my chair, I ask, "Ma, Lena, what brings ye by?"

It isn't like the distillery is on the way to the kitchen. It's a good five-minute drive, and they never make their way here. Ma smiles as she comes toward my desk. Something tells me I am not going to like what she is about to say. "We came up to tell you that we are having a White Ball!"

Yup, I don't fuckin' like it. Groaning, I say, "For fuck's sake, why?"

"Declan! Language!" she scolds as Lena giggles.

I roll my eyes. "I'm sorry, Ma, but why? Why do you have to do this?"

"Because we want to! It is set for a month from now on the nineteenth. Lena is going to help you find a date."

She claps her hands happily. I make a face as Lena snickers, her eyes gleaming with mischief. "The hell she will. I don't need help finding someone to come with me, Ma!"

She waves me off, smiling. "Well, in case you do, she said she'd help."

Lena smiles. "Yeah, Dec, I'm sure one of my friends would love the chance to date the Whiskey Prince."

Like a child, I stick my tongue out at her and she does it right back, grinning ear-to-ear. Glaring at her, I say, "Not a hope! I'm well capable of doing that myself!"

"Okay, well, good. Tell Kane the same, and please make sure you bring someone. Your da is very adamant on seeing you with someone since you've been going out so much."

"Yeah, I guess there is something better than the food at the Céad Míle Fáilte, huh, Dec?" Lena teases and I want to tell her to fuck off, but I don't want to get in trouble with Ma. So with a smile, I say, "Maybe so."

She laughs as she heads for the door. My ma gives me a tight smile before saying, "Please make sure you bring someone."

"Ma! I will, sheesh, off with you. I have work to do, and I don't want to discuss this anymore."

She rolls her eyes as she turns. "So much like your da, and for all that is good and holy, will you make sure she wears white!"

And then she is gone. I'm glad too because I was about to be even more of an arse if she wasn't. God, they drive me up the wall, and I wonder why I was glad to see them. Getting back to work, my mind is clouded with thoughts of Amberlyn. I wonder when a good time would be to ask her about Casey. I hope that, like Fiona implied, things will go south quickly so I can swoop in and show Amberlyn what a man really is. I still worry about her being with him, dating him, but I feel like Fiona has it under control. I want to question her decision to allow her cousin to date a rapist piece of shite, but that is her business, not mine. But the moment he does something wrong to her, it will be my fucking business.

Fuckin' tool.

When the door opens, I look up to see Kane coming toward me with my bottle of whiskey and two cups. I glance at the clock. It's nowhere near time for us to be done, and while I'm not one to oppose drinking during work hours, I still have a lot to do.

"Trouble in paradise?" I ask since his face is long too.

He doesn't answer as he falls in the seat in front of me, pouring us both a shot of whiskey before raising his glass up. I meet his in the middle and then bring the cup to my lips, taking a good, hearty swig of the warm liquor. Letting out a noise of satisfaction, I put down my cup. "What's up?"

"Don't get mad, okay?"

I let out a breath, taking another swig before I shake my head. "I hate when you say that because I know I'm going to get mad."

He nods. "Sure, sure, but you have to understand that I took care of the situation. Plus, I would have told ya sooner, but I got drunk as hell last night, slept at the pub, and was late to work. I've been swamped with work all day, and I haven't had time to get back to you about it. I didn't want to say this over the phone either."

I'm irritated by the time he is done talking. "Fuckin' hell, what?"

He takes a quick drink of his whiskey before meeting my gaze. "Amberlyn apparently called things off with Casey last night."

He pauses. I'm not sure why that would make me mad, but before I can ask him, he says, "And he attacked her."

I am out of my seat within a second. Leaning on the desk, my arms taut, I ask, "What the fuck? He did what?"

"He got ahold of her, dug his nails in her face, and made her kiss him, I guess. She kneed him in the balls. That's when I came in, fuckin' clocked him one, threatened to kill him if he came anywhere near her again, and that was it. She's all right, a little shook up, but she's a trooper."

My nostrils flare as my nails bite into the desk to the point where I am convinced they might just pop off, but I don't care, I am going to kill Casey fucking Burke.

"Now calm down, Dec. I told you, I took care of it."

"No, I'm going to fucking kill him," I say, coming around the desk, but he stops me.

"Won't do ya any good. I took care of it. He touches her again, you get him then, but now, it won't do anything but make you look crazy. Let it go."

I shake my head as I take in a deep, long breath. "I hate him."

Kane nods. "I know, we both do."

"Why would he do that to her?"

He shrugs. "He fancies her, I guess."

"Great way of showing it!"

"She called things off, and he got mad. I don't get it."

That doesn't soothe my anger. "I'll kill him. I swear to fuckin' God, he touches her again, I'll go away for her."

Kane laughs as he pats my shoulder. "I know it, and I'll sit right there beside you in the cell."

That causes a grin to grow on my face. He really is my best friend, but I can't appreciate that the way I should with the anger still coursing through my veins. I shake my head as I let out a long breath. Looking up at Kane, I ask, "Why didn't she tell me? I saw her today, I asked about her face, and she didn't tell me anything about it. Fiona is lying to me too. Why are they lyin' to me?"

Kane shakes his head. "I don't know."

That's not a good enough answer for me. "Well, I'm going to fuckin' find out!"

Passing by him, I go out the door and out to where Cathmor is waiting for me by a tree. Kane is running behind me, coming to a halt beside me. "What are you doing?"

"I'm going to go see Amberlyn and find out why she lied to me."

"Now?"

"Seems like as good a time as any," I reply before I greet my horse.

"Well, it just seems like you're mad. I think you might want to calm down."

"Well, it's either her or Casey. Pick one."

"Ugh, neither? Let's get drunk," he suggests, but I know I can't do that. If I do, I'm bound to do something stupid. I shake my head, looking back at Kane.

"I'll calm down before I get there. I need to know why she lied to me. Why she didn't tell me what was going on. Why doesn't she trust me?"

I have so many questions, but I don't want to sound like a total eejit, spilling my heart out to my best friend. I feel like I did the day before when she told me she was going out with him, like a failure, something I don't like. I don't understand what I have done not to earn her trust. I thought I had been really open with her, but maybe I haven't. I don't know, but I know I need answers and I need them now.

Thankfully, Kane doesn't say anything more, and within seconds, Cathmor is carrying me to where I need to be.

And that's with Amberlyn.

eleven
Amberlyn

I just want to go back to bed.

My head is pounding, and I just feel empty. Add the stuff that is happening with Casey and Declan to the fact that today is just a "bad Mom and Dad day," and that means I am just having the worst day ever. I woke up feeling like shit. Utter crap. I miss my mom, I miss my dad, I hate what Casey did, and I hate how things have played out with Declan. The night before has played over and over in my head, and I keep trying to figure out if there was a way I could have prevented it from happening.

Maybe I should've never gotten involved with him. Maybe I should have listened to the warning signs when they were flashing in my face. The first time he kissed me without even knowing my name should have told me that he wasn't the guy I was meant to get involved with. Instead, I used him to distract me from my feelings for Declan, and I can't believe how utterly stupid that was. I should have just left it alone, and let everything play out. Instead, I made bad choice after bad choice, and now, I just feel stupid. Downright dumb. I don't even know what I was thinking. He isn't my type, and I still took the risk when it wasn't the right one to take.

Blah.

I've always seen myself with someone like my dad. My dad was so respectful, worked hard to provide for his family, and loved with everything inside of him. There wasn't a day, and still isn't one, that I didn't know he loved me. It was all in his eyes and the things he did. He would buy my mom flowers just because, and he would leave little notes for me. He was never too tired to do things with my mom and me. We were his world, and I always said I would be with someone like him.

The main thing is that I want to be wooed, I want to be wined and dined, and I want the romance that my mom had. What a whirlwind it was! She didn't like my dad at first, said he was obnoxious, but he wouldn't give up. He showed up relentlessly wherever she was. He'd sing to her with a whole crowd around them. He'd bring her tokens of his love, little sweet nothings she called them, that made her fall for him completely. He promised her the world, and he gave it to her, she said, the day I was born.

Clearing my throat, I look away from the customer talking to me to collect myself. This isn't the place to reminisce about my family, but I just miss them so much. It seems like I never stop thinking about them. Sometimes I wonder if I would be the same person I am now if I had both of them today. I know I probably wouldn't be in Ireland, but would I still be the naïve girl that I am? Never been thoroughly kissed by a man, never been in bed with one, or even touched in a sexual way. I don't know why I am thinking so much about being a virgin, but since last night, that's the second thing that has been flooding my thoughts.

All I could think as Casey was forcing himself on me was that I was going to be raped my first time. I know it happens to women all the time, and I hate that more than I can ever express, but I always pictured my first time, like every other girl, all romantic and sweet with the man I love. Or even hot and passionate in the back of my longtime boyfriend's car because we didn't have anywhere to go since both our parents were home. I never got that though. I never really did anything wrong. I was always the perfect daughter. I'm not saying I want to start doing crazy shit, but I just want to stop feeling like my life has been nothing up to this point.

Because I know it hasn't. I cared for and loved my mother until her dying breath. I was and still am a straight A student. I know how to run a household, and I know how to love because I watched two of the most unbelievable people in the world do it. I just hate that I let myself get in the position I did last night, and more than anything, I hate that I pushed Declan away today.

I should have told him about Casey, maybe not all of what happened, but I just couldn't. I am so embarrassed, and I'm positive he'd think I am as stupid as I feel. A stupid, naïve girl who isn't worth his time. It was bad enough that I turned him down despite my gut feeling not to, but now I put myself in a position with Casey. One I don't like. I mean, I get that flowers are good things to send when you need to apologize, but I am sure that Kane's message was clear when he told him to stay the hell away from me. I guess that Casey didn't fully understand that.

Instead, he spent money on a beautiful bouquet of yellow daisies and wrote me a note that he really shouldn't have because I do not intend to speak to him ever again. Even though I threw the flowers and card away, I'll never forget the words he messily wrote to me.

Amberlyn,

> *I am sorry for the way I acted last night. I never meant to hurt you or make you feel that I forced you into something you did not want. I assumed you felt for me what I feel for you and acted on the feelings. I hope that we can move on from this and maybe you will consider giving me another chance. I know that we just met, but I just feel this insane attraction to you, and I hope you feel the same.*

Casey.

I still can't believe he actually thinks I want to have anything to do with him. He scared the living shit out of me, and I don't think I'd ever be able to be with him alone. I don't know if I believe the stories that I have heard since. Of course, it is still only a rumor, but I was there to feel him dig his nails in my face, and that alone has me not wanting to be anywhere near him. The mere thought has me physically shaking as I fill my regular's pint.

"You all right?"

I look up at Fiona. "Sure. Just supertired."

She moves around me, filling her own pints. As she does, she leans in and whispers, "I heard you crying, Amberlyn. I know you're not. You can talk to me."

I move around her to pass a pint before grabbing another. "I know I can but not now. I'm fine."

She looks around, cupping my shoulder in a loving way. "All right, we won't be busy much longer."

"I hope not." I sigh as I put a fake smile on my face when my favorite college guy comes to the bar.

"I love you, Amberlyn. Marry me?"

I smile. "Sorry, Brian, I'm not in the marrying mood tonight."

He looks deflated for only a second before he asks, "Mrs. Maclaster, are you and your husband still together?"

My aunt Shelia laughs loudly from where she is working the register. "Of course, we are, Brian. Go on before I call your gran!"

Brian's eyes widen before he scurries off with the pint I filled. He is always here for a good laugh, but tonight I just don't feel like laughing. Letting out a sigh, I reach for the plates my uncle placed on the food counter and serve them to table nine. My patrons are all grinning and thanking me, but then, suddenly, they fall silent and their heads turn toward the door. Weird. I look around and see that everyone is doing the same thing, which can only mean one thing.

Turning, I find Declan standing in the middle of the door, breathing heavily, with his face red. He looks around the pub, and when his eyes fall on me, meeting my gaze, I can't catch a breath to save my life. Honestly. His blue eyes are flaring with anger, his brows meeting together, and his sweet mouth is in a straight line. Instantly, my heart speeds up and a weird feeling settles in my stomach.

He knows.

"I need to talk to you, right now," he says in a very steady, but forceful voice.

I raise an eyebrow as everyone's eyes shift to me. "Okay?"

"Now."

I scoff. "Well, you're gonna have to give me a minute. I have to finish serving these tables."

"No, I need to talk to you this instant. Please."

I roll my eyes as I walk past him to get the plates I couldn't carry. "Like I said, it's gonna be a minute."

"Amberlyn," my aunt scolds as I reach for the plates. "Declan would like to speak with you."

"Okay?" I ask. "I have tables to serve."

"We can take care of that," she says, pushing Fiona toward me, but I shake my head, holding the plates out of Fiona's reach.

"But I can," I say, taking the plates. "He can wait."

"No, he cannot," she urges me, her eyes wide.

But I stand my ground. I have to work, and I don't answer to Declan's beck and call, unlike everyone else in the damn town. "Yes, he can," I say, passing by him and setting the plates down. I know I have mixed up everyone's orders, but I doubt they even notice. They are all just as shocked as my aunt.

"Anything else?"

No one says anything, and I roll my eyes before glaring at Declan. "Fine, you've rendered the pub speechless. I guess we can go outside. Might as well do it in here though, since I can guarantee you everyone will be listening."

Declan crosses his arms across his chest, his eyes burning into mine. "I'd like to speak to you in private, please."

I pass by him and go out the door he left open. When I hear it shut behind me, I know he followed. I start for the field by the parking lot so that Declan can have the privacy he asked for, since I am going nowhere near the alley I was in with Casey last night. When a gorgeous white and black horse comes into view, my mouth drops open.

"Who rides a horse to the pub?" I ask, reaching out to pet him. He neighs a greeting, rubbing his nose into my hand.

"I do. That's Cathmor."

"Of course you do," I say. I mean, really? A horse? He comes riding across the field on his mighty steed to have it out with the woman who crossed him. It is so eighteen hundreds-ish that it isn't even funny. Doesn't he know that we live in the twenty-first century? I let out a disgruntled noise, knowing I'm being a bitch, but I don't like the way he came in demanding to speak to me. Dropping my hand from the beautiful horse, I turn and make my way to the field. Once there, I whip around to find myself face-to-face with Declan. My breath hitches as his eyes watch me, his chest rising and falling, and his mouth still in such a straight line. I wish he'd smile more. He makes me nervous when he is staring at me like this.

"Amberlyn—" he starts to say.

I cut him off before he can finish. "Before you say what you need to, I'd like to say that I don't like the way you talked to me. I am not beneath you. You don't demand anything of me or push me around!"

His head falls to the side, his eyes still locked with mine, but then he nods. "I'm sorry. I let my emotions take over."

"Thank you," I say, mimicking his stance and crossing my arms across my chest as I look away. "Now, as you were saying?"

He chuckles. It has me looking up at him quickly, surprised. His mouth is turned up in the most beautiful smile ever. His anger and his standoffish stance are gone, and what is left behind is breathtaking. His eyes are so light, even in the darkness, and his smile radiant. I am in awe as he says, "I love how you treat me. It is refreshing. I also admire the fact that you can't be pushed around. I respect you, Amberlyn, a lot."

That has me dropping my arms and tucking my hands in my pockets. "Thank you."

"I'll admit that I'm spoiled and usually get what I want, but you've never treated me that way. I like that you put me in my place. I should have never spoken to you like that. Thank you for reminding me of that."

"To me, you're just a regular guy, like I've said before."

"I know and I like that, but I don't like being lied to, Amberlyn."

I look up quickly. "I never lied to you."

"No? Then what would you call it? Withholding information?"

I shrug as I look away again. "Okay, maybe I did withhold some information, but it wasn't like you came out and asked."

"Maybe so, but I don't like what happened, not one bit, and it is taking everything out of me not to go find him and fuckin' kill him," he says, his accent flaring more so than before with his voice laced with anger.

"I know."

"Why did you lie to me? I thought we were friends, at least."

I shrug again as I shake my head. "I just felt so embarrassed. Like, how stupid could I be? Why did I go out with him alone after what Fiona told me about your sister? Why did I allow him to get so close to me—where I was in reach of him grabbing me? You know? Is it my fault because I allowed him to kiss me before without really putting up any kind of boundaries?"

He is shaking his head before I can finish talking. Stepping closer, he says, "No, he is trash, filth. Amberlyn, you did nothing wrong. He did. A man should respect a woman. Something that Casey Burke obviously has no clue on how to do."

I know he is right, but I still doubt the fact, even though everyone has told me the same thing. I just feel so stupid and wish I were a better judge of character. "I just don't want to look bad in your eyes, and I feel like that is exactly what happened. I not only turned you down, but I went out with a guy you obviously hate. I mean, how do we come back from that? Do you even want to be anywhere near me?"

When his hand cups my chin, I look up, surprised to find him much closer than he was a second ago. Looking deep in my eyes, Declan holds my face tenderly as he says, "You'll never look bad in my eyes, Amberlyn. I'm smitten with you, if you haven't noticed. I have been since the moment I saw you. I never want anything to happen to you. I'm sorry about what happened, but I can promise it never will again. Not while I'm around. And the answer is yes… I want to be near you, very much so."

I can only blink as he holds my gaze, his other hand coming up to cup my cheek. "I'd like to take you out to dinner and get to know you. See if this thing I have for you is real because, yeah, you did turn me down, and you did go out with someone I despise, but that's all in the past, done with, over. All I care about at this moment is your lips forming the word *yes*."

I know my eyes are wide and my mouth is hanging open in complete shock as I dumbly ask, "Really?"

His mouth curves up as he nods slowly, his lips only inches from mine. "Yes, I promise it will be worth your while."

I don't doubt that at all. "Then, yes, I'd like that."

He smiles as he drops his hands from my face and takes my hands in his. Bringing my knuckles to his lips, he kisses each one before looking back up into my eyes. He leans in, his mouth so close that my lips part as I await his kiss. I can feel his breath against my mouth as he whispers, "Tomorrow?"

I'm breathless as I agree. "Sure."

"Wonderful. Let me walk you back to the pub."

Wait, what? His fingers intertwine with mine, and I'm still gasping for breath, unsure on what just happened. "You're not going to kiss me?"

I. Did. Not. Just. Ask. That.

Oh my God, someone kill me now. What the hell is wrong with me? I close my eyes, covering my face with my free hand, but Declan laughs as he uncovers it, taking my chin between his forefinger and thumb. Holding my gaze, he says, "Not yet, but did you want me to?"

My heart skips a beat as I smile, looking deep in his eyes. "Yeah, I do."

He smiles. "Good to know. Yes, of course I want to, but I want to wait."

My brow comes up as I look at him questioningly. "For?"

"The moment it will mean the most, when you'll least expect it."

Breathlessly, I grin like a fool as my heart swells in my chest. I'm glad he didn't kiss me because now I want to wait for that moment too. I don't know why, but as he holds my gaze, I know it will be a moment worth waiting for.

As long as it's with him.

twelve
Declan

"What are you grinning at?"

I glance over to where my sister is watching me from the doorway. I am sitting in my favorite chair in my library, getting lost in the world of *The Hobbit*. I don't know how I forgot how much I love this book. It's been years since I've read it, and I feel like a kid again—lost in the world of dwarfs, hobbits, and the dragon, Smaug. It's great, and I wish I did this more often. Usually, I work all the time, and I've decided I need to make more time to read. Instead of only doing it when I am nervous and trying to distract myself. I am doing that now, to pass time before I have to go pick up Amberlyn.

Amberlyn.

Ugh, just thinking her name has my heart palpitating in overdrive. I was so mad before I found myself in the field with her. Alone. Just us. Her eyes set on mine, and all my anger was gone. Feeling her so close, holding her hands, and looking so deep into her eyes had me wondering why I waited so long for this moment. I should have just jumped in from the beginning, but that was in the past. Now all that matters is that in no time, I'll be getting lost in her aquamarine eyes. I am giddy. Something I've never felt before, but looking into my sister's knowing eyes, I feel that my giddiness might be short-lived.

"Nothing," I lie, because there is no way I am sharing my thoughts of Amberlyn with her, or anyone for that matter. I haven't even kissed the girl, and she can turn me into a blabbin' eejit. I want her, desperately. I want her lips on mine; I want to feel her body against mine as we lay in bed, talking and getting lost in each other's bodies. I have never been this far gone with a girl whom I've just met, but I find that I am. It's scary and causes my heart to feel like it is blowing up in my chest, but there is something about Amberlyn that hits me in my core.

Pressing my lips together, I glance back at my book but I watch her out of the corner of my eye. She is wearing jeans and a T-shirt, not something she'd wear to go out in public, which means she is having a "lazy day" as she calls it. Usually she's so made up, every single detail so perfect that she looks like a Barbie doll. When I say that, she gets mad, but it's the truth. It makes me nervous because I know that's not her. She does it for my ma, for Micah, since his family expects her to look pristine at all times. She's so young, but she already has so much on her shoulders. Sometimes I wonder if she is really doing what she wants or doing only what everyone expects of her. I refuse to do that, but then, maybe I am because I'm doing exactly what my da wants of me. But that can't be right because I'm not doing it for him; I'm doing it for the distillery. It's my home, my business, and I won't have another person run what's mine. I'm what's best for it, and I'll do anything to keep it.

Lena sits on the arm of my chair, leaning into me as she wraps her arm around my shoulder. "I know it's something, Declan, or someone maybe?"

I shake my head innocently. "I don't know what you are talking about."

"Fiona Maclaster maybe?"

I scoff. "No, Kane's goin' out with her."

That must have stunned her, which means that not too many people know about Amberlyn, but they will after tonight. Even though it has my skin breaking out in goose pimples and my heart beating out of control, I know that once I bring Amberlyn to Thornton's, everyone will see us and report it as news when all it's supposed to be is my first date with the most gorgeous girl in Ireland. But I try not to think about it. Instead, I'll enjoy stumping my sister and my ma too, since I know she sent Lena in to spy. "Then who are you seeing at the Céad Míle Fáilte?"

I shrug my shoulders. "No one."

"Oh, ya liar!" she accuses as she smacks my forearm. "Fine, fine, keep it to yourself. Are you going to bring her to the White Ball?"

I don't want to answer, but before my brain can tell my mouth that, I say, "If she'll have me."

"Ha! I knew there was someone!"

Fuckin' hell. "Yeah, so?" I ask as I look up at her. Her eyes are dancing with laughter, her grin unstoppable, but when her eyes meet mine, her grin falls.

"No, I'm happy," she says with her palms up to me. "I want you to find your Mrs. O'Callaghan. This is awesome."

"Don't go putting that thought in your head. It's our first date. I could find her annoying after tonight."

I doubt that, but it could be true. Lena gives out a laugh as she shakes her head. "No way, not with the way she makes you smile."

Maybe so. Pushing into her playfully, I smile when she hugs me tightly. Pulling away, she leans back as she rests her head against mine. "Have you talked to Kane lately?"

"Of course, saw him earlier today."

"So you know that he and Casey got into it?"

I pause before moving my head out from beneath hers to look up at her. "Got into it? Way I heard it, Kane knocked him the hell out."

"Yeah, that's what I mean."

"Then yeah, I heard. Why? How did you?"

"One of my friends said she was in the shop the other night and he was saying how our family has ruined him. He can't even get a date with a fuckin' American."

I shrug, my heart picking up in speed with anger. I hate that fuckin' gobshite. "It isn't our family—it's him. It's his fault he's a fuckin' wanker, and maybe it's the way he treats women that keeps him from getting a date."

She nods slowly as her eyes glaze over. I always hate when Casey's name comes into the conversation. It makes my beautiful sister look so hollow. I place my hand on hers. "Don't let him bother you one bit."

"No, no, I'm not. It's just I hate when he runs our names through the mud when really he has no right to. We don't go around running his name." She pauses as her eyes meet mine. "Well, at least I don't, nor does Ma. It's mainly you and Da."

"He's a fuckin' fucktard. I hate him."

"I know. I just wish we could all let it go. It happened so long ago," she says sadly.

"It was only three years ago," I say, and I can feel my skin burning with anger. "You don't care for him still, do you?"

She shakes her head quickly. "Hell no, I just hate how it went down. I really don't know what happened, and I don't even know what has been said is true. All I know is that I left with him, and I wake up cold, wet from the rain, and raped. It's scary and still hurts me inside, you know? I love Micah, I do, but I don't know. I just feel like a part of me is still missing. The part Casey took, and it scares me that I'll never be the person I was."

I hold her hand in mine and nod. "You've grown, Lena. You've learned from your mistakes. It has made you a stronger person. You are still healing from it, and you're going to overcome all of it. I believe that because you're amazing, Lena."

She lets out a long breath as she nods. "That's what Micah says when I tell him this."

"Then believe him, because it's the truth."

She smiles as she leans into me again. "I just think that hearing about him, talking about him, messes with me and makes it worse. I wish that he would just leave town. I told Da this at dinner because I'm so over him, but even Da agrees. If he hasn't left yet, he won't. Not with his ma here, God bless her soul. Such a wonderful woman, such a shitty fella."

"Yeah," I agree as I shake my head. I would love nothing more than to never see him again, but like my sister said, it won't happen unless we leave. Casey's ma is very sick, has been for years, and he is the only one who can take care of her.

"So I asked Micah if we can skip town once we are married and he agreed. I haven't told Ma and Da yet."

I nod as a grin pulls at my lips. "That's good. I doubt they'll mind. They'll have to understand the reasoning behind it."

And I know I'm right. This is the first summer Lena has stayed home since it happened. Usually she goes off to Germany with her friends or family, but since meeting Micah, I've slowly seen my sister come back to life. He may be dumb as a rock, but he treats my sister like a princess, so he is all right in my eyes.

"Yeah, I hope. Oh well, if they don't! We are the rebels of the family, I think!"

I laugh as I agree. "Maybe so, but I know I can't leave."

"Then you better get married before I have to stay here and Micah runs the business."

I scoff as I shut my book. "I'd turn over in my grave before I'd let that happen."

"I know. You love it too much."

"I do."

She looks down at my book, reaching for it and flipping carelessly through the pages. I want to ask her to be careful, but before I can, she says, "I don't think Da will give it to Micah."

I shrug, reaching for the book to keep it safe. "I'm not sure one way or another, but I don't plan to find out. I am doing what they want. Let's hope it works out."

"With the girl from the pub?" she asks with a wink.

A smile pulls at my mouth as I shrug but reality sets in because I may want that to be true at this moment, but all it is right now is attraction. I don't know her deepest, darkest secrets, I don't know what makes her tick, and I don't know what her wants are for the future. We could want two totally different things, and as much as I hope that doesn't happen, I can't help but think about it. It scares me, but at the same time, I try to push those thoughts away because I want to enjoy her. I want to live in the now.

With her.

So looking back at my sister, I grin as I slowly shrug. "Maybe."

When I pull up to the Maclasters' house, I park behind Fiona's little Bug and turn my car off. I run my hand through my thick, curly hair, knocking my beanie off. I consider leaving it off, but only for a second before I pull it back down on my head. Letting out a long breath, I tap my fingers on the steering wheel, willing myself to go get my date. I've been thinking that I might not like her after tonight, but what if she doesn't like me? What if she thinks I eat loudly? Or maybe that I don't smile enough like my ma says? What if I say something stupid and she runs the other way?

Fuckin' shite.

My knee is bouncing, my heart pounding, and my hands feel clammy. I was fine driving over here, excited even, but now, I feel like I might vomit. When I see the curtain pull back and Mrs. Maclaster peek out, I know I've been seen and have to go in. Throwing the door open, I step out and head toward the door. Before I can knock, it flies open and Mrs. Maclaster grins up at me.

"Declan, how nice to see you," she greets before stepping out of the way to allow me to come in. I give her a curt smile before stepping inside and meeting Mr. Maclaster's gaze. I reach my hand out and he takes it strongly, squeezing my hand as he holds my gaze.

"Howya, Mr. Maclaster."

"Howya, Declan. Good to see ya."

"You too," I say, dropping my hand from his and tucking it in my pocket.

"Amberlyn should be down any second. They have been fussin' over hair and makeup all afternoon."

I nod as I look around the Maclasters' home. It is an old stone home with beautiful, large windows with a wonderful view of the lake. The furnishing makes the house homey and inviting. A smile plays on my lips when my gaze falls on a picture of Fiona and Amberlyn hugging tightly. It has been taken recently because it isn't even in a frame yet, just leaned up against an old, Celtic cross. They could honestly pass as sisters with how much they look alike—both so beautiful. "That's a nice picture."

They both nod, Mrs. Maclaster's grin wide and full of love. "Yes, our girls. They are something, that's for sure."

I couldn't agree more. When the sound of someone coming down the stairs catches my attention, I turn to find Fiona and then Amberlyn. Like an angel from heaven, Amberlyn is breathtaking. In a pair of tight, light pink slacks, she has on a black, lacy top that she has covered with a matching pink blazer. But the outfit wasn't what had my tongue thick in my mouth. It was the shoes—

sexy, black, and high, making her legs look long and lean. A smile pulls at my lips as her eyes meet mine. Her eyes are done up very dramatic, something that I haven't seen on her before. Her hair is in a mess of curls down her shoulders and her lips are full, pink, and glossy. I want nothing more than to lick every bit off her sexy, sweet mouth. Fuck, she is intoxicating.

Her mouth pulls up at the side as she walks over and stops before me. "Hey."

"Hey," I say breathlessly. "You look gorgeous."

Her cheeks dust with color as she smiles. "Thanks, so do you," she says as her eyes run lazily over me. I am dressed nice enough, I guess, in a pair of khakis and a blue button-up shirt, but in a way, I feel inferior to her, which is crazy since I've never felt like that before. I've never thought someone was better than I am, but at that moment, getting lost in Amberlyn's eyes, I feel that way. I'm not sure I deserve to spend the night with this beautiful woman.

"Well, be home by midnight, please."

We both look over at Mr. Maclaster, and I notice that a grin is playing on Amberlyn's mouth as Fiona smacks her da on the arm.

"Da! She's twenty years old! Let her be!"

But I don't think Mr. Maclaster cares how old Amberlyn is. He wants her home, and I respect that. I go to say that as Mrs. Maclaster blurts out, "Yes, don't listen to him, Declan. You do what you'd like with her. Bring her home whenever."

The room falls silent except for Fiona's giggles as Amberlyn gawks at her aunt and Mr. Maclaster sets her with a look. I have no clue what to say to that, so I look back at Amberlyn as she rolls her eyes. "No, I'll be home at midnight, and he won't have his way with me! Jeez, Aunt Shelia!"

Fiona is still laughing as Mrs. Maclaster sets her with a look. "He's Declan O'Callaghan… He'll do what he pleases."

"No, he won't," Mr. Maclaster and Amberlyn say at the same time.

"Yeah, I won't," I agree.

I doubt anyone is listening to me as Amberlyn says, "I don't care if he's the Pope. Jeez, can you believe this lady?" she asks me, but I don't answer as she steps to her aunt. "And to think, you're my favorite aunt ever?"

Mrs. Maclaster's face is red, but her smile is still beaming. Kissing her cheek, Amberlyn leans to Mr. Maclaster and kisses his cheek before saying, "I'll be home by midnight."

He nods before setting me with a look. This is really weird. I don't do this. I don't date, and to have a set limit on when I have to bring a woman home is a little weird, but I don't have a problem doing what is asked of me. I want them to like me.

"Ye have fun!" Mrs. Maclaster calls as we head out the door after Amberlyn hugged Fiona bye. Once the door shuts, Amberlyn laughs. "If this is what it would have been like when I was younger going on my first date, I'm glad I waited. My dad would have been worse than my uncle, and my mother probably would have cried."

I glance over at her. There is a smile on her beautiful face, but I can see the pain in her eyes, and the laugh isn't a regular Amberlyn gut-busting laugh. "You didn't date when you were younger?"

She shakes her head. "Nope, I took care of my mom. She was sick for a long time before she passed."

"So what, this is your first date?"

She smiles nervously up at me. "Officially, yeah."

I smile, too. Why does that make me feel so good? When she stops suddenly, she glances back over at me before pointing to my Mercedes CL65. "No horse?"

I scoff as I reach for the door. "Not tonight."

"Darn, I was hoping to be whisked away on horseback. I even wore pants," she teases with a wink. I smile as I shut the door and head around the car.

Sitting down, I put the key in the ignition. "It does have a 510-horsepower engine though."

She giggles, and the smell of her fills the inside of my car. It's intoxicating, a mix of flowers and shampoo. I love it and want to nuzzle my nose in her hair. Turning the key in the ignition to make sure I don't, I glance over at her as she says, "That will be fine then. Whisk me away, Declan."

She does a very flourishing wave with her hand like she is royalty as she leans back, her face bright with a smile as her eyes stay locked on me. I can't get enough of her, and the nerves from before are gone as I nod with a grin pulling at the side of my mouth.

"I hope to."

thirteen
Amberlyn

I'm nervous.

So freaking nervous that my knee is bouncing out of control as I ride in Declan's very expensive car. I'm not sure if he's had it long, but it smells new and has me afraid to touch anything. I glance over to admire him; he looks simply scrumptious as always, but then I notice that damn beanie. I wish he wouldn't wear it. I love his curly hair. Shaking my head, I say, "Still with your trusty beanie, I see."

He smiles over at me sheepishly, causing my body to catch fire. There is something about this man's smile that makes me come completely undone. He has dimples, and his teeth are so straight and white, which makes me realize that I must have a thing for straight, white teeth because I am hot just watching him smile. I grin as he reaches up, pulling the beanie down some. "I thought about leavin' it off, but then I remember that I don't like my hair."

I reach out, but he moves out of my way, sending me a grin. "Take it off. I like your hair," I plead, giving him a little pout.

He scoffs. "No way. That pout is cute, hot even, but I need my hat."

"Why?" I ask, my body liking that he said I was hot a little more than it should.

"'Cause, I just like it on."

I roll my eyes, letting out a breath as I lean back, mock pouting. "Fine."

He laughs as he takes my hand in his. The warmth of his hand is consuming and soon I forget about the beanie as his fingers lace with mine. "This is okay?"

I nod quickly because I like the way my hand fits in his. I've wanted this, and I am soon watching as his thumb moves across the back of my hand. A smile is pulling at his lips as he drives. His eyes are on the road, and I wish they were on me. I have been a wreck all day. I tried to work to keep myself from thinking about tonight, but when it came time for me to get ready, I was basically shaking with nerves. Fiona helped, and I have to admit I look hot as hell, but even knowing that doesn't calm the butterflies in my belly.

Silence stretches in the car, and I'm not sure if that is a bad thing or good. I am comfortable, happy even, but what if he is bored and I need to talk to make him feel better? I've learned very quickly that Declan is a man of few words, and I am fine with the silence, but I'm not sure if he is. I want to make him comfortable with me because I am with him. He makes me all giggly, and oh my goodness, how I love this feeling.

When we pull into the valet of Thorsten's Restaurant, my door opens and I reach for the hand that awaits me. I smile at the valet and then glance over to see Declan right there, his arm out for me to take. I want to giggle from the sheer chivalry of it all as I take his arm, but I push that giddiness away as he leads me inside. This place is like a castle, so huge and beautiful, stone walls with golden furniture. It's superfancy and a part of me feels like I didn't dress nicely enough. I also think that if I touch anything, it'll break, so with my other hand, I reach over to hold on to his wrist. He sends me a sweet grin before looking up at the host.

When he sees us, he stands up straighter than before and comes to meet us. "Mr. O'Callaghan, it's wonderful to have you tonight and your beautiful date, of course."

"Thank you," Declan says very sternly, but when he looks over at me, his eyes dance as he says, "She is beautiful, huh?"

My lips curve into a grin as I lean into him, wanting to hide my face, but before I can, we are being led to our table. I want to take in the fancy décor, the beautiful, large windows and gold tablecloths, but as we walk, people who are walking too stop to look at us. Even people who are eating stop to stare. Even some of the waiters and waitresses pause to glance at us too. Well, not us, but Declan.

When we come to our seats, he pulls my chair out for me and I sit down, placing my clutch on the table as I met the gaze of all the people in the restaurant. Nervous, I push my hair off my shoulders before clasping my hands in my lap. My heart is knocking into my ribs, and I can't help but look around as everyone stares.

"Amberlyn?"

I glance up to meet Declan's gaze. His eyes are narrowed, his cheeks flushed, and his beautiful lips are in a straight line. His nervousness is coming off him in waves, and I hate that he is nervous. I wonder if it is all the watchful eyes because I know they are making me nervous. "Yeah?"

"Would you like wine?" he asks, nodding his head toward the waiter that I didn't realize was standing there.

"Oh, what are you having?"

"Whiskey."

Of course. I smile as I nod. "Well, I guess I need to have a glass too."

That makes his lips twitch as he nods, and the waiter is off to fill our orders. Taking in a deep breath, I try to look at the menu but I can feel eyes on me, and it has me clumsily flipping through the menu. When I knock the candle over, I groan as I reach for it, putting it back up. When I glance up to see if Declan saw me do it, I find that he did and his lips are curved up at the side as his eyes dance with laughter. I bite into my lip as my face reddens. I shrug and then look back down. Letting out an annoyed breath, I try to read the menu, but all I can think of is the people staring at me.

When a glass is set down before me, I reach for it, downing the bitter liquid in one gulp. I want to puke afterward, but as the liquor warms my throat and chest, I keep it down with the hope it calms my nerves. Placing the glass down, I look over to find Declan with his glass paused at his mouth. Even the waiter is staring at me, and shit, so is the rest of the fucking restaurant. Damn it!

"Sorry," I breathe, tucking my hands in my lap, my shoulders falling forward in embarrassment.

Declan smiles, and I swear that I'm in a Taylor Swift song because all I see are sparks flying. There is something about those ice-blue eyes plus that smile that make me feel like I'm soaring through the air. Soon I forget about everyone in the room. The only person here is him.

"Don't apologize," he says before downing his glass too. He lets out a gasp and then grins over at me. "Future advice… it's meant to be sipped, not knocked back."

"I'm nervous," I admit.

He nods. "I am, too."

"Everyone is staring."

He nods again but doesn't take his eyes off me. "I know. I hate it."

It's at that moment that I actually realize that since we've been here, he has only looked at me and the menu, never around us. He is wound tight, his shoulders taut, the veins in his hands and arms showing. I hate that, and the fixer in me wants to make him feel better. Without really thinking, I reach over and take his hand in mine. It's clammy, but I don't care as I lace my fingers with his.

"It's always like this, huh?"

He nods. "Yeah, but tonight I have someone so beautiful to look at I don't even know anyone else is here."

That sends the butterflies in my belly into a frenzy. I squeeze his hand as the waiter comes to our table again. "Are you ready to order, Mr. O'Callaghan?"

Declan nods, his eyes still on me as he asks, "What would you like, Amberlyn?"

I order a chicken dish because it was the only thing I thought I'd like, while Declan orders something crazy. With his fingers still locked with mine, I watch as the waiter sets new glasses of whiskey on the table before taking a small sip. Declan winks at me before saying, "Better. Savor it. It's a beautiful age, this one. I think it's a 1966."

"Wow," I say and he is right. It is pretty good just sipping it rather than just throwing it back like a madman. "It's really good."

"I'll take you on a tour at the distillery…have you sample the best whiskey in the world," he says with his eyes shining with pride.

I smile. "I can't wait."

"Me neither."

Biting into my lip, I grin, but before I can say anything, someone appears at our table. I look up to see a tall blonde with her breasts falling out of the front of her dress and hips and legs that could make a grown man cry. She is hot. I can admit that if I were a guy, I'd do her. That's how hot she is.

"Declan, I am shocked to see you after so long. How are you?"

Declan looks up reluctantly and the smile is gone, replaced with a straight line. "Fine, Marci, thank you, and yourself?"

"Fine, it's wonderful to see you."

"Yes, you too. How are your parents?"

"Fine, thank you."

"That's good. Give them my best."

"I will," she says, and then an awkward silence falls over the table. It's like she doesn't see me and that's fine, but I wish she'd go away. "Oh, well, I just wanted to stop by, say hi, maybe get a picture with you for old times' sake?"

Seriously? What the fuck? I glance over at Declan to see what he will say, and thankfully, he is shaking his head. "I'm sorry, I don't think so. And I'm sure my date would have something to say about that."

Damn right, I would!

"With who?" she asks, actually looking confused.

I raise my hand and she looks over at me, her fake eyelashes shooting up to her forehead. Looking straight on, I decide that she isn't very pretty. "Me. Amberlyn Reilly, nice to meet you."

"Oh," is all she says before looking back at Declan. "I didn't know that you were seeing anyone."

"Yeah, it's not anyone's business but mine."

"Do your ma and da know?"

Declan sets her with a look, his eyes narrowing as he says, "Yes, why does that matter to you?"

"Just wondering. Guess I'll leave you be."

"That would be great," he says, and inside, I cheer him on. What a bitch. She glares before she stalks away, and then Declan is looking off to the side. I watch as he nods his head, and then the waiter appears. "Sir?"

"Yes, can I please have our food to go? Or you know what, cancel it," he says before standing up and throwing some money on the table. He closes the distance between us and holds out his arm. I stand without questioning him, taking his arm as he leads me out. "I'm sorry for cutting our dinner short, but since she came up to our table, everyone will. We need to get out of here."

"Oh, okay," I say as we walk out of the restaurant to the car that awaits us. After being seated inside, he soon enters and then we are off. I want to say something, but he is on the phone and I don't want to interrupt him. I feel like it's my fault we left. I don't know why because I did nothing wrong, but I feel like he was embarrassed by me or something. Was that why he didn't want people coming to the table? Fuck, why am I so insecure around this guy?

When we pull up to a pub I don't know, he parks the car and lays his phone down before looking over at me. "I'm sorry. I shouldn't have taken you there. That is a life I used to have, and then I gave it up because of eejits like Marci. I apologize."

"It's okay," I say with a shrug. "Are you taking me home?"

He shakes his head. "I didn't plan on it. I still have five hours," he says, pointing to the clock, his brows touching each other as his gaze holds mine.

"Oh, I figured since we left, you didn't want to spend time with me."

"Huh? What? No, I hate that place. I wanted to impress you, but it kind of backfired."

I smile. "You don't have to take me to some fancy restaurant to impress me, Declan. The place was nice, but I'm fine with just this pub. As long as I'm with you, I don't care."

He nods, a smile playing on his lips as he looks over at me. "Well, we aren't eating here either. I figured we'd get some food to go and go out on the lake."

My heart flutters in my chest as I reach over and slowly pull his beanie off. It has been taunting me all night, and it's just us now. Nothing to be embarrassed about. When I place the beanie in my lap, he grins at me as I say, "That sounds wonderful."

LATER WITH the lights from Declan's car allowing us to see, we sit on the dock of the O'Callaghan side and dig in to the food that he ordered for us.

"A burger and fries is more my thing than whatever the hell that chicken dish was."

He laughs. "Yeah, it was probably a bad idea all around taking you there. The food isn't that good."

"Maybe, but the whiskey was fantastic."

He nods in agreement. "It is, but lucky for you, I had the pub owner throw in a bottle for us," he says, pulling it out before filling up two plastic cups. "Perks of being the *Whiskey Prince*."

I laugh. "Yeah. I guess it does have its perks, while any other time, it's just weird."

He shrugs. "It's my history; I don't mind it much until I'm out. When I'm on this land, it doesn't bother me."

"The staring bothers you, huh?"

"Yeah, and the way everyone thinks that they need to tell my parents everything. Oh, and the lies they put online and in the papers. It's really stupid."

"I bet. I still don't get it."

He doesn't say anything as I take a bite of my hamburger. The flavor bursts in my mouth, and I smile happily as I eat. When I look over at him, I can see, even with the limited light, that his brows are pulled together. He is picking at the bun of his hamburger, too. Shit. "Did I say something wrong?"

He looks up and shakes his head. "It's not that. I'm just worried that my birthright is going to be a problem between us."

I lay my burger down. "How do you mean?"

"It seems like a big deal to you. Is it?"

"No, not at all," I stress. "I don't care. I just hate how everyone makes a big deal and makes you uncomfortable when you are just like every other guy in the world."

He shrugs. "I want to say that it doesn't bother me, that I understand it, but sometimes I feel like I'm lying. I don't like the attention. I've always been sheltered. I went away to private school until I was fourteen, and I hated it. The older kids used me for money, and the younger kids used me to get in with the older kids. I never really made friends. All I had was Kane, but that was only when I was home during the summer. The only reason I went to a public school was because I begged my parents to let me go to school with him. I've always felt comfortable with him, and they agreed. I guess because most of the school was using their money. So then, I'm in school with everyone who Kane is close with, and I go from being picked on and hated to being worshiped. It was weird, and I guess it got to my head because I went fuckin' crazy. Kane and I tore this town up, and I didn't care about my name, about my title, or anything, for that matter. I was having a blast with my friends I thought were cool, but then it got to be too much. I was always at parties, girls all over me, wanting to marry me, and soon I realized that these people weren't here because they liked me but because of who I am. And then Lena was raped."

I don't touch my food as he talks, and when Lena's name leaves his lips, I can see the pain in his eyes. It physically hurts me. I want to scoot over and, I don't know, hug him, but in a way, it feels like he doesn't want that. So I listen as he goes on.

"My da flipped, as you can expect, and so did my ma. It was time for the charades to stop and time for me to be a man. So I did, but because I was scared I was the reason that Lena had been hurt, since Casey was my friend, I stopped everything and didn't leave anymore. I lost all faith in humanity because how could someone hurt a beautiful fifteen-year-old girl and use someone they claim to like? So I turned into a hermit, as Kane says, and I hate that I did because now when I go out, everyone is going to be all over me. No one knows why, and everyone wants to suck up to me, but I want nothing to do with them. I'm older now. I know what I want in friends and in the person I want to date. I know what's important—my family, my distillery, and my heart. I think when everything happened, I needed that time to heal because when Lena was hurt, it wasn't only who that suffered the aftershocks of it—it was the whole family. You know?"

I nod and hate that my eyes are filling with tears. I can understand exactly what he means because I did the same thing. I hate how much pain his family has been through. Everyone sees them as this big, rich family that is basically royalty, but no one looks over the walls to make sure they are okay. It's sad, and I hate that this has happened.

Taking in a deep breath, I say, "Yeah, I do. When my dad died, a piece of me died too, and when my mom went through chemo and all the cancer shit she did, I felt like I went through it with her. Each day weighed on me, like it did her. I offered to shave my head because we shaved hers, but she wouldn't let me. She said if she couldn't have her hair, she wanted to admire mine."

When a tear runs down my cheek and splashes on my hand, I look down as I take in a deep breath.

"Don't hide," Declan whispers before lifting my face so he can see me. "That is really amazing of you, to want to do that for your ma."

I smile. Man, I miss her, and I would do it all over again. Everything. "Yeah, but sometimes, I think I didn't do enough. Maybe I could have saved her somehow, but then I know I couldn't have. I was the best daughter I could have been because I wanted her to be happy and proud of me. I worked so hard, didn't do anything but focus on my studies and take care of her. I don't have any friends back home because I didn't have time. I went to school, came home, did homework, and did anything she needed. My senior year, I was homeschooled. I didn't have a prom, homecoming, nothing. I did everything for her, and I was a nobody to the kids my age. Don't think I regret any of it, because I don't, but it's sad to think that when I left, no one knew, no one missed me, because I didn't have time for anything or anyone but her. And if I hadn't come here, I'd be alone, trying to figure out how to live life without my mom. I know she knew that, and that's why she asked me to come here."

Moving our food, Declan slides beside me. Taking my hands in his, he kisses each of my palms before looking deep into my eyes. "I believe that you are the strongest person I know, Amberlyn. Your ma was right to ask you to come here. It may very well be for my own selfish reasons, but because of that, I thank your ma every day. You know why I came out after hiding away for three years, right?"

My eyes are cloudy with tears, and my heart feels like a vise grip is around it as I look deep in his eyes. I haven't shared any of that with anyone else but Fiona. I can't believe I just blurted it out like that either, but it's just different with him. I feel so at ease with him. Slowly, I shake my head. "No."

"For you. I saw you across the lake that day when you were sunbathing, and I knew I had to know your name and the color of your eyes."

Hearing him say those words has me breathless as he holds my gaze, his ice-blue eyes shining. "Then I met you and had the pleasure of being on the receiving end of that beautiful smile of yours, and the more I learned about you, the more I thank God I came off this damn land."

If he wanted me to smile, he succeeded. My grin is huge as stray tears roll down my cheeks. "And if you left now, I'd miss you. Terribly."

Leaning toward him, I rest my head to his. "I'd miss you, too."

He smiles, and I can't help but smile back, even though I want to break down and cry for both of us. Grinning, I say, "Good thing I don't plan on going anywhere."

"That is a good thing."

His mouth is still curved in a contagious grin as he reaches up, slowly moving his thumb along my bottom lip, causing gooseflesh to cover my skin despite the hot weather. His eyes are so dark, locked with mine, and when his tongue comes out to wet his lips, I ask, "Are you gonna kiss me now? *Oh-dear-God-why-did-I-just-ask-that!*"

I say it as one word before I close my eyes in complete and utter humiliation. Declan's laugh runs down my spine, and it doesn't help my embarrassment one bit. If anything, it makes it worse as I open my eyes to look at him, and what I find makes me smile. His face is so close to mine, his eyes bright and playful.

"Really though, why do you keep asking? Do you want to kiss me or something?" he jokes, pulling a nervous laugh from me.

"Something like that," I joke back with a grin, but then I shake my head. "I need a filter."

"No, I like that you say what you think," he says, cupping my face. With his eyes locked on mine, breathing is not an option. As he leans toward me, his lips coming for mine, I hold my breath and close my eyes tight because thank sweet baby Jesus, he is going to kiss me. But then his lips meet my nose in a sweet, soft kiss, and my eyes spring open as he pulls away. Deflated, I ask, "Not the moment, huh?"

He reaches for his burger and takes a huge bite before shaking his head. After swallowing, he grins over at me. "Not yet."

"This better be some amazingly awesome kiss," I tease as I pick up my own burger.

He winks, his eyes dark as he says, "Best damn kiss you'll ever have. I can promise ya that."

I want to say he has that right since I've kissed only one guy, and he had weird braces that stuck me in the lip. Instead, I just nod and eat my hamburger happily because this was probably the best first date ever.

fourteen
Declan

I hate board meetings.

They are stupid and pointless, in my opinion. I am the youngest person in here, while my da and our colleagues are all in their late fifties. Usually, I don't say anything. I can be found at the end of the table, taking notes and taking in everything my da is saying. This will be my company one day, and when that happens, I want to be able to fall into the seat my da is sitting in and lead like he does. He is a powerful man, knows what he wants for the company, and what he doesn't. He is vocal about his opinions, and everyone respects him.

I want that.

But today, instead of taking notes and listening attentively like I should, my thoughts are on a certain lady with freckles that dust every inch of her. I haven't seen Amberlyn since I dropped her off at eleven thirty, two nights ago. I didn't make it to the pub yesterday because one of our pot stills went on the fritz, and then today, I have this damn meeting. I'm pining for her.

Pulling my phone out of my pocket, I hold it under the table and quickly text her.

I'm stuck at work. I won't be in today.

I go to tuck it back in my pocket when it vibrates with a new message.

You're slacking, slacker. Haha. No worries, just means you owe me dinner or something.

Doesn't that sound like a perfect idea? Smiling, I write her back.

Tonight? You free?
I can be if you are asking.
Yeah, I am.
Then yes, I'll see you…when?
Six.
Awesome. J

"Declan, what do you think?"

I glance up, tucking my phone in my pocket. "I think it's good," I say, even though I don't have a clue what is going on.

"So you agree on an increase of two percent for the distributors in the US?" my da asks.

I shake my head, leaning on the table. "Why are we raising the prices at all?"

"Because they are making a double profit off us. Where have you been?"

I shrug. "Not listening, I guess. Excuse me, I was distracted."

Da nods. "Would you like us to wait until you are done?"

"No sir, I apologize."

"That's fine, please read the proposal and give us your opinion."

I glance down at the file in front of me and know that all eyes are on me. Biting into my lip, I read quickly and agree that the distributors' prices need to go up. Looking down at my da to find he is watching me, I try not to be nervous as I say, "Yes, but it needs to be more. At least four percent so that we are both equal, and send a suggested price because they don't have that yet. Since we are the best whiskey in the world, they are taking advantage of it. Send a suggested price and then a cap of what they can sell. If they don't like it, that's fine. We are the leading whiskey brand in the United States behind Jack Daniel's. I know they are banking from their distributors, and we can too."

My da nods as a satisfied smile covers his face. Pride is shining in his eyes as everyone at the table nods in agreement. The nervousness I was feeling is gone as a triumphant feeling takes over. This is what I love; this is what I was meant to do. I may hate being trapped in this room with these stiffs, but I love the feeling I get when I do something right. It's almost as satisfying as being close to Amberlyn.

"I agree. Ryan, write it up and get it together for the distributors all over the world. Good job, Declan."

Everyone sends me a nod before getting up and leaving the room. Standing up, I follow everyone out and soon fall into step with my da. "Good job in there, but stay off that phone."

I nod. "Yes, sir. It won't happen again."

"Good. Everything going well in the distillery?"

"Yes, very well. Kane is doing a great job," I say as my da stops, turning to me.

"I knew he would. He takes after his own da, hardworking. He'll do well in the production room. I believe that. I hate to lose Paul to retirement, but Kane is the perfect replacement."

"I couldn't agree more," I say. He nods as he looks down at his phone, reading an email from what I can see. Usually I don't talk about things I want for the business because it might start a fight due to my marital status, but for some reason, I'm feeling brave. I clear my throat before saying, "Da, I was wondering if we could send my whiskey into beta testing?"

He looks up from his phone to me. His brows are pulled together, and his eyes no longer hold the pride they did before, more like annoyance now. "Come into my office, please."

Fuck me. Reluctantly, I follow him into his office and fall into the seat before his desk. I just wanted a simple yes or no answer.

"She's American then?"

I look up, confused. "Excuse me, what?"

"The girl you've been seeing, Amberlyn Reilly, twenty years old, born in Nashville, Tennessee. Her ma and da were born here, but they left after getting married, both deceased. She is Shelia and Michael Maclaster's niece. Works as a bartender at the pub across the lake."

Holding my da's gaze, I nod. "Yes."

"She's American, Declan. That won't work."

My fingers bite into my thighs. "Why is that?"

"Because she doesn't come from old money like us."

Flabbergasted, I take in a breath before protesting. "That wasn't part of the requirements."

"Maybe so, but I won't accept her. Call me a snob, but I want you to be with an Irish girl—old money, pretty, and good for you."

I don't know why, but rage takes over within seconds, and I want nothing more than to pick the chair up and throw it through the window. I roll my eyes and stand up, holding the file that I have like a shield over my heart. "That's the stupidest shite I've ever heard, and I refuse to listen to this any longer. You said get out, meet people, fall in love, and get married so I can have the business. I am doing that. I refuse to have you go and add different stipulations. I also refuse to allow this to bother me now because I don't know what will happen with Amberlyn. So this conversation is over. Forget I asked about my whiskey. I'll do it once I own this fuckin' company."

I stalk out of the office, slamming the door behind me. I chance a glance at my da to find him with his mouth hanging open and his eyes wide. That's right, be fuckin' surprised 'cause you are a wanker!

How dare he?

Stomping through the offices and out into the fresh air, I let out a long breath, sucking in more air as my heart pounds in my chest. Lacing my fingers behind my head, I replay our conversation as I fill my lungs with air, letting it out in a swoosh each time. I focus on Cathmor, who is waiting to take me back to the distillery, but I can't move right now. My da may very well kill me once he sees me again, but I just don't get it. The nerve of him. The rules are pretty much set in stone. I get married…I have the company, nothing about her race, her origin, or anything. As long as she is female and has my last name, I am good. Why the fuck would he throw that at me? Damn it. And why am I letting it bother me so much? I am not asking Amberlyn to marry me today; I haven't even kissed the woman yet.

"You say that you won't let what I've said bother you."

I glance back at my da and stiffen at the sight of him. He still has the power to make me feel like he did when he scolded me when I was six years old and was found breaking windows with rocks. It was all Kane's idea, of course, since my nanny was a bitch, but I was still the one who took the brunt of the punishment. I swallow loudly as I nod. "Sure, I won't."

"But you are, I know you are, and that shows me that she does mean something to you and that this is more than you are letting on. It won't last. She doesn't believe in what we do, who we are. She isn't what you need."

"You don't know what she is," I snap, my heart pounding so fast in my chest that it hurts.

"It doesn't matter because I know you, and you believe in family, in traditions, and she doesn't have that."

Taking in a deep breath to keep myself from cussing my da out, I look up at him. "Da, you don't know her. Nothing about her. She loved her family, she has traditions, and she is the most beautiful person I've ever met."

"So you love her."

I balk, my heart racing at speeds I didn't know it could go. My palms are soaking wet, and I feel faint. I hate arguing with my father, but I hate that I might be lying with the answer I am about to provide him. I don't know what I feel. "No, but I care for her, and I know that this is nothing to bat your eyes at. She is special, and I feel that our relationship could be something to treasure. I'd like the respect from you to see what it is."

Looking away, he shakes his head slowly before letting out a long breath. "I hope you aren't making the same mistake your sister did. She got involved with someone who was not in our social standing, and look what happened. Thank goodness she found Micah."

Sometimes my da can be a real snob. Is that all he cares about? Someone's social standing? Someone's money? What about who they are? And fuck, am I like him? Looking him over, I am disgusted, not only with him, but with myself. I'm like him in so many ways, and I can't believe I've allowed that to happen. I don't agree with his views. I want to be successful, but because I'm savvy, not because I chose people with money over anyone else. I don't want to be a snob, a stuck-up arsehole. I want to be someone whom Amberlyn can like, maybe one day fall in love with. Having my da say this has put everything in perspective for me. I have to make sure I never end up like him—bitter and hating anyone who isn't us. Not that I owe him anything else in this conversation, but I still feel that I have to reiterate how important Amberlyn is.

"She is nothing like that slick git, Casey Burke. She is special," I say confidently. "You'll see."

WHEN I pull into the pub later that night, my da and the conversation we had are the last think I'm thinking of. Amberlyn is center stage, shining, flooding my thoughts with every detail I can remember. Which is basically everything about her. I've missed the way her hair cascades down her shoulders, the way her eyes shine, and the way her lips purse when she is in deep thought. God, my hands are shaking. I want to see her so bad. At this point, I don't care what we do. We can sit in the car and talk and I would be happy, which will be what we do if Plan A doesn't work for her.

Reaching for the door handle, I go inside, and the loud, boisterous pub goes quiet at my entrance. Popping up from behind the bar, Amberlyn grins as her eyes set on mine. My chest aches at the site of her. She looks angelic. Her hair falls the way I like it down her shoulders, wild and curly, her eyes bright with only a little makeup enhancing them. Her lips are glossed to perfection, and a sweet, pink color dusts her cheeks. When she comes out from behind the bar, she is wearing a pair of fitted jeans and a green see-through shirt with a tank covering the pieces I've been dreaming about. As she reaches me, a slow grin forms on my lips.

"Hey."

"Hey there," I say as my hands shake at my side. I want to envelop her in a hug, nuzzle my nose in her hair, and get lost in the intoxicating smell of her. "You look beautiful."

She smiles sweetly, the pink of her cheeks darkening. "Thank you. Let's go before my uncle comes out here and threatens you or something."

I chuckle at that as she takes my hand, lacing her small fingers with mine and basically dragging me out the door with only a wave to Fiona. I wave, too, and receive a grin as the door slams shut. Once we are outside, she whips around, wrapping her arms tightly around my middle. My eyes drift closed as I hug her in closer, loving the way she feels in my arms. She is small, but she fits me perfectly. Taking in a deep breath, I get drunk off the smell of her hair. I love it, crave it, and when she pulls back, I stop her by holding her tighter.

"Not yet," I whisper.

"I don't like sharing you with anyone else."

I know what she means. I hate the onlookers, too, but this…this is wonderful. I can feel her smile on my shoulder as she hugs me tighter. Squeezing her one last time, I pull back and look down at her beautifully flushed face. She bites into her lip as her head falls to the side, her eyes locked on mine. "What if I kiss you?"

I pause, surprised. "What?"

"You won't kiss me until the perfect moment, as you say, but what if I kiss you?"

I grin as I shake my head, letting my hands drop from her waist to put some distance between us. "I won't let you."

She scoffs. "A willing girl's lips coming toward you, and you won't kiss them?"

"Nope," I say, taking another step back for good measure. She laughs as she follows me, trying to close the gap between us, but I am quicker. Turning around, I run to the car with her chasing me, our laughter filling the air. When I reach my car, I unlock it, but before I can get in, she jumps in my seat and looks up at me with her lips pursed in the air.

"Kiss me," she mumbles through her pursed lips. I laugh, but damn if I don't want to. I wouldn't stop though. I'd give her the best fuckin' kiss in the world, and I refuse to do that in the cab of my car.

"No way," I say, reaching for her wrist to pull her from the car, but she bats me away playfully, her eyes sparkling with mischief.

"I'm not moving until you kiss me," she says, crossing her arms under her breasts to push them up. Not sure if she did it on purpose, but of course, I look at her delectable chest through the sheer green fabric before looking up at her pursed lips. Swallowing loudly, I cross my own arms before I do what we both want. "Come on, you've got me begging for a kiss from you. How pathetic."

I laugh as I lean down, bracing my hands on her knees, which results in my being closer than I can handle. Her eyes are dark, swirling with want, and when her pink tongue comes out, wetting her plump lips, I almost groan loudly. "Instead of begging, you could just be patient," I suggest, my lips itching to be on hers.

"Yeah," she says breathlessly, "but I'm not very good at being patient when I want something."

Yup, my dick is so hard that it hurts. Swallowing again, I lean toward her. My heart is pounding, and my knees feel like at any moment they could give out. As much as I want to get lost in her luscious lips, I know I want to wait until the moment she'll remember forever. Going for the side of her mouth, I grin before pursing my own lips to meet at the sweet spot where a dimple lays, but before I can, she turns her head, meeting her lips to mine. Heat explodes everywhere, and I can't breathe. Fuck, there is no stopping me now. Her lips are as soft as I imagined, plump, and taste sweet like her. Pulling back, I stand up, reaching for her before she can say anything, to set her to her feet. Her eyes are locked on mine, and when I drop my mouth to hers, she gasps as I try to deepen the kiss, running my tongue along her bottom lip, hoping for entrance.

Thank God, she gives it to me.

Pushing my tongue in her mouth to play with hers, my fingers bite into her hips as I bring her closer to me. I want her to know her little game just turned into something bigger. When her hands run up my chest and lock behind my neck, I groan against her lips at the mere pleasure of her sweet hands on bare skin. This has to stop before I do something that neither of us is ready for. Pulling my lips from hers, I inhale deeply as my eyes lock with hers. Her face is flush, her lips swollen, and fuck, she looks so damn edible.

"Whoa," she breathes, her breasts touching my chest as she takes long pulls of air.

I nod in complete agreement. With that kiss, I was supposed to blow her away, but I'm the one who is having a hard time breathing. "Told ya to wait."

She laughs. "No way, that was perfect."

I smile, leaning my head against hers. "And to think, it's only the start of our date."

"Well, damn, this is gonna be some date then, huh?"

I nod as I lace my fingers with hers. "Damn right, it is."

Pulling her to me again, I brush my lips on hers and smile. "I'm more than likely going to do that more often than needed."

She grins as she goes up on her tippy toes, placing a small kiss on my lips. "And I'll more than likely enjoy it each time."

Running my nose along hers, the thought of staying in the car and making out the whole time seems like Plan C, but I think I owe her more than that. So, pulling way, I kiss her knuckles before pulling her toward my car. "I better take you on this date."

"Yeah, before we end up making out in your car the whole time, huh?"

I nod. "Exactly."

fifteen
Amberlyn

Declan makes my heart race.

Like seriously. This feeling is new and exhilarating. It has me grinning so hard that I'm afraid my face will stay like this permanently, but then I am okay with that because he put it there. We haven't said anything since the "knock you on the ass" kiss he gave me. I mean, words can't describe the way he rocked my world. My heart is still pounding in my chest. My lips are still tingling, and my body is humming with awareness for him. I want to reach out, cup his neck with my hand, and slowly trace the veins in his neck with my thumb.

It's been two days since the night we sat on the dock and spilled our souls to each other. Since that moment though, I've never felt so free in my life. Declan is honestly the best listener in the world and makes me feel safe when I'm with him. Since leaving me that night with only a kiss to my palm, I've thought of him constantly. When he would text me, I'd get this grin on my face and then do this disgusting, girly giggle before answering him back just as fast as I could. Nothing matters but texting him back and waiting for his reply. It's pathetic, but it is what it is. I can't help it. I've never felt like this before.

Like I'm flying.

With a content grin on my face, I reach out, lacing my fingers with his. When he squeezes my hand and sends me a wink, I'm breathless. He looks good every day, but after that kiss, he looks hot. Like superhot. He has that damn beanie on, but his eyes are dark, his lips puffy from our kiss. He's wearing a thin, white tee with a grey striped one over it with fitted jeans. When he glances over at me, a smile pulls at his lips, and his eyes are radiant as they hold mine for a split second before looking back out at the road. He makes me feel so warm, from the inside out. I tried to explain it to Fiona, but she was too busy gushing over the almost kiss and how silly I was to wait for one. She was the one who suggested I just do it. I have to admit I am buying her a gift card to the tanning place tomorrow because her idea was spot-on.

I don't know where we are going, and to be honest, I don't care. I sit contentedly in the car as we drive down the weaving roads along the countryside. When we come to the large gate that surrounds his property, I wonder if we are going back to the dock. That's fine with me, I love it there, but instead of taking the road to the pond, he takes another one, and soon we are lost in the lush greenery of his land. It's spectacular, and I can't wait to see the main house, or anything for that matter. Declan promised to take me on a tour of the distillery, and I wonder if that is what we are doing. When we pull up next to a large barn, I peer out the window, in awe of the massive building.

"That's a big barn."

He smiles as he gets out, grabbing a bag out of the back before coming around to help me out of the car. "Yeah, we only have about an hour and a half before it gets dark, so let's get Cathmor and get going. Do you have a problem riding in the dark? We might have to after we eat."

"Oh, we are riding?"

He nods before glancing down at my feet. I know he is thinking the same thing I am since I am wearing flip-flops. "Yeah, I forgot to tell you to get boots or something since you basically pulled me out of the pub and devoured me," he says before winking at me. "But I'm sure you can fit in Lena's boots."

"Okay," I say, but then he looks back at me, his brows together.

"That's okay, yeah?"

I nod my head earnestly. "Yes, of course, I'm excited. The last time I rode, though, was before my mom got sick, so it might take some getting used to."

He smiles, his eyes filling with compassion as he laces his fingers with mine. "It's like riding a bike. Come on."

I go willingly, and when we enter the barn, I am completely astonished. It is state of the art and the poshest barn I've ever seen. There are about six horses, all tucked in their little living quarters. Their stalls are bigger than my room, big troughs are full of fresh veggies, and then there is one with water. It's so nice that even I wouldn't mind living here.

When a pair of boots and socks appears in front of me, I reach for them before smiling up at Declan. He's gushing with excitement, and it fuels my own. Dropping the boots, I lean over to slide the socks and then boots on. When I stand, I am pleased they fit.

"Good?" he asks.

I nod. "Perfect fit."

"Awesome, okay, let's go," he says, leading me down to a stall that holds a gorgeous, white mare. I smile when she comes toward me, running her nose along my face for a kiss. My mom loved horses, said when she was younger she wanted to own a billion of them and love each one. She never got the chance, but that didn't mean we didn't ride a lot. Those were some of my favorite memories. We'd all pack lunches, go rent some horses, and spend the day riding before having a nice lunch by the lake. It was fun. With my throat tight, I look over at Declan to catch him watching me.

"You okay?"

I nod. "Sure."

"We don't have to ride. We can go somewhere else if you like."

I shake my head. "No, it's not that. I did this with my mom and dad a lot. I was just thinking of them."

"Oh, that's awesome," he says before wrapping an arm around my shoulders. He brings me in close before placing his lips on my temple.

"Yeah, it was."

He moves his nose against my temple, and my eyes drift closed. He feels so good against me, and I never want him to stop touching me. I don't get what I want because he pulls away, opening the gate and letting the white horse out. Suddenly, three people are around the horse, getting her ready to ride as Declan looks back at me. "This is Belle, Lena's horse. She's a good girl, huh, Belle? So pretty."

I reach out, running my fingers along her silky skin. "Hi, Belle."

She lets out a happy horse noise, and Declan grins back at me. "She likes you." When he reaches for me, I gasp as he brings me in close. "So do I," he whispers against my lips. Before I can smile, his mouth is on mine, and I swear it's heaven being kissed by this man. When I hear someone clear their throat, I pull away. I can't believe I forgot that three people were in the room with us.

"Mr. O'Callaghan, do you want us to suit up Cathmor too?" one of them says, and Declan nods.

"Yes, please, thank you," he says it so sternly, but when he turns, there is a smile on his face. "So you know how to get on, right?"

I laugh as I go around Belle, reaching for the saddle to pull myself up. "I have a feeling you just want an excuse to touch my ass."

Declan's cheeks warm with color before setting me with a look. "You're on to my master plan, I see."

"I am."

He laughs. "Are you sure you can get up there?"

I send him a look that tells him not to doubt me before pulling myself up and settling into the saddle. I give him a smirk, and he laughs.

"Okay then," he laughs before walking over to where his horse waits for him.

"Is that all, Mr. O'Callaghan?" the same one from before asks. He is an older man, while the two other men are young, my age even.

Declan nods. "Yes, thank you."

"Thank you," I say, and then they all look up at me. They look so shocked that I thanked them, but soon they are smiling at me.

"Sure thing, ma'am. Have a nice ride."

I smile just as Declan says, "Ayea, Cathmor."

His beast of a horse starts out the door, and I guess Belle is used to following because she does just that. Soon the warm, setting sun is shining on us as I follow Declan away from the barn. It's so beautiful out here. Don't get me wrong, I love my aunt's land, but Declan's is awe-inspiring. It's so beautiful with lush greenery and big trees that cover most of the grounds. The lake is off in the distance, and I love the way it looks with the sun setting along it. I can see the massive castle, too, with smaller castles behind it. It's an intimidating thing, seeing all this, but when Declan's eyes meet mine, none of it matters.

All that matters is him.

When we are a good distance, he looks back at me again, sending me a grin before clucking his tongue at Belle. She trots toward him, and he grabs the reins to stop her beside him and Cathmor. "Ready to ride? Belle is fast."

"Sure," I nod, my heart racing a bit from the adrenaline coursing through my veins. It feels great with this beast beneath me, but I'm nervous to ride her to full power.

He laughs. "You don't look ready, *mo stór*."

My brow goes up. "Did you just call me a store?"

He shakes his head, chuckling before he reaches for my hand, bringing me close to him. "No, never, it's something my da calls my ma. It's Irish."

That sends chills down my spine. Leaning closer, I run my nose along his, squeezing Belle with my thighs to stay on. "What does it mean?"

He cups my chin and smiles, his eyes holding mine. "My treasure."

Yup, warm and fuzzies go nuts inside me as I get lost in his eyes. As he presses his lips to mine, I close my eyes and think how freaking romantic this is. The sun is setting, and I'm on horseback with a freaking prince. How the hell does this happen to someone like me? Pulling away, Declan kisses my nose before letting me go. We share a smile before he says, "Right then, let's go."

I nod as excitement fills me. Declan hollers something, and then Cathmor is off. The next thing I know, Belle is racing through the countryside right along with him. Breathless, I hold on tightly, my hair flying as the wind whips me in the face. I know I'll have crazy hair once we stop, but I don't care. This is exhilarating! He was right when he said it would be like riding a bike; it is, and I love every second of it. We cut around the pond, riding fast, and soon I pull ahead, but only for a second before Declan cuts me off, sending me a grin before kicking Cathmor to go faster. I kick Belle and she digs in, hauling ass as we race for what seems like hours.

When Declan slows down a bit, I pull the reins, having Belle do the same. We are trotting alongside each other when Declan asks, "Fun?"

I quickly nod. "Blast."

"Great, she's fast, huh? You're a good rider."

I smile. "Thank you. Yes, she's beautiful."

"She makes Lena nervous. She's more of a Barbie doll, our Lena is, so I usually take Belle out since she won't."

"That's too bad. She's beautiful."

He nods in agreement before asking, "You ready to eat?"

My stomach picks that moment to rumble, and I smile. "Yeah, I'm starved."

When we stop at a little, rock garden-type thing, Declan dismounts Cathmor before coming over to help me. My feet hit the ground and then I am wrapped up in his arms, his mouth moving against mine. I hold on tightly to him, basking in the feel of his lips on mine. When he parts from me, he kisses me one last time before saying, "I have to admit, Amberlyn, you look fuckin' hot on that horse."

I giggle as my face goes hot. "So do you."

He winks at me before backing away, taking my hand in his. Once settled on the grass between all kinds of rocks with our subs, chips, and of course, a beer, we enjoy our dinner before I say, "This is fun."

"Good," he says with a nod. "I was hoping you'd enjoy it."

I send him a grin before taking a big bite of my sub. After swallowing the bite, I ask, "How was work?"

His face changes then as he shrugs. "It was work. I actually got in trouble for texting you today during the meeting."

I laugh as I reach over, swatting at his arm playfully. "Don't do that!"

He nods. "Oh, I won't be doing that anymore, but my da knows about you now."

That stops me mid-bite. "He does?"

"Yeah, we were on a blog, I guess, and he did a background check on you, not to freak you out or anything."

I roll my eyes. "'Cause getting a background check done on me without any notice isn't going to freak me out, right?"

He smirks at me. "Right."

I shake my head, biting into my lip before asking, "What did you tell him?"

"That you are the most beautiful woman ever and to mind his business."

I grin, my heart fluttering in my chest. "Well, that was nice."

His eyes are dark as he nods. "It's the truth."

Grinning, I take a bite before looking around us. I wonder what his dad found? It makes me nervous. I don't know why, but it does. Declan doesn't seem affected by it, so maybe I shouldn't be either. No big deal, right? Trying to let it go, I enjoy my dinner.

"Do you miss the States?"

I look up at him and shrug. "No, yeah, I don't know. Sometimes I do. I'm actually really happy here except for one thing, that is."

He looks up questioningly. "What?"

"Goober. I can't find it anywhere in this damn country."

He looks at me, confused. "What the hell is Goober?"

I laugh. "It's like strawberry jelly and peanut butter mixed together in one jar. It's my favorite. If I'd known you guys didn't carry it here, I would have smuggled some in."

"That's disgusting! One jar?"

"Yes! It's the most amazing thing ever."

He laughs from the gut before shaking his head. "If you say so."

"I do!" I exclaim, throwing a chip at him, which he catches in his mouth. I glare before popping one in my mouth as he just continues to laugh. It's a euphoric noise, one that curls my toes and has me giggling along with him. He is so beautiful like this. I feel free, and I hope he feels it, too, because as I watch him, my nerve endings tingle and my heart races. Something is happening here, and I might not know what it is, but I like it.

A lot.

"I'm pissed at Kane."

I look over at where Fiona is furiously cleaning the bar. Her face is red, along with her limbs, and her lip is curled up in frustration.

"I would have never known that by the way you threw your phone across the bar," I say, but then wish I hadn't when she sets me with a look.

"He's a fuckin' eejit, I tell ya! We've been dating for what…almost three weeks, no, a month maybe, and this dude won't admit that we are together! He says don't rush him. I'm about to fuckin' kick him, is what I'm gonna do."

Running my fingers through my hair, I hate that I don't know what to say as my fingers get tangled in it. "Yeah, I don't know. Fiona? Does he give a reason?"

"No, just that I don't need to rush things, but I like him, thought he liked me, so doesn't that mean we are together? I mean, shit."

"Yeah, I agree," I say. Inside, I am thankful that I'm not in the predicament she is in. Declan has made it known that he likes me. I mean, we are only dating, but if I did want to commit to something, then at least I know he'd be all for it. The night before is still playing over and over again in my head, just like all the times I have spent with him do. We spent the night kissing and cuddling under the stars before riding back to the barn. He then took me home, walked me to the front door, kissed me thoroughly, and then left, promising to text me once he was home. And he did. It was perfect. God, I'm crushing bad on him.

"It's bullshite is what it is. I swear, the man is going to drive me crazy."

I nod. "Yeah, but I doubt you'll stop seeing him."

"Nope, but I swear to God, Amberlyn, he sees another girl, I'm gonna throttle him."

"I'll help," I promise, and like I wanted, she smiles before wrapping me up in a tight hug.

"You're too good to me."

"Always will be, too," I say, sending her a grin and then restocking the beer. We only have a few folks in the pub today, mainly older ladies who are enjoying tea and Aunt Shelia's chocolate cake. I'd already had two pieces…okay three, but it's the best dang cake I've ever had! I kind of hope that Declan comes in for a piece. I texted him earlier about it, but he hasn't responded yet. He usually doesn't during the day—he is busy at the distillery—but I'm still hopeful.

As Fiona walks around to make sure our patrons are taken care of, I clean the barstools and mop. We are getting ready for the Friday dinner rush, and since tonight is bound to be busy, we are working quickly so that we can both go back home and nap. As I wash out the mugs and glasses Fiona has laid on the bar, the door sounds and I look up, wanting to glare at the asshole who comes in twenty minutes before we close. However, I freeze when I see it's Casey.

"Howya, Fiona."

Fiona pauses, her eyes wide, but she doesn't say anything. Casey doesn't seem worried about it though. His eyes are on me as he comes toward the bar. "Howya, my beautiful sunshine?"

"Casey," I say, diverting my eyes toward the glasses I'm washing. "How can I help ya?"

"I came to see if ya got the flowers I sent?"

I nod. "I did, thank you. They were nice."

He doesn't say anything, and I don't look up. I am hoping he'll catch the drift, but he doesn't apparently. "Did ya read the note?"

I nod once more. "Yeah. I did."

"I really am sorry," he says, a little louder than a whisper.

Knowing that I can't ignore him much longer, I look up and brace my hands on the sink as I look into his eyes. I can see Fiona watching me out of the corner of my eye, and I know she is there since I have to nip this in the bud now. I need to tell him the truth, even if I feel like my voice is shaky. My heart is clanking against my ribs, but I have to do this. "Thank you, and I forgive you, Casey. I didn't set boundaries or something, but still, I don't feel the way you do."

He waves me off. "Sure you do. We just have to get over what happened and move forward. I wanted to give you some time. I think it's been enough, don't you?"

Not nearly enough, but I don't say that. Instead, I say, "I'm sorry, but I don't, and I can't get over it. You hurt my face and you scared my family and me. Nothing is going to happen between us."

"Because of Lena O'Callaghan?"

I shake my head. "No, because of you! I don't feel comfortable around you."

Holding my gaze, he seems to mull that over before he nods. "Then I'll have to work to make you comfortable."

Before I can say that, no, that's not what I am trying to say, the door opens again. When I glance over his shoulder, my stomach drops.

Declan's face breaks into a grin until Casey turns to look back at who I am staring at. The grin is gone, and I swear it is so quiet the only thing you can hear is one of the older ladies' breathing machines. When Declan looks back at me, his eyes are full of anger, but before I can say anything, his heated gaze meets Casey's again and he says, "What the fuck are you doing talking to my girl?"

sixteen
Declan

My body tenses and I feel my teeth grind as my gaze meets Casey's look of surprise, but he still doesn't seem to care that I'm talking to him. I want to kill him. Tear his limbs one by one from his body and then beat him with the bloody ends. Yes, I may be overreacting, but I hate this man and wish him to the nine circles of hell. I feel I have good reason for my hatred, too. He is a fuckin' slick git!

Putting a smirk on his face, he leans against the bar and throws a thumb toward Amberlyn.

"This is your girl?"

"Yes, that's what I said, you fuckin' arsehole," I say as I start for him. Within seconds though, a hand comes around my bicep, stopping me. I look back to hit whoever has a hold of me, but when my heated gaze meets Kane's cool one, I pause. Kane slowly shakes his head as Casey says, "She didn't tell me that. Maybe it isn't true?"

I whip my head toward him to tell him that it is fuckin' true, but Amberlyn beats me to it. "Actually, I never got the chance to."

Casey looks back at her, his brows up. "You're seeing stiff-ass Declan O'Callaghan?"

She nods. "I am."

"So he's the reason you won't go out with me?"

She shakes her head. "That…and because I'm not comfortable around you."

"I told ya I could make you comfortable, if you'd give me the chance, sunshine."

"The fuck you will," I sneer as I head for him, basically dragging Kane along with me. "Call her sunshine again, and you'll never see the light of day, ya arsehole!"

"Dec, calm down," Kane tries, but I'm not listening.

"No," I say, pulling my arm out of his grip and going toe-to-toe with Casey. "You stay the fuck away from her. She doesn't want anything to do with you, ya sick fuck."

He still stands with a cool expression and a smirk. I want nothing more than to knock the look off his face, but I doubt Kane will let me get that far. I can still feel him beside me. As Casey turns fully toward me, I hold his gaze. He is bigger than I am by a foot, but in no way, shape, or form am I scared of this wanker.

"You looking for a fight, Dec? Because I feel you are, and I have no problem finishing with you. You've been a constant pain in my arse for years."

"And I'll continue being one until you leave."

"I'm not going anywhere, friend, so get used to seein' me. Also, you better be careful because I might try to steal your girl."

Amberlyn scoffs. "In your dreams, buddy."

He glances back at her, but I don't move, my gaze locked on him, waiting for the moment to swing. As he looks back at me, Casey glares. "What do ya say, then?"

I have a lot to say, but before I can, Fiona comes between us, pushing Casey.

"That's enough is what I say. Get the hell out, Casey. You're not welcome here anymore."

He laughs. "What the hell? You don't mean that."

She nods. "I do. Don't come back."

"Because of that wanker? You're taking his side? I thought you were my friend."

She takes a step toward him, a look of pure disgust on her face as she says, "I was until you laid your hands on my cousin. You're dead to me, Casey Burke, and you are no longer welcome here. Now off with ya. Don't make me go find my da, or he'll let Declan have a go at ya."

A look of distress comes over Casey's ugly mug, but for only a second before he glances up at me. "Fuck you, Declan."

Heat bubbles in my chest and I'm ready to go, but when a hand comes over mine, I glance down to see it belongs to Amberlyn. "Don't. Let him go."

I nod, and when the door slams shut, I let out the breath I was holding. "Fuckin' eejit."

Kane laughs as he sits down. "Jaysus, Dec, you dragged me at least a yard!"

I smile grimly. "He's an arsehole, makes me crazy."

Lacing my fingers with Amberlyn's, I bring them to my lips, placing a soft kiss on her knuckles before looking deep into her eyes. Her hair is up today in a tight bun, her eyes are dark with makeup, and her lips lush and pink. Leaning forward, I brush my mouth over hers as her hand comes to rest on my cheek. I want to deepen the kiss, but we have an audience, so reluctantly, I pull away, smiling slightly. "Hi."

She smiles. "Hi. Great entrance there."

I grin bashfully. "I only came to tell you I was madly thinking about you all day, not with the intentions of all that. I apologize."

Her lips curve further before she runs her thumb along my bottom lip. "No worries, but I am confused on something."

Her eyes are teasing, her lips plump, and all my anger from before is gone, replaced with pure lust for this beautiful woman. "And that is?"

"When did I become your girl?"

I smile, my cheeks dusting with color as I pull her closer to me. "The moment I kissed you. You didn't get the memo?"

She shakes her head, biting into her bottom lip as she holds my gaze. She says, "No, must have lost its way to me."

"Must have," I say, bringing our mouths together again. This time I don't care about the audience, and I hate that the bar is between us. I want to feel her against me, get lost in her kiss, but before I can, I hear someone clear their throat, causing us to part quickly.

"No making out in the pub," Mr. Maclaster says sternly. "Or anywhere I can walk in, for that matter."

Dropping my hands from Amberlyn's face, I nod. "Of course, I apologize, sir."

He nods before looking over at Fiona. "Burke leave?"

"Yes, Da."

"Good. Is that the Kane you're dating?"

I look back at Kane to see him look up from where he is playing on his phone. His eyes meet Mr. Maclaster's and he stands, his hand out. "Yes, sir. Kane Levy. It's nice to meet you."

"You too. Same rules apply to you as well."

"Yes, sir," Kane says quickly as he drops his hand, tucking both in his pockets. Mr. Maclaster looks around the pub and then nods at us before walking away without another word.

"Well, that was awkward," Amberlyn says with a laugh.

Fiona nods. "Hell yeah, it was. My da is something."

Something scary, I think, dropping down in the seat. "What are you doing tonight?"

Amberlyn looks at me sadly. "Working. It's Friday."

I nod. "I know, but after."

"After? Like two in the morning after?"

I didn't realize it would be that late, but I nod anyway. "Yeah."

"I don't know, going to bed probably."

"Can I come see you before that? For only a bit, I won't keep you long."

She shrugs as a smile plays on her lips. "Sure, but I'll be boring."

"Never," I claim as I reach out, taking her hands in mine. "I want to see you."

Our hands lace together but then she asks, "How about now? I feel like an ass pulling you out of bed at two in the morning."

Leaning toward her, I say, "You can pull me out of bed any time ya want."

When heat flushes her face, I smile, but she pushes me away. "No, seriously, let's go hang now. I have a couple hours before I gotta be back."

I feign hurt as I say, "You don't want to hang out with me tonight?"

"Oh, shut up," she says, smacking my arm before removing her apron. "Fiona, I'll see you tonight."

"Yeah, see ya later."

She comes around the bar, stopping in front of me, and I smile. She looks hot even in a pair of shorts and a pub tee with her green toes wiggling in her sandals. "You ready?"

I wrap my arm around her shoulders. "Yeah, let's go."

We head out to the car and pull out of the drive before I even glance over at her. She is smiling, looking so contently happy, that I find myself feeling the same.

"Why don't you want me to come later tonight?" I ask, even though I am glad to see her now. The only reason I wanted to see her was because I thought she had to work.

"Because it's late, and after a Friday shift, I am so tired. I usually crash. Plus, this way we have plenty of time to spend together before I have to go back to work."

"I understand. I just wasn't sure if there was another reason behind it."

She takes my hand in hers. "Not at all. I just want to be coherent when we spend time together, and at two a.m., I won't be."

I nod. "I get it. I'd probably be sleepy too. We'd probably end up falling asleep in the car."

"If that happens, I can guarantee you my uncle will kill us if he finds us."

I laugh. "I think you are right, so for now, we'll go exploring."

"Exploring?" she asks, wagging her brows at me.

Heat flushes through my body straight to my dick. I take in a deep breath before shaking my head. "Naughty girl, get your head out the gutter. I mean the distillery."

"Oh, that's what I thought you meant," she said with a smile. "I'm excited."

"Me too," I reply, taking her hand in mine. I then ask, "Can I ask you something?"

She nods. "Sure, what's up?"

"You weren't mad were you…when I said you're my girl?"

She glances over at me, smiling. "Not at all. I like you, Declan, a lot."

Relief washes over me. I may have jumped the gun there, but I am glad she feels the same way I do. "Okay good, 'cause I feel the same."

She grins as she squeezes my hand, holding our hands with her free hand. "It's not too fast, right?" I ask, and she shrugs.

"I'm not sure. I've never had a boyfriend, so I don't know how this is supposed to work. In books, they meet, have sex, fall in love, get into a fight, break up, and then get back together. So, I mean, I don't have much to go on."

Something in my chest lurches before I glance over at her. "You've never had a boyfriend?"

She shakes her head, a worried look on her face. "Never had the time. Sorry, that's not a problem, is it?"

"No, not at all. It's just I don't want to rush you into anything, and I don't want you to feel like you have to date me because I want you to."

She laughs. "I am not dating you because you want me to. I am doing it because I want to. All I know is that I want to see you, I get giddy when you text me, and I love being around you. So that has to mean something. If it means we are together, then we are…and I'm okay with that. For a first boyfriend, I think I hit the jackpot," she says with a wink that hits me straight in my gut.

Suddenly stopping the car, I reach over, taking her beautiful face in my hands before smothering her with a kiss. She responds the way I want her to, melting to my touch. As our kiss deepens, I find myself completely immersed in her. I am utterly gone when her lips touch mine, and I'm curious to see what will happen once we take it to the next step. Not saying that we are anywhere near ready for that, but of course, my body is. But I have to control that, even if it is the hardest thing I'll ever do.

Pulling my mouth from her, I kiss the side of her mouth before sitting straight in my seat. Pulling at the crotch of my jeans to adjust, I let out a breath. "You kiss like a dream, Amberlyn."

I glance over at her and she is blushing, the color so beautiful it takes my breath away. "Really?"

"Yeah," I say with a nod.

"You're not too bad yourself, big guy," she says, sending me a cheesy grin. I laugh.

"Okay, enough before I ravage you and I don't get to give you the tour."

She smiles innocently as she giggles. "You're the one who attacked me."

"Yup, sure did," I agree as I bring the car back on the road. Within minutes, with my hand securely in hers, I pull into my spot at the distillery. Getting out, I come around to help Amberlyn out as one of the workers comes up, like they always do.

"Sir, should I fetch Cathmor?"

I shake my head as I notice that he is the same guy who has been working for me for a year, and I don't even know his name. How sad. "No, not today. I'm sorry; I didn't catch your name."

The man looks at me, surprised, before answering, "Matthew."

I hold out my hand. "Matthew, thank you, but not today. I have to take her home afterwards."

He shakes my hand slowly, his eyes full of bewilderment, and I smile. "Sounds good, sir. Let me know if you need anything."

"I will. Thank you."

As we walk in, I am thankful my da works in the offices and not in the distillery. I don't want to introduce him to Amberlyn yet. I'm afraid she'll run the other way once she meets him. I know everyone is watching me, and more than likely, he'll know within seconds that I am here—with a girl—but for right now, I'll enjoy the way she looks with the stone wall behind her, how she's smiling, and how fuckin' gorgeous she looks in my favorite place.

I didn't realize how much I was going to enjoy having her here. As we walk through the distillery, I explain how to make the whiskey and what we do. She seems very interested and hangs on every word I say.

"So it takes three years for the grain to be ready?"

I nod. "Yup, and the grain has to be grown in Irish ground for it to be considered Irish whiskey. Since that is the only thing we make, that's the only way it works, but some places can outsource. We do not though. We are strictly Irish."

"No way. I would have never guessed, being in an Irish distillery," she jokes. I chuckle as she leans into me.

Wrapping an arm around her, I take her to the malting room and explain the process. A lot of our workers are working hard, turning over the barley. "This is a constant process. They are in here twenty-four hours, for eight to twenty-one days, depending on the germination. Kane has it down to a science. That's why he is the boss in here. I used to do this when I was a kid."

"Looks like fun," she says with wide eyes. "Hard though."

"No, not at all. Come on."

"Huh? What?"

"Come do it with me," I say, pulling her along. She comes willingly, smiling as we reach for rakes leaning against the wall. Picking a section that doesn't look as if anyone has gotten to it, I show her how to rake the barley over and over again. She catches on quickly and soon she is laughing, just enjoying the process. I love how she lives. How she jumps in with no cares, no worries—she just lives. She is so happy, and it's mind-boggling with all the tragedy she's been through.

When we are done, we clean up what mess we made before heading to the malting room, the grinding room, the brewing room, then the aging room, until we are in the distillation room.

"This is my favorite room."

She looks around before glancing back at me and asks with confusion lacing her voice, "Why?"

I try to look at the room through her eyes. It is basically just a room with huge pot stills but to me, it is home. This is where Kane and I would hide from Lena. Where I smoked my first fag. Where I kissed my first girl and drank my first shot of whiskey. I was eleven, and my grandda had to hold a bucket to my mouth since I was vomiting so bad. This was my home…my place…and it is unbelievable to share this with her.

"Because I love how quiet it is, and I love how beautiful it is. It also hides my whiskey."

"Your whiskey?" she asks with a grin.

I nod as I reach for my bottle, bringing it out for her to see. "Yup, took me seven years to brew it."

"Wow," she says, taking the bottle from me. "Is there like a barrel of it?"

"Yeah, but I haven't gotten permission to manufacture it yet."

She unscrews the top, taking a swig, and then grimaces as she tries to smile. "That's strong."

"Yeah, but good right?"

She takes another swig, moves it around in her mouth, making a face as she swallows. Laughing, she hands me the bottle. "I mean, yeah, the best whiskey I've tried all day."

Pride flushes through me as I lay the bottle down. I know she isn't lying or teasing me, her eyes are sincere and her words mean the world to me. Taking a step toward her, I wrap my arms around her waist with all the intention of showing her how much that means to me. "Really?"

"Yeah, I mean, it's good, spicy. Why can't you sell it? Does your dad not like it?"

I lean my head against hers, not wanting to get into my family drama. "It's a long story."

"I have another hour before I gotta be back," she says, moving her nose against mine.

"Maybe another time."

She nods, moving her hands into the back pockets of my jeans. I close my eyes, holding her tighter against me. "Okay, well, when you want to tell me, I'll listen."

"Thank you."

She smiles before looking up at me. "What do you want to do now, then?"

Desire is swirling in the depths of her aquamarine eyes. It's such a sight to see. One that hits me square in the chest. She is so beautiful, so amazing. My da has no clue what the hell he is talking about. "I can come up with a few things."

Her eyes drop to my lips as her breathing hitches. She whispers, "Would it involve you kissing me?"

I'm lost. Completely and entirely lost in her eyes. My heart feels like it is coming out of my chest. My body is tingling, and I want nothing more than to do what she just asked. So I do. Capturing her mouth with my own, I kiss her, hard. She molds herself to me as I bring her off her feet and closer. She wraps her arms around my neck while I hold her around her middle, kissing her with all the pent-up lust I've kept hidden from her. Every second I'm around her is another second my control is tested. She drives me wild and makes me feel so free. I've always felt like I'm in a cage, but with her, it isn't like that. I don't have to hide who I am. Even when we first met, she had such a welcoming smile and inviting eyes. I've always felt at home with her.

Dropping my hands to her thick ass, I squeeze her against my growing erection, and she gasps against my mouth. Moving my tongue with hers, I want to groan in satisfaction when her hands come up, knocking my beanie off before tangling her fingers in my hair. She feels so good. So perfect. Removing my mouth from hers, I run my lips down her chin, her throat, to the valley of her breasts, kissing each one softly before I run my tongue slowly up the hollow of her neck. Her gasps of breath fill the room as I go crazy with lust.

Fuck, I want her, and I don't know how to stop.

"Whoa! My bad," I hear Kane say.

I didn't mean I wanted to stop!

Inwardly, I groan as I remove my mouth from her neck as she cries out, "Eeek!"

She hides her face in my neck as I slowly drop her to her feet. Turning to look at my sheepishly grinning best friend, I say, "This better be good."

He shrugs. "Your da is on the way here."

I had every intention of killing Kane Levy, but now I want to buy him a pint. I nod as I put some space between Amberlyn and me. "Thanks."

"No problem," he says before disappearing out of the room.

Once the door shuts, Amberlyn looks up at me and I'm utterly speechless. Her hair has somehow fallen out of the bun it was in, her lips are swollen and red, and her eyes are bright with excitement and lust. Taking in a deep breath to compose myself, I smile. "*Mo stór.*"

Her face reddens more as she breathes against my lips. "That's superhot and totes-ma-goats sweet."

I scoff. "What the hell is 'totes-ma-goats'?"

"Totally awesome," she says, and then she kisses me again. I love the taste of her mouth, it's sweet, like candy, and I want to feast for hours…but we have to go. Pulling away all too soon, I cup her face.

"As much as I want to sit here and kiss you until my lips are raw, I have to take you back before my da gets in here."

Her face falls as she says, "Oh, okay."

"Don't think that," I say, because I can see it in her eyes. She might possibly think I'm embarrassed by her, when that is so far from the truth it isn't even funny.

"Think what?" she says with a shrug.

"That I don't want you to meet my da. Well, that is kind of true, but it's not because of you. It's because of him. He can come off strong, and I want you to like me."

Moving her fingers with mine, she says, "I already do. No stopping it now."

Cupping her face, I smile against her lips before kissing her hard. Once we part, I whisper, "Good to know, but I don't want to test that theory today. Let's go, another time."

She nods, but I don't move until she smiles. It only takes a second before her lips curve and she grins. Kissing her nose, I lead her out of the distillery and then to the car, thankfully without any run-ins with my da.

seventeen
Amberlyn

"You're a fuckin' arse is what you are, Kane Levy, and I am done with you. Stay the fuck away from me."

Kane throws his hands up and shakes his head. "You are overreacting. She's a friend."

"A friend? You kissed her!"

"I kiss all my friends!"

With that statement, I know that Kane Levy is a dead man. Fiona's eyes go wild as she throws the bottle of pop she has at him. He ducks out of the way and tries to reach for her, but she dodges his grip while I just sit here and wish like hell we could leave. Why I agreed to ride with her to the park to find Kane is beyond me. I felt like it was my duty though. She is my best friend, and when they beg you to go see if the guy they are dating is cheating on them—you go. I just wish we wouldn't have found Kane with another girl.

"Fiona. Please, calm down!" he says, reaching for her and pulling her to his chest. She slams her fist into him and pushes him away.

"No, you won't cheat on me and then expect me to be like oh, no big deal!"

"I am not cheating, but also, I won't point out that we're only seein' each other, so even if I was here getting it on with Ellen, it wouldn't be cheating. I'm not doing anything wrong here."

I want to jump out of the car and wrap my arms around Fiona because I can see she is about to lose it. Her eyes fill with tears and her lip wobbles as she slowly nods her head. "Yeah, you're right," she breathes. Kane smiles before reaching for her, but she swats him away. "We aren't together. How stupid of me to assume the guy I've been going out with, slept with, and slowly fallen for could actually feel the same for me, but don't worry… You'll never have to bother yourself with me again."

"Whoa, Fiona, stop," he says, taking hold of her wrist to stop her. "We are seein' each other. I never said we were going out!"

"Yeah, I forgot to tell my heart that."

With that, she turns and gets in the car, slamming the door before jamming the key in the ignition. I reach over and wrap my arm around her shoulder, leaning into her as she takes in a deep breath, tears falling down her sweet cheeks. As the car takes off, I spare a glance at Kane to find him watching her, his face sullen and his lips parted. I look away just as his eyes meet mine, and I hate this. Nothing is coming to mind to say to her. I've never had my heart broken by a guy. I've never experienced the pain of rejection, so I have no clue what to say. Sitting up, I look at her profile, her nose red, her eyes swollen, and her lips wobbling as she sobs.

I want to make the pain stop, but I don't know how.

"Fiona, I'm sorry."

She shakes her head. "It's no one's fault but his. Or fuck, mine, for falling for someone who didn't want what I did."

"What can I do?"

She tries to smile, but it doesn't reach her eyes as she takes my hand. "Just be here, okay?"

"Yes," I promise.

"Grand."

She drives faster than normal back to the house as her soft sobs fill the car, leaving me feeling helpless. Thankfully, my aunt and uncle are at the pub working, so we are able to hide in her room with ice cream, popcorn, and soda, watching horrible chick flicks in our PJs at two in the afternoon. With Fiona's head in my lap, I braid her hair as we watch *The Notebook*. My nose is running from my tears, but damn, this is one of the greatest love stories ever put out.

"I want a love like this," she whispers, and I nod.

"Me too. I want the kind of love that you run across a field for. Like in *Pride and Prejudice* when Mr. Darcy beelines for Elizabeth."

"That's a good one. We should watch that next."

I couldn't agree more. Smiling, I say, "Sounds good."

She moves her head to look up at me. "I would have run across the field for Kane. I thought that he was it. How stupid am I? It's only been a month, and I almost fell for him! No one does that. No one falls in love that quickly. I am so naïve."

"Why do you think that?" I ask.

She shakes her head, sitting up before wrapping the blanket around her. "Because love is complicated and hard. It doesn't come easy. You have to work for it. My feelings were lust, and I confused them for something more."

I pause for a second, and I know she doesn't mean any of that. She is just trying to cover up her hurt. Knowing that, I ask, "Do you think that it's lust for me? And Declan, I mean?"

Her brow comes up. "You've fallen for him?"

I shrug. "I don't know. I don't think so, not yet, but I think I could."

"Yeah, well, be careful. He is the first guy you've ever been with. You'll sleep with him, everything will change, and you'll think he is the one. The next thing you know, he's sleeping with the fuckin' bitch down the road! Love is stupid, Amberlyn. Don't get caught up in the ridiculous notion of it all. It turns smart women into dumbasses who do stupid things. Just don't do it."

With that, she suddenly gets up and goes to the bathroom, slamming the door behind her. I am stunned by what just happened, but more than that, I'm worried. Even with knowing she is just saying all this because she is upset, I can't help but wonder if she is right. What if what I've been feeling since meeting Declan is just lust? I mean, I've never slept with anyone in my life, and maybe my body is like "Hey, you might want to get me off, and I am making you think you like this guy so you'll do it." My body knows that I won't do anything like that unless I love the person. What if it is all a trick? Oh my God, have I lost my ever-loving mind? Am I actually sitting here thinking my body is trying to deceive me to get laid?

Really though, I need to remember that Fiona is heartbroken right now and not really speaking the truth. She's hurting, and this thing with Declan is different. I've been dating him for two weeks now, and each day is something new and beautiful. He makes me feel alive, and I can't stop smiling when I think of him. I like how easy it is around him and most of all, I like that when we talk, both of us listen, and we have real conversations. It's not just small talk with us. We learn about each other. I like that. I like him.

When my phone sounds, I look down to see that it is Declan. *Speak of the devil*, I think with a grin as I read his text.

Haven't heard from you today. Are we still on for tonight?

Not sure, I type sadly.

What do you mean?

Letting out a breath, I write back quickly. *Fiona and Kane got into it, and well, she is all heartbroken. I'm in my PJs, watching movies with her.*

Oh shite. That sucks. I haven't talked to Kane today. His friend is in town or something. I'm not sure.

Yeah, we saw them kiss.

I wait for his text back, but then the phone rings. "No way," he says when I answer.

"Yeah."

"Like what kind of a kiss? Because Ellen is a lesbian."

Hmmmm… Before I can answer, he says, "She was his sister, Amy's best friend in school. We lost Amy a couple years back, and when Ellen comes in town, they always get together for old times' sake. Surely, Fiona knows that, right?"

Oh, this is a crapshoot. Shaking my head, I say, "I'm not sure she does, but it's more than that. He won't commit to her."

"What? Really? Every time I talk to him, he is all about her."

"I don't know. She is a pain in the hole," I reply, mocking the way Fiona always says the angry sentiment.

He laughs. "I love it when you go all Irish on me. That's hot."

I smile as my heart flutters. "Well, thanks, but yeah, I don't know, Declan. I'll have to talk to her."

"Talk to me about what?"

I look up to see Fiona. Her face is red, and she looks like hell ran over twice. Shrugging my shoulders, I say, "I'll call you back."

"Of course, my love. Call me soon."

Yup, heart is fluttering like crazy as I say, "I will."

Hanging up, I tuck my phone in my lap. "Everything okay?"

"Yeah, ignore me, okay? I'm a crazy bitch, just broken over him. He's a pain in the fuckin' hole, I tell ya."

I smile. "I know, are you okay? Do you need something?"

"I need you to go on your date with Declan. I don't need someone to sit with me. It's a broken heart, not cancer or some shit."

Her words stab me a little bit, and I'm pretty sure my face gave me away. "Fuck, sorry, Amberlyn, just go. I'm a danger to society right now. I suck."

I smile as I stand, going to her for a hug. "Not at all," I say as we part. "But remember, the sun will shine tomorrow and so should you."

She nods. "And I will. Today though, I'm gonna cry and act like he ruined me."

"I also think you should talk to Kane, I think there is more to the story," I say, not wanting to tell her what Declan said. We aren't getting in the middle of this, and Kane's story or reasoning is not for me to tell. He needs to tell her. I just hope she'll listen.

She rolls her eyes. "Maybe one day, but not today. I'm too upset."

"I know, hang in there," I say before kissing her cheek. I hug her once more before leaving her room to go to mine. Glancing up at my mom's letter, I pause as I read the words I just said to Fiona. She wanted so much for me, and I pray I am doing everything she wanted. Running my fingers along her writing, my eyes cloud with tears, but I hold them back as I whisper, "I miss you."

Swallowing the lump in my throat, I turn and go to my closet for an outfit as I call Declan back. He answers after only two rings.

"Hey."

"Hey, I am getting ready now."

"Awesome, I was a little bummed I might not get to see you. I'm glad that changed."

My mouth curves as I reach for a cute, floral-print sundress. "Me too. What are we doing tonight?"

"It's a surprise."

I bite into my lip as I lay the phone down, pulling the dress over my head. "I happen to like your surprises a lot."

"I know. I have the house to myself tonight, and I thought I'd show you my favorite part."

"Really?"

"Yeah, I'm sure you'll love it."

I pause, the spot between my thighs quivering as my heart speeds up. The last two weeks have consisted of a lot of hot make-out sessions with Declan. While my body catches on fire at the mere thought of him, I don't know if I'm ready for that. Swallowing loudly, I try to stay calm as I ask, "Awesome. When will you be here?"

"I can leave now."

No, I need more time. "Wait like twenty minutes," I say as I quickly button up the front of my dress.

His laughter fills the line. "Fine, that's grand. I'll be there soon."

"Awesome."

Hanging up the phone, I beeline for Fiona's room, my heart pounding in my chest. She looks up at me as I enter, saying, "That's a nice dress."

"I think Declan thinks I'm having sex with him or something."

"What?"

"Yeah, he said he wants to show his *favorite* part of the house, he's sure I will love it, and his parents aren't home."

Her brow rises. "Are you ready for that?"

"No."

"Have you told him that you're a virgin?"

"No, again."

"Okay, well, you said that you didn't set boundaries with Casey, so you need to with Declan, or be ready for what he might want. You have the holy hot oven. He can't do anything without your permission. He isn't a sleaze."

"You're right," I say with a nod. "But what is a holy hot oven?"

"Your vagina."

I scoff. "You're crazy."

"Yeah, I know, but don't worry. He likes you a lot. He isn't going to do anything to fuck that up. Just tell him once he starts getting all hot that you're not ready."

"Yeah, you're right. Okay, I gotta get ready."

"Knock 'em dead, kiddo," she calls after me. I smile as I run to my bathroom, doing my makeup soft with pastel pinks to match my dress. Running my fingers through my hair, I try to tame the mass but fail miserably. I could throw it up, but I've found that Declan likes it down, so I leave it before finishing my makeup.

I am putting on lip gloss when the door sounds. Slipping on some pink ballet flats, I snatch up my purse before running down the hall to the stairs.

"See ya!" Fiona calls.

"Bye! Call me if you need me."

"Okay."

Running down the stairs, I reach for the door and smile when Declan grins at me. Wearing tan shorts and a yellow tee, his sun-kissed skin glows. He is wearing a pair of aviators and that damn hat. I want to burn the fucking thing, but damn, he looks amazing. Leaning toward me, he places his lips firmly against mine, stealing my breath. Pulling away way too quickly, he laces his fingers with mine.

"Hi."

I grin as I swing our hands like a child. "Hey."

"Ready?"

"Yeah," I say without hesitation. I may have been nervous before, but like Fiona said, Declan would never force me into anything I wouldn't want to do.

The car ride to Declan's is quick, both of us speaking of our days. He had meetings and then some drama in the malting room since Kane wasn't there today. I told him again about finding Kane, and he still didn't understand why we found them like that. He had tried calling Kane, but he wasn't answering.

"I think we should leave it alone, you know? Even though he is my best friend and she is your cousin, I don't want them to come between us. So let's not talk about it, okay?"

I nod in agreement. "Yeah, sounds like a plan."

He smiles. "Good, because I don't need my girl getting pissed at me."

I laugh. "Won't happen."

"You say that now. I'm a little weird."

"It's okay, your charm makes up for it. Plus, I'm weird too."

He grins over at me as we drive through the gates of the O'Callaghan property. I take in the rolling hills of green, the lush trees, and the beauty where the horses are out grazing the field as we drive up a hill. When I look forward, the massive O'Callaghan castle is in view. Breathless at the beauty of it, I take in every single stone, the large, stained glass windows that cover every inch of the castle, and the general splendor of Declan's home. It's breathtaking, beautiful, and a little scary.

"It isn't haunted, right?"

Declan laughs as he shakes his head. "Not our wing. My grandda claimed at one time his part was by his great-grandda, but I haven't found any activity, and believe me, Kane and I looked when we were kids."

"I don't doubt that," I say as he parks. Someone opens the door for me and helps me out before wishing me a good afternoon.

"Hello, thank you."

The man, I think his name is Matthew, smiles before Declan takes my hand. "Thanks, Matthew."

"You're welcome, sir."

Tucking my hand under his arm where it rests on his bicep, he covers it with his other hand as we walk through the large, stone doors. "Are you hungry?"

I shake my head. My stomach is hurting from all the ice cream and popcorn I devoured. "Not right now."

"Awesome, we can get right to it then."

My insides clench as my heart speeds up in my chest. Gasping for breath, I allow him to lead me through the gorgeous home. The furnishings are from the 1900s, classic and classy. There are pictures everywhere, big ones of Declan and who I assume is Lena. She's as beautiful as he is, big blue eyes, long, light blond hair, and skinny as a rail. When he said she was more of a Barbie doll, he wasn't much off. She's perfect.

While it is a beautiful home, without the pictures of Declan's family, I wouldn't believe anyone lived here. It is immaculate. Nothing out of place, not like at home where Aunt Shelia's yarn is everywhere or where the fireplace is cluttered with Uncle Michael's hunting stuff. While the B&B side is nice and tidy, our living quarters are well lived-in.

Not like this.

This is too nice.

But then again, everything about Declan is always so put together. His car, his horse, his office, his home, and the way he acts around others. The only thing that isn't is his hair, but he always keeps that hidden. While I like all of him, I like it better when he lets himself go and doesn't worry one bit about the repercussions. Like when he almost fought Casey. I've never been so hot in my life. Or when he picked me up and kissed the stuffing out of me, his control slipping with every passing second. So fucking hot. Thankfully, though, he seems more himself when it is just us, and in a way, I like it like that. It's like I get to keep all that part of him to myself.

I'm selfish like that, I guess.

As I lean into him, we head through the different corridors while Declan gives me the tour.

"The house is massive, as you can tell, but my family lives in the North Wing, which is eight rooms, twelve bathrooms, two dining rooms, a huge kitchen, and three studies. It also has my favorite part of the house."

"Wow," is all I can say as I take in every single detail of the house. I'm still blown away at how gorgeous everything is. "How many people work here?"

"On the whole grounds? Over fifteen hundred, but that includes the distillery."

"Good Lord."

"Yeah, I live here with my ma, da, Lena, grandda, and grandma. I don't see my grandparents much. They are traveling with my uncle and his family. I think they are in England right now. Lena usually goes with them, but she stayed home this year. When my da retires, he'll travel more, too."

"So then you'll have the whole house to yourself? Or will you travel, too?"

He shakes his head. "Yeah, it will be all mine."

"Wow. This is a lot of house for one guy."

He bites into his lip as he nods his head. "Yeah, but by then I'll be married."

I looked up, my brow raised. "Oh."

I have no clue why I just got jealous, but I am. It's a horrible feeling, one that feels like it's on fire in the middle of my chest. Biting into my lip hard, I push the feeling away as we reach a huge, white door.

"So this is what I wanted to show ya."

Excitement takes over, and I bounce on my heels. I may have been nervous before, but I'm pretty sure this isn't his room. For one, the door is as big as a car, and for another, he would have said "This is my room," right? Shit! Letting go of my hand, he takes both handles in his hands and pushes the doors open. I swear, what I see brings tears to my eyes.

"Please, pinch me."

Declan laughs as he shakes his head. "It's real and my favorite place on the whole grounds, beside my room in the distillery."

"Good God," I mutter as I set inside. The sun warms me from above, but I ignore it because all I see are rows and rows of books. It's a library, a huge, beautiful library. Large marble pillars hold up another floor of books, and there is seating everywhere. It's like a book nerd's Holy Grail. "It's like the *Beauty and the Beast* movie."

"That's what Lena said when we were growing up."

"Oh my God," I say in complete awe. "I've never seen anything so beautiful."

He comes up beside me, and I look up into his eyes. He smiles before saying, "I was thinking the same thing."

My cheeks rush with heat as my heart completely blows up in my chest. It's not lust. I mean, yeah, it's there, but this is more. My heart may very well be his. Looking away shyly, he says, "I figured you'd love this as much as I do. I mean, the books in here date back to the early 1700s. Voltaire, James Joyce, Samuel Beckett, Oscar Wilde, W.B. Yeats, C.S. Lewis, Jonathan Swift, Daniel Defoe, loads of Jane Austen… I know your favorite."

He must have seen my face light up. "Oh my God, Declan, I am in complete awe. This is amazing."

"I'm glad you like it. Come on, let's go check out the Jane Austen. I think I have a first edition *Pride and Prejudice*."

I halt and throw my hands up in utter shock. "No way!"

"Yes," he says, his eyes sparkling as he reaches for my hand. "Go see for yourself."

He does have it and when I touch it, a stray tear runs down my cheek. Like everything else in this damn house, it is impeccable, but I can see the wear where someone has read it. Along the front reads *Charleston*, and I can't believe I am holding this.

"Oh my God, I can't wait to tell my mo—" I stop before the whole word leaves my mouth. My grip tightens on the book, and I take in a sharp breath, trying to compose myself, but I can't stop the tears from gathering in my eyes. Or falling as my heart feels like it is being ripped out of my chest. My mom would have loved this. She wouldn't have believed me, but I won't get that chance to tell her.

When Declan's arms wrap around me, squishing me into his chest with the book between us, I want to try to save the book, but I can't. I can't do anything because I need his comfort.

I need him.

eighteen
Declan

My lips dust her hair, her temple, and snuggle into her neck as she takes deep breaths, crying into my shoulder. My heart is breaking for her. She tries so hard to be so strong, but the smallest things can just break her sweet, beautiful heart. It honestly kills me because I have no fuckin' clue what to do. Laying my head against hers, I hold her, no words coming to mind on what to say to her. I've never experienced that kind of loss, and I feel a little lost as to how to help her. The book she is holding is stabbing me in the chest, and since I don't plan on moving any time soon, I slowly remove it, putting it beside us as she continues to sob.

I will hold her forever if she wants me to.

The room is completely quiet; the only sound is her sobs. Then, very faintly, I hear her whispering or maybe singing. It's so faint, but it's there. I'm not sure if she wants me to hear it, but I want to know, so I get closer to find that she is singing. The song is an old song that my grandda and da would sing when they were shit-faced, "The Parting Glass." I know that my voice is shite, but soon I am singing along with her in the hopes that it helps. Removing her face from my shoulder, she looks up at me with her eyes red and full of tears as her beautiful mouth moves with mine. She sings better than I do, but I don't think this is the time to tell her that. Soon her tears have stopped falling, and our voices carry throughout the whole room. It's beautiful.

When the last note leaves our lips, I cup her face in my hands and lean in to press my lips to hers. She wraps her arms around my neck, holding me close as she takes over the kiss, running her sweet tongue along my lips. My mouth opens and slowly we play, our tongues teasing each other as my heart beats out of control. When she pulls away, I follow her, wanting one more kiss. Her mouth is so sweet, and I want her to know how much I care for her, that I am here for her. She smiles against my lips, but only for a second before she begins to move her lips with mine, deepening the kiss. Parting only for air, I run my thumb along her jawbone, taking in every single feature of her. The freckles, the pain in her eyes, the redness of her lips and nose, the beauty that is Amberlyn.

"Don't look at me, I'm a mess. God, I'm so sorry," she says, looking down at where the book lays.

"Never," I say, bringing her face back up. "You're beautiful, and don't apologize, Amberlyn. I know it has to hurt, and I don't want you to hide that from me."

She picks the book back up and smiles at it before looking up at me. Her eyes are watery again as she says, "My mom would have loved this. She wouldn't have believed that I touched it. Thank you, thank you for giving me this moment."

"Shh," I whisper, kissing her temple again. "She sees you now. She's in your heart. Hell, I don't know if what I'm saying is helping Amberlyn. I'm so sorry."

"No, you are. I'm sorry," she says, waving me off. "This happens sometimes. I just lose it."

"And I'll be here to help you find the pieces and put you back together," I promise.

"That is the nicest thing anyone has ever said to me," she whispers. Slowly a tear rolls down her cheek and I catch it, wiping it on my shorts before kissing her lips once more. Mainly because I want to, but also because I have no clue what to say. I didn't plan to say that to her. It just left my lips. Once it was out there, I knew it was true. I wanted to be the person to wipe her tears, to hold her when she cried, and to be the person she confides in. I want to be the person who helps her heal.

I think I've fallen for her.

I look up from where I am staring a hole in the ground. My chest hurts, feels like it is cracking open, and I don't know what that means. Everything is tingling, and I feel dizzy as I hold her gaze. I know she asked me something, but I can't seem to comprehend what it was. I feel like she's just kneed me in the gut, and as I look in her eyes, I can't help but wonder if she feels the same way.

"I'm sorry, what?"

"The bathroom? Can I go clean up?"

"Oh, sure, sorry. Right there."

"The library has a bathroom?"

She says it in awe, and I smile sheepishly. "Yeah."

She smiles as she lays the book down like it's a newborn baby before heading to the bathroom. Once the door shuts, I take in a lungful of air and let it out in a whoosh, repeating the motion as I try to figure out what I'm feeling. Could I have fallen this fast? Surely not, but I sure do think I have. For fuck's sake, what if she doesn't feel the same? Normal people don't fall this quickly, and I'm not sure what I am feeling is real. All I know is that when I look into her eyes…all I see is home. My home. Oh man, I'm fuckin' long gone!

When she comes back out, her face is washed clean of makeup and tears. Sitting beside me on the sofa, she reaches for the book again, slowly running her fingers along the binding and words on the front. "It's so beautiful."

"It is," I agree. "Do you feel better?"

She nodded. "Yes, thank you. You're pretty amazing, Declan."

"You are, too," I admit. Thankfully, she flashes me a winning grin as she looks down at the book.

"I can't believe I am holding a first edition of my favorite book."

"All the first editions are on this wall. My great-great-gran was really into books, so she collected a lot, spent a good deal of money on them, too. My grandda joked that she was the reason we were broke in the eighties."

She laughed. "You guys were broke?"

"Apparently." I laugh with her.

When she stands, I stand with her and follow her to the shelves that are full of some of the best books I've ever read. When I wasn't running amok with Kane, I was reading or sitting under the desk in my da's study, listening to him work. But all in all, reading was a big part of my life. Even when the other kids called me a nerd, I ignored them and escaped to a place where I could get lost in the worlds these amazing authors provided me with. And while each of these books blew me away at one time or another, watching Amberlyn discover each one will forever hold a special place in my heart. She is mesmerizing, gasping and squealing over each one she finds that she loves. It seems that we loved most of the same ones, and with each book comes a story of her ma and da. It is nice and a really great way for me to get to know the Amberlyn before she came to Ireland.

When she finds *The Hobbit*, I can see the tears in her eyes as she falls onto the couch and looks up at me. "My dad bought me this book when I was ten. My mom was so mad because she said I was too young for *The Hobbit*, but he disagreed and so did I!" Her laughter is intoxicating as she slowly flips through the ancient pages. "I stayed up for eighteen hours reading."

"I did it in ten, ha!" I tease, and she laughs as I sit down beside her.

"Whatever. How old were you?"

"Fifteen."

"Ha! I still beat you."

"Maybe."

"No maybe about it," she says, playfully pushing me. "What's your favorite part?"

"I'm actually reading this again now, and to this day, it's Smaug. Everything about him is my favorite."

She nods, her face so bright and beautiful. "I love Bilbo. He said some of the greatest things that I still hold close to my heart."

"Like?" I ask, and a sweet smile covers her lips.

Clearing her throat, she says, "*It's a dangerous business, Frodo, going out your door. You step onto the road, and if you don't keep your feet, there's no knowing where you might be swept off to.*" I watch as she slowly hugs the book, and when she looks up at me, she whispers, "I told my dad that it was my favorite part of the book because it was all about the adventure, getting mixed up in all the awesomeness of the earth, and he smiled. To this day, I still remember what he said."

She bewitches me. The love for literature and her father is evident on her beautiful face.

Smiling, I ask, "What did he say?"

"He said it might be a dangerous business but to still allow myself to be swept away. He asked me to never lose my love for adventure, to experience everything that makes me smile. To love with all my heart and to get lost in the things that make my heart race." She pauses for a second, and then slowly her smile falls as she lets out a long breath. "My mom always said I was a lot like him. That I had this very carefree, adventurous part of me while still keeping my head on straight. When I would come home crying because people would tease me for reading all the time, she promised that one day someone would love that about me."

Moving my hand onto her knee, I squeeze it as I say, "I think she is right."

Her lips curve as her eyes leave the book to look at me. "Really?"

"Yes, because I do love that about you."

Her eyes brighten as she leans into me, her nose moving with mine. "Thank you."

I move my hand up her neck to cup her jaw as I smile against her lips. "Another thing."

"Yeah?" she asks.

"I love that quote, too, but also your da was completely right. If I didn't allow myself to get swept away, I wouldn't have found *mo stór*, would I?"

She giggles as she cups my face. "I don't think I'll ever get used to that. Every time you say it, it gives me goose bumps."

"Grand," I whisper against her lips, "That's what I want."

Without another word, I take her lips with mine. She slides hers across mine before she slowly parts her sweet lips for me to deepen the kiss. Threading my fingers in her hair, I hold her close as I move my mouth with hers. My heart is freaking out in my chest, beating so hard as I drink from her succulent lips.

Pulling away, I hold her gaze as I take the book from her lap and lay it on the table. Running my hands down her arms, I take her waist and pull her against me before I slowly lean us back against the couch so that we are facing each other on our sides.

"Is this okay?" I ask since she looks a little worried.

But she nods, thankfully, and that's all I need before I pull her against my chest for a long, hot kiss. I can feel her heart pounding in her chest, and I know mine is beating at the same pace. She feels so good against me, and I can feel my control slipping. I know I need to get that in check, but I can't stop, not yet. Our legs tangle, both of us wanting more from the other as we kiss and tease each other. I want her to touch me, to discover my body, but her hands stay tucked at my neck as she assaults me with her lips. I'm not sure what that means, but I have to have more. I have to touch her.

Tearing my mouth from hers, I kiss down her jaw to her chin before running my tongue down her neck. She lengthens it for me, giving me more room as her gasps fill the room. Her hands are shaking, but somehow, she snakes them up my neck to my head where she pulls off my hat, throwing it to the side before she is tangling her fingers in my hair, causing me to groan against her neck. My dick is harder than a rock, and I know she can feel every inch of me, but I am too lost to worry about it.

Kissing down her neck, I run my tongue down the valley of her breasts. I want more, but her dress isn't allowing it. Pulling away, I look into her heavy-lidded eyes and I swear I could come at the sight of her beautifully flushed face. Taking in a deep breath, I ask, "Can I unbutton these?"

I tug at the buttons on her dress, and she lets out a breath. "What is gonna happen if you do?"

I can only blink as my gaze stays locked with hers, not really sure what I should say here. I go with the truth. "I am going to kiss and nibble on your breasts."

"Are we going to have sex?" she asks, and my dick strains against my shorts from hearing her say that.

"I don't know. Do you want to?"

She bites into her lip, and I know she doesn't. She isn't ready, and that's fine. So before she can answer, I say, "No, my love, we won't. We'll only go as far as you want. Let me know when you want to stop. Okay?"

She nods, and I drop my lips to hers for a long, lusty kiss. When we part, I ask again, "Can I unbutton your dress?"

"Only if you take your shirt off," she whispers. Sitting up quickly, I pull my shirt up and over my head before throwing it on the floor. Her eyes graze over my chest before reaching out to touch me softly. Closing my eyes, I take in a deep breath when her lips touch my burning hot skin. Tangling my hand in her hair, I gasp for breath as she nibbles and teases my skin with her mouth. Her lips are a gift from God, and everything inside me is tight as she licks along my shoulder, tracing my tattoo with her silky tongue. It becomes too much, and I know I need to take this back over. Bringing her mouth to mine, I kiss her long and hard before I lay her back on the couch. Her eyes holding mine hostage as I slowly flick each button open with my fingers until her breasts are unveiled to me. And boy, what a sight they are. Silky, pale skin trapped behind a white, lace bra, her bright pink nipples standing at attention. Cupping one, I run my tongue along it, kissing it before doing the same to the other. My fingers find her tight bud and I squeeze it, making her squirm against me before taking her mouth with mine again. She is so hot, so sexy, and I never want this to stop.

Running my lips down her neck again, I lick and feast on her breasts as my hand runs up her leg to her thigh. I can feel the heat from between her legs, and I want to bury myself in her, but I know that can't happen. Not now, not today, but that doesn't mean I can't feel her as long as she's okay with that. Tearing my mouth away from her breast, I pull back some to look in her eyes as my hand travels up her thigh, cupping her ass. She moves her hand up to my face, running her thumb along my jaw as her eyes hold mine. Her movements are jerky and sort of make me think she is nervous.

"You're so beautiful," I whisper, not only because it's true, but also to ease her nerves. Like I wanted, she smiles before meeting my lips with hers. Kissing her, I press myself into her, causing her to gasp against my lips. She kisses the side of my mouth, then my jaw, and my eyes drift shut as she runs her lips and tongue down my throat. I move my hand to her hip, squeezing her as she nibbles at my neck, teasing me the way I did her. When she rubs herself against my raging hard-on, I almost cry out. Instead, I take her chin in my hand and kiss her long and hard. Our kisses are demanding, hot, and I'm not sure how much I can take.

Parting only an inch, I whisper, "My love, I have to touch you."

"Yes," she says as a breath.

Biting into her lip, her eyes lock on mine. I know she trusts me because she lies on her back, her hands coming to her sides as she watches me. Her hand is so close to my dick, and I want her to touch it, but my need to touch her is greater. Moving my hand down her breast, over her belly, I pull her dress up to see that her underwear matches her bra. Biting into my lip, my hand shakes as I trail a finger slowly along the lips of her sweet pussy. She gasps, and I look down to find her watching me. With my eyes locked with hers to watch for hesitation, I move her panties and slowly slide my finger inside her dripping wet folds.

She gasps again, biting her lip as I find her clit, slowly moving my finger against it. My dick is throbbing in my shorts. My breathing is labored and matches hers as I move my finger in figure eights around her clit. Her moans are deafening and they drive me wild, assaulting every single part of me. I want her so fucking badly that I can't see straight as I pick up speed, needing to bring her to release. I drop my lips to hers, capturing her moans in my mouth as she squirms underneath my hand.

Fuck, she is hot.

It doesn't take long before her nails are digging into my chest as she seizes up, her body going completely still as she comes. As she pants against my lips, I remove my hand and bring her in close, kissing her nose and her temple before taking her mouth with mine. Slowly, we kiss, and I swear my heart is coming out of my chest it is beating so hard. I've never almost gotten off by watching a girl come, but Amberlyn nearly brought me there. My cock is straining and it hurts, but seeing her come like that, so beautifully, makes it all worth it.

Pulling away, she cups my face as her eyes search mine, and I know this is as far as we are going.

"I don't know what to say…" she whispers.

"Say nothing. Let's rest here together for a bit."

"Are you sure?" she asks, and I nod.

I know that later I'll have to take care of myself, but all this was worth the blue balls I'm suffering at this particular moment. Pulling her skirt down, I bring her in closer, kissing her temple before closing my eyes. A moment passes, and I can feel her watching me. When I open my eyes, she smiles.

"You really know how to show a girl a good time."

My lips curve as I ask, "You think so?"

"Oh yeah, libraries and an orgasm are the epitome of a good time for a girl."

I laugh as I nestle my nose in her hair. "I'm glad you are having a good time, my love."

She giggles as she cuddles closer into me. "The best."

I couldn't agree more. As I watch her close her eyes to go to sleep, I can't help but think the thought I had earlier that I was falling for Amberlyn was completely mad. I wasn't falling—I already have fallen…

Completely and entirely in love with her.

nineteen
Amberlyn

"So let me get this straight."

I look up from where I'm washing dishes and smile at Fiona. She stands before the sink with her hands on her hips and a confused look on her face.

"Declan O'Callaghan got you off in the middle of his *Beauty and the Beast* library, and afterwards he said, let's have a rest for a bit?"

I shrug as the smile from the night before still plays on my lips. My heart hasn't slowed down in pace since Declan walked me to my door and kissed me goodnight. After our nap, we got up and had dinner. I was still on my little orgasm cloud, but even so, I couldn't help but feel weird throughout dinner. It wasn't how it was supposed to be, all romantic and just the two of us. It was like being in a restaurant. There was no privacy, and Declan seemed to be all tensed up when his staff was around. He didn't smile once the whole time we ate. I tried to make him smile, laugh, *anything*, but it didn't work. It was like he was shielding himself from his staff, and I hated every second of it, but once they were gone, he was my Declan again. Holding my hand, kissing my knuckles and whispering sweet nothings to me. I'm still not sure how I feel about that, and a part of me wants to question him about it, but for now, I'll enjoy gushing with my cousin.

"Yeah, it was sweet. It's like he knew that I wasn't ready to go forward."

Still with a scrunched-up face, she asks, "So you didn't suck him off or anything?"

I drop the dish I'm holding, suds flying everywhere as I yell, "Jesus, Fiona! I have never even touched a penis, and you want me to suck it?"

Fiona laughs as she nods. "Well, yeah, he got you off, you get him off. Turnabout is fair play, ya know."

"No, I didn't know, and the mere thought of it scares the living shit out of me," I say dryly, and she rolls her eyes.

"It's not a big deal. You just take his dick," she says, grabbing a cucumber and holding it up for me to see. "And you put it in your mouth, like this—"

Before she can do it though, I reach for the cucumber, throwing it back in the bowl. "Fiona, I love you, I do, but I am not in the mood to learn how to give head by watching you suck on a cucumber. Let me bask in the goodness of my first orgasm brought on by a guy, please. We can do lessons later."

Her laughter follows me as I go out to the bar. I swear she is crazy. Reaching for all the condiment holders, I bring them to the back to refill them with Declan flooding my thoughts. I still can't believe it happened, and above all else, I can't believe how patient and sweet he was with me. I was nervous, scared, and a little freaked out, but he took care of me, asked for permission, and pleased me in such a beautiful way. It was perfect. He was perfect. I've never felt that good in my whole life. I've had an orgasm before, brought on by a good romance novel and myself, but the way he felt, his strong arm, skilled fingers between my thighs, still has my toes curling in my shoes. But my favorite part was still touching my lips to his beautiful body. He was so hard, so hot…

My body feels all tingly, and I love the feeling. I can't wait for the next time we do it, and maybe I'll do what Fiona has suggested. The thought makes me shiver with anticipation, but I'm sure that Declan will be patient and coax me through the experience. He was just so amazing afterward. When I was tucked in my bed, still giggling over it all, he texted to wish me goodnight, and I swear another piece of me fell completely for him.

I know, it's insane, but he is making it so easy to do it, and that scares me. I don't want this to be some quick romance, and it's over. I obviously like this guy, a lot, and I can see myself falling head over heels in love with him. I know I can, but I'm worried that I'm rushing this and that he won't feel the same in the end. I could throw all my chips in while he folds. It's a scary thing, this love shit, but I can't help but want every single scary part of it… As long as it's with Declan.

Cutting up the limes, lemons, and oranges, I put them in their respective areas while Fiona preps the stuff for the salads. Aunt Shelia should be in soon to start cooking for the dinner rush, but for the time being, both of us work quietly, lost in our own thoughts. While I think of Declan, I know Fiona is thinking of Kane. She's still hurting, and as much as she tries to act like he doesn't matter anymore, I know she is lying. I heard her crying when I got in last night, and I think her feelings are deeper than she has let on. I think she does love him.

"Have you spoken to Kane?" I ask.

She glares over at me, shaking her head as she angrily cuts the cucumbers. "Fuck no, fuckin' eejit."

I smile even though she is upset. I just love how thick her accent gets when she is angry. "Has he tried texting you?"

"Yeah, a bunch, and I've ignored it all."

"Oh."

"Yeah, screw him," she mutters before going back to work. I do the same, and I'm almost done when she asks, "Have you told him?"

I look up from where I am stuffing cherries in the little bins. "Told who what?"

"Declan…have you told him that you're a virgin?"

I shake my head. "No, why should I? I don't want to admit that I'm extremely inexperienced. That's embarrassing."

"It would probably be a good idea. It is something you share with someone you're involved with."

"It's only been a month though."

"He got you off, Amberlyn. He'll expect more and more and so will you. Then you guys will get to the moment of penetration, you'll freak out, he'll be like, what's wrong, you'll start crying, and then your first time is a fuckin' mess."

I can only blink at her. "You've given way too much thought to my first time."

She smiles. "Of course, it should be magical—rainbows and sunshine and unicorns doing it or something."

I roll my eyes as I scoff. "Oh my goodness, Fiona."

"No, really, you need to tell him. Give him time to prepare."

"Prepare?" I ask, confused.

"Yes, he has to make sure to ruin you for the rest of the male race."

My eyebrow cocks. "Is that what happened with your first time?"

She laughs. "Fuck no, he did me in the girls' bathroom and thrust so hard that I hit my head on the bathroom mirror, shattering it! Everyone called me 'thrust and bust' after that."

I can't even hold in my laughter. "Thrust and bust?"

"Yeah," she says, shaking her head. "It was horrible. Thankfully, I moved on from the horrid experience and had some pretty great ones. Kane was the best, though. He could have me screamin' in two-point-one seconds with just a little touch. Jesus," she says, her eyes falling shut some.

"Wow," I say, and then she snaps her eyes back open.

"Fuckin' eejit! We are having sex and we aren't together? I'm no fuckin' slag, damn it!"

"No, you're not," I agree.

"Arsehole."

"For sure," I say.

When she glances up at me, she grins and I smile back, but then her smile drops as she sets me with a look. "You have to tell him though."

I shrug my shoulders before I pick up both trays. "I don't see a reason to tell him that I'm a virgin. It isn't like we are having sex."

"Yet," Fiona adds pointing a knife at me.

"Yet," I say with a smile. "When the time comes, I'll tell him."

She nods and goes back to cutting, but when I turn to head to the bar to put everything up, I see the last two people I want to see at that moment. Declan is standing with wide eyes, looking completely gorgeous with a jar of what looks like Goober. While I am excited to see him and even more excited to see a jar of Goober, I can't help but assume he heard what I said. And judging by my aunt Shelia's expression, it's safe to say she did, too.

And there go the trays.

Fuck me.

Crashing at my feet, fruit goes everywhere as Fiona yells, "What the hell—oh crap." I look back at her with wide eyes, my legs drenched in the juices while my face burns with embarrassment, and all she does is shrug.

"Hiya, Ma! Declan."

Declan doesn't say anything as Aunt Shelia comes to my rescue, fussing over me and helping me clean up. I can't look at him. My heart is pounding in my chest, my hands shaky, and I have no clue what to say. I planned this to be different. I thought we'd be lying in the afterglow of my first time, and I would tell him that way. I'm beyond embarrassed by my inexperience, and I sure as hell didn't want my aunt and boyfriend to know this.

I feel him near before I see that he is helping clean up the condiments. He grabs both trays and stands as I do before placing them on the table. Sparing a glance, I find that he is watching me, his face as red as mine. His lips are in a straight line, and I'm not sure what his expression means. There is no reason for him to be mad, maybe shocked, but I don't know. I hate the way I feel. I hate that all eyes are on me. It's like I have a huge, red V on my chest that everyone is staring at. That I'm some kind of fucking alien. Blah, it's mortifying!

"Well, this is awkward," I mutter, and Fiona laughs.

"What is?"

I swear the look I give her could kill her on the spot. She laughs again and before I could throw something at her, Declan says, "Can I please talk with you, Amberlyn?"

Ugh, not what I want to do. I send Fiona a pleading look that she just smiles at. "I wonder what he wants?"

"I'm gonna kill you," I say. This time, I do throw a lemon at her. That she, of course, dodges. I swear, the next time she is in an embarrassing situation, I'm going to make it ten times worse. I know she is probably trying to play this off as not a big deal, but the tension in the room can be cut with a knife. "Sure," I say, still without looking at Declan. I then, grudgingly, pass by him without another word. He follows me through the pub and out the side door.

Once outside, the afternoon sun warms my face as I lean against the wall, kicking at the ground as Declan shuts the door. Biting into my lip, I chance another glance to see that he is still watching me. His eyes are dark and set on me, leaving me breathless. Breaking away from his gaze, my eyes fall to where he is holding a jar of Goober.

"Why are you holding a jar of Goober?" I ask.

At the same time, he asks, "You're a virgin?"

Both of us look away as I let out a long breath. This is so freaking awkward, and I hate that. Looking back at me, he meets my gaze and I smile. "I told you I never really had time to date or anything like that."

"I know, but you never mentioned that you were a virgin."

"So what, you thought I slept around?"

"Well, yeah," he blurts out, running his hand through his hair.

"Wow, thanks," I mutter, rolling my eyes.

"Sorry, I didn't mean it that way. I'm a little shocked here. I wish you would have told me."

"I didn't think it mattered," I say with a shrug. "It doesn't matter."

"Yes, it does. To me, it does. I haven't met a virgin since secondary school."

I let out a breath as I look away. "Oh my God, you make me sound like a rare gem. It's not a big deal. Lots of people are virgins."

"You are a rare gem, Amberlyn. To me, you are," he says, taking a step toward me. "And you being a virgin doesn't change anything between us, but I still wish you would have told me. I wouldn't have done what I did last night. I would have waited."

I glance back up at him. "Why? It was amazing. See, this is why I didn't tell you. I didn't want you to be weird about it. You say it doesn't change anything between us, but I bet you before you knew, you were ready to bang me. Now that you know, you want to be all proper and gentlemanly about it, and I still just want to bang you. Just because I haven't done it doesn't mean I don't want to. I do. It's just I never had time, and I also wanted it to be with someone I care for, love even."

I let out a long breath and suck one back in. When his hand comes up to my face, gently tipping it back so our gazes meet, I look up to see that his mouth is curling up at the side. God, he is so beautiful. "I still want to bang you, Amberlyn."

My face breaks into a grin as I let out a small laugh. "Nice to know."

"But, like you, I want your first time to be with someone you love."

Oh hell, I almost said it, I did, but thankfully, before I could utter those three words, Declan says, "I want that to be me, of course, but that takes time. This is new; we are new. We are testing the waters, and they are pretty great, I think, so let's act as if this never happened. Let's just let things happen, okay?"

"You're the one who made a big deal about it."

His mouth breaks in a grin as he says, "It took me by surprise, that's all, but I'm good now. All I care about is being with you."

"Me too," I say, leaning into him.

"So we'll forget this all, just be us."

I nod. "That sounds great."

"Grand. I think so, too," he whispers, and it's safe to say that Declan's accent is the hottest thing ever. It's been almost two months of knowing him, and still, to this day, the certain things he says can bring me to my knees. He is just so freaking hot. As he leans his head against mine, we share a smile, and I can't help but think of those three words. He wants to wait though, which means he doesn't feel the same as me. Yet.

Kissing my nose, he smiles as he asks, "Can I be honest?"

I smile. "Of course."

"I like that you want to bang me," he admits, giving me a goofy grin that makes my insides flip.

A girly giggle escapes my lips before I say, "Well, after last night, how can I not? I can't wait to have your hands all over me."

His eyes darken as he leans into me. With a low groan, he says, "You test my control, Amberlyn. I'm usually so in control of everything, but with you, I'm a mess."

Reaching up, I take ahold of his shirt and yank him toward me. "Good, I like you that way."

I seal my mouth on his and he kisses me earnestly, causing my heart to feel as if it is coming out of my chest. Moving my tongue with his, I run my hands up his chest to his neck where I wrap my arms around him, bringing him down closer. When we finally part, only for air, I smile. He grins back, kissing the side of my mouth before pulling back some to hold up the jar of Goober. I squeal as I take it and then ask, "Where did you get it?"

"I ordered it for you. I have a whole case at the house. All for you."

My heart tightens in my chest as I open the jar and scoop it on my finger, plopping it in my mouth. I smile as the flavors explode on my tongue. Ugh, Goober, how I've missed you. "God, I love this stuff. My dad and I were obsessed with it. My mom thought it was disgusting."

"I'm with your ma."

I smile as I take another scoop, holding it up to his lips. "Try it."

"No way," he says, his face scrunched up in disgust.

I pout, my lip out, as I say, "Please?"

He laughs as he shakes his head. "Your pout won't work. We've talked about this before."

I glare. "Yes, it does. I got you to kiss me last time." He goes to protest, but I stop him. "Please," I say, jutting my lip out even more.

His eyes darken and then he takes my finger in his mouth, sucking the PB&J off. Biting the tip, his eyes stay locked with mine as he moves the Goober around in his mouth before swallowing. Shrugging his shoulders, he says, "It's okay."

I smile triumphantly. "Told ya."

"So you did. Come here," he says, dropping his lips to mine. I go to deepen the kiss, but he pulls away, cupping my face, looking deep in my eyes. His thumbs caress my jaw as he holds my gaze, his eyes searching mine. I'm not sure for what, but I love the way he looks at me. Like I'm the only girl in the world.

"I brought the Goober because I wanted to sweeten you up a bit before I asked you something."

I laugh. "I'm already sweet."

He nods as he drops his lips to mine for a quick kiss. "I was supposed to say that."

I laugh as he presses into me. The feel of every inch of him silences me as he says, "But I need to ask if you'll be my date to this ball my ma and sis are throwing."

I smile. "Of course I will. I'd love to." I pause, watching him for a minute. His shoulders are so tense, and he's working his lip. "Why do you look nervous? Did you think I'd say no?"

I laugh as he smiles back, running his nose along mine. "I don't know. I don't want to go. It's stupid and my family is intense. There is a chance that you'll hate them."

I shake my head, holding his jaw in between my fingers. "I'm sure they are great. Just like you."

His mouth pulls up at the side as relief floods his beautiful face. "I don't know about that, but I do hope you like them."

"Me too."

He grabs my waist, pulling me closer, desire swirling deep in his blue eyes. Looking at my lips, he bites his, squeezing my waist as he brings me even closer. Dropping his head, his lips meet mine, and I swear everything inside me turns to mush as he kisses the living crap out of me. I love kissing him. I love the feel of him, the way our bodies fit together. It makes me breathless and giddy all in one. I never want to leave this moment. It feels so perfect being wrapped up in his arms, but when I hear yelling from inside, I pull back, cocking my head toward the sound.

"I have nothing to say to you," I hear Fiona say.

"Who is she talking to?" I ask, breaking away from Declan before taking his hand in mine to pull him with me. He comes willingly as I say, "She sounds really mad."

I start for the door as Declan says, "I think Kane was coming by."

"Oh no," I groan as I open the door to find Kane and Fiona with only the bar between them.

"Give me a chance to explain, Fiona, come on," Kane pleads.

Fiona shakes her head. "There's the door, don't let it hit you on the arse."

"Fiona, baby, look at me, come on," he says, leaning across the bar to reach for her. She swats him away, but then he gets ahold of her hands, bringing her to him with the bar still keeping them a good distance apart. "I don't want to be apart from ya, baby, but I was stupid and scared because…because… Fuck, baby, I'm just not good enough for you."

Fiona pauses then as her face freezes in shock. "What?"

"You deserve someone who is gonna be something. Me, I'm a fuckin' malter. I don't have jack shit going for me. I live paycheck to paycheck. I come home smelling like crap. You don't want that. You're going to school, getting your degree in marketing, baby. How you gonna feel telling folks that your man works at the O'Callaghan Distillery, racking fuckin' grain?"

Shaking her hands from his, she reaches out, taking his face in her hands. "I'd be proud 'cause you're mine. I don't care if you live paycheck to paycheck as long as you do it with me. I don't care that you'll come home stinking because more than likely, I will, too. But none of that matters because I'm not asking you to marry me, Kane. I'm askin' you to be with me, love me. The rest will fall in place later. Right now though, I just want you."

Kane smiles as he covers her hands with his. "Really?"

She nods. "Yes, you big lug. I'm mad about ya, and I don't care about anything else. Just you, just us."

Kissing her nose, he whispers, "I'm sorry, and I promise, Fiona. I wasn't getting off with Ellen. She's my friend."

She nods, leaning her head against his. "I believe you."

"I'm sorry I hurt you, baby," he whispers, kissing the side of her mouth.

"It doesn't matter now that I have you in my arms."

He smiles before taking ahold of her and pulling her across the bar. She laughs loudly, and my heart constricts in my chest as I watch them kiss like they haven't in years. When they part, Fiona holds his face, her eyes bright as she says, "Don't do something stupid like that again. Just talk to me, don't hold it in. Okay?"

He nods. "Okay, so I guess we are together, huh?"

She laughs before smacking his arm. "Yup, together or nothing."

"I pick together," he says with a wink.

"Good choice."

"I think so, which means you have to be my date to this dumb ball the

O'Callaghans are throwing."

Fiona eyes him, and I can't help but grin like a fool as she asks, "Is that why you came to apologize, so you'd have a hot-ass date?"

He looks at her stone face as he answers, "Well, yeah, can't expect me to go with someone ugly, do ya?"

She smacks him again as I laugh out loud along with Declan.

"You arse!" she accuses with a grin.

He smiles as he brings her in close. "No, I apologized because, even though you just want me, I want a future with you. I'm mad about ya, Fiona. So mad."

I cup my hands together against my chest in such a girly way, but I don't care. I'm a sucker for this gushy stuff. Fiona eyes him for a moment before pressing her lips to his. He kisses her long and hard, holding her so tight I'm not sure she can breathe until she pulls back, grinning.

"I feel the same way," she declares. "I'm in deep."

Kane smiles as he holds her close. "Grand, baby."

Still smiling, Fiona looks over at me and asks, "Are you going?"

I nod quickly. "Yup!"

"You know what this means."

Confused, I ask, "What?"

"We have to go shopping!"

twenty
Declan

I can't wait to see you.

A grin curves my lips as I text Amberlyn back. *I'll be there in an hour.*

"Declan, son, did you find a date for the ball?"

I look across the table at my ma and nod as I tuck my phone back in my pocket. "Sure did."

"The American?" my da asks in a snooty way, and I hate the way he asks that. Like Amberlyn is beneath him, when really, she is ten times the person he'll ever be. It's moments like this that I lose all respect for my da. He is supposed to be supportive, proud of the woman I chose to be mine, but instead he ridicules her when he doesn't even fuckin' know her. It's beyond frustrating.

"Da, she has a name, Amberlyn, and yes, she will be accompanying me to the ball."

Da makes a face as if something stinks, while my ma and Lena beam.

"She is so pretty. I can't wait to meet her," Lena says with a grin.

I smile back at her. "She is beautiful, really something great. Even though I'd rather walk through fire than go to this ball, I know she'll make it bearable."

My ma waves me off as she laughs. "Oh Declan, it will be fun. Don't you worry."

"I highly doubt that, Ma, but all the same, I am coming and I am bringing someone."

I reach for my water and take a gulp. I feel my da watching me, and I know that he isn't done with the subject.

"Even though I don't feel she will last, I look forward to meeting the person who is entertaining you right now."

My nails bite into my palm as I clench my fist. "She isn't just entertaining me. It's more than that, Da. I fancy her, a lot."

"That's wonderful, Declan," my ma says, trying to defuse the situation, but we are both so headstrong that neither of us will back down.

"She isn't marriage material, and you know that."

"I do not. I feel she is and you will see."

"You're right, I will. When she sees the expectations of you, she'll run. An American is not meant for this kind of life. You have to be bred for it. Cleary, she has not. It isn't easy being an O'Callaghan."

"Got that fuckin' right," I mutter.

"Declan!" my ma scolds as my da glares.

I don't care though; I want to rip his head off. "You don't know her. So how can you sit there and make these accusations when ya haven't even met her. Da, don't you want me to be happy?"

He holds my gaze as he nods slowly. "Of course, but with the right person. She is not it."

"She's it. I swear, all she has to do is smile and I'm grinning while my heart feels as if it is coming out of my chest. She makes me feel so good inside and complete. I didn't want to leave these grounds for the last three years because I've been so scared of trying to fall for someone who is going to use me and screw me over, but all it took was seeing her across the lake, and that was it for me. I was off to go find her. She is special, and not that you deserve to see that, but you will."

Ma and Lena both look at me with wide, loving eyes, while my da's eyes are hard and not the least bit affected by my declaration of love for Amberlyn. I don't get it. How can he not see how much I've changed? How I'd face a place full of people just because Amberlyn wants to? I'd do anything for her.

I love her.

"You love her? After a month? Please," Da scoffs. "That is preposterous."

Shit, did I say that aloud? Looking across the table, I shake my head as I hold his stone-hard gaze. "No, it's not. It's the truth. She does something to me, something that no one has ever done. I love her, Da, and I want you to respect me on that. I think I've been the prodigal son. I've learned the business. I've loved my family first and always been loyal and true to you. Can you not give the girl I love a chance? You are dismissing her on her background, and that's not fair."

I stand, throwing my napkin on the plate as my ma says, "Declan, please sit, finish your dinner."

I ignore her, my eyes set on my da as I continue, "I've always respected you, always looked up to you, wanted to be the man you are, but if this is how you treat people, I'm sorry, I don't want to be you. I want to be better. Amberlyn is special. She owns my heart, and because I love her, you should do the same. If you can't, then you don't love me."

"Now Declan—" he starts, but I shake my head, stopping him mid-word.

"I've said my piece, and I don't want to hear that you think you know what's best for me. I am a grown-ass man. I am capable of knowing how to choose someone to love and trust. All I need now is for you to accept her, and until that moment, I don't think we have anything else to say to each other."

Turning, despite my ma's pleas and Da's demands, I leave the room and head for the door. Once outside, I greet our front doorman as he opens the car door for me before wishing me goodnight. Starting my car, I head out of the driveway, and once on the open lot, I kick the car into high speed, racing down the road. The speed calms me and I am thankful for this outlet, but I just hate how much I let him get to me.

Does it really matter if he likes her? No. It doesn't. As long as I love her, nothing else should matter, but a part of me wants him to. I want him to look at her and know she was made to be mine. I want my ma and sister to love her, for them to get along and want to do things together. A spot of tea here, shopping there, anything for them to bond. To know that she was sent to Ireland to love me, to be with me. That the stars mapped out our love.

It's true, and I don't care how sappy it sounds. When you know, you know, and I refuse to allow anyone or anything to derail that. People search their whole lives for someone they feel is their soul mate, and I found mine across a lake. I wasn't looking, I didn't even want to find her, but there she was, and I couldn't bear the thought of her being anyone's but mine. She drives me wild. Her body, her eyes, her mind, her laughter—she is the whole package. One that I refuse to let go of. All I need now is for her to feel the same way, and life will be grand.

Letting out a breath, I pull into the pub and notice it is packed. I wouldn't expect anything else, but I guess a small part of me hoped they'd be dead so Amberlyn and I could escape away. Locking the car door, I head inside, greeted by silence when everyone sees that it is me.

"Howya, Declan."

I look up to see Mrs. Maclaster grinning at me, and I smile back. "Howya, Mrs. Maclaster."

She winks before balancing a tray on her hip with plates. "At the bar tonight? Or would you like a table?"

"The bar, please."

She cocks her head up toward the bar and says, "On with ya then. Amberlyn should be out in a bit."

"Thank you," I say, heading to the bar where my girl stands with a grin on her face and her hands full of plates.

"Hey you," she calls as she passes by me, winking playfully. The smile on my face can't be removed as my fingers run along the small of her back, the silk of her shirt teasing my fingertips.

"My love," I whisper, and she flashes me a grin before going to deliver the plates to her patrons. I watch as she moves, talking and joking with the elderly couple before going to a group of ladies. I know they feel at home, loved even, because that is the way you feel when Amberlyn is around. You just feel good. She looks amazing tonight, too. In shorts with a white, see-through blouse layered over a green tank, her hair is pulled up in a bun and she is wearing thick, dark-framed glasses that are covering her sparkling eyes. I'm not sure if they are prescription, but I love the hip look she is portraying. When Fiona passes by me, I see that she matches Amberlyn, wearing the same glasses but with a yellow shirt. I smile at her as I settle into the barstool, receiving one back before pulling out my phone, checking my Facebook until Amberlyn appears.

When she places a pint in front of me, I say with a grin, "I needed this."

She smiles before coming up on her tippy toes, leaning over the bar to place a sweet kiss on my lips. As we part, my grin grows as I say, "No, I needed that."

As I cup her beautiful face, we share a smile before she falls back on her heels.

"Everything okay?"

I shrug. "Family drama."

"Anything I can do to help?" she asks, her head falling to the side, her eyes genuine.

I shake my head, lacing my fingers with hers. "Just being here is helping."

"You don't talk about them much."

I shrug. "There is nothing to talk about."

She bites into her lip before squeezing my hand and asking, "Are you hungry?"

I nod. "Yes, please."

"Special? Fish and chips."

"Yeah, sounds good."

"Awesome," she says, letting my hand go to fill my order. I play on my phone while I wait. It doesn't take long, and soon she returns, laying my plate on the bar.

"How long until you're off?" I ask, munching on a chip.

"Gotta get through the rush and then I can go. Tomorrow though, Fiona is going out with Kane so I probably won't be able to see you," she says sadly with a shrug.

I smile, running my finger along the back of her hand. "I'm not going to lie, that sucks."

"I know." She grins as she moves away from the bar. "Enjoy your dinner."

"Thanks, love."

As I eat, I watch her. It's hard not to. She is intoxicating and takes up whatever space she is in. I love her laugh, the way she moves, and the way she has a quick comeback to the drunks in the bar. Sometimes I feel like I'm enveloped in her carefree way, and I love it. I wish I could be half of what she is. I am still so mad, frustrated with my da, but like I said earlier, she makes it better. Nothing bothers her. She takes everything with a grain of salt and always sees the brighter side. I wish I could do that. Instead, I dwell on things and I constantly think of things I cannot change. I want to learn to be like her, I want to grow with her, and to constantly be surprised by her. She is simply amazing and thankfully, all mine.

It takes longer than I would have liked for the rush to slow down. It's well past eight before we are in the car, heading toward the movies.

"I'm sorry," she says for the hundredth time.

"Love, its fine. We'll just make the later show."

"I know, but I feel bad you had to wait so long."

"It's no big deal," I say, squeezing her hand. Out of the corner of my eye, I see her yawn and ask, "Do you still want to go?"

She nods earnestly. "Oh yes, I can't wait. I'm just worn out."

"Are you sure? We can go back."

"No, I want to go. I want to be with you."

I bring her hand up to kiss her knuckles before letting it drop back in my lap. We arrive at the movies just in time for the later showing like I hoped. Getting out of the car, I come around and wait as she fools around with something before getting out.

"Hey, do you have your wallet?" she calls at me.

I glance over at her and slowly nod. What is she worried about my wallet for? "Yeah, why?"

"Can you hold my bank card?" she asks, holding it up for me.

"Why?"

"I don't want to bring my purse in, and my shorts don't have pockets."

I blink and can't believe what I was thinking. This is Amberlyn, not some fuckin' gold-digging bitch. Taking her card, I smile as I tuck it in my pocket. "You don't need it."

She laughs. "I like popcorn and stuff."

"And I'll buy it. It's a date, Amberlyn," I say, taking her hand in mine.

"I know that, and you are obligated to buy my ticket, but I can get the popcorn with extra butter, M&Ms, and a pop."

I pull her against me, kissing her temple before saying, "Or I can get it all and you can hush?"

She glares up at me, her eyes gleaming with mischief. "Are you telling me to shut up and let you be the man here while I am the girl?"

I laugh. "Yes. Now come on, we are late."

She laughs along with me, probably knowing I won't budge, and once inside, I pay for everything before settling into our seats to watch the latest action flick. It is good, but it's better with Amberlyn in the crook of my arm. When it ends, we head through the lobby toward the car while people stop and stare. I hate it. I want to apologize but in a way, I know it would do no good. My da's words play in my head, saying that she isn't made for this life, but I know she is. So I don't say anything because she needs to get used to it if we were going to be together, but when someone pulls out their phone and takes a picture, I can't help it and say, "Sorry, people are staring and taking pictures. I hoped it wouldn't be this busy."

I feel so self-conscious, as if at any moment she is going to throw her hands up and storm away, hating this thing I call life, but to my surprise, she grins up at me, and God, I love her eyes. They are so bright, so playful, and I swear, everything about her drives me insane.

With a shrug, her eyes narrow in such a matter-of-fact way as she says, "They stare because we look so good together, duh! Or they're jealous because I'm with the hottest guy ever."

When she winks, my heart explodes in my chest. Not knowing what to say, I let my body do the talking by turning, stopping her mid-stride, wrapping my arms around her waist, and pulling her to me. Her eyes go wide before I drop my mouth to hers, kissing her so hard and deeply that nothing else matters but her sweet lips. Slowly our mouths move together, and all I can think is if people weren't staring before, they sure are now. Parting, I press my lips to hers lightly before whispering, "You are the best thing that ever happened to me."

A slow grin spreads over her face before her hands travel up my chest and around my neck. I can feel her heart pounding, her eyes are bright, and I feel like she is trying to say something without really saying it. Twirling her fingers in the hair at the nape of my neck, she smiles. "I've never felt like this."

"Me neither," I say, taking her mouth with mine. I know for sure that people are staring, along with taking pictures, but I don't fuckin' care. I also know that my ma and da will probably get wind of this before I get home, but, at this moment, nothing matters but holding this woman in my arms and getting lost in her kisses.

"Do you want me to take you home?"

Amberlyn looks over at me and shrugs. "Up to you. I'm not tired now."

I laugh as I turn onto the road that will lead back on her aunt's property. Driving out on the grass, I park under the tree by the lake.

"We could have walked," she jokes as she throws the door open.

"Yeah, but then we wouldn't have anything to lie on."

She looks at me questioningly. "So what? We are lying on the car?"

I shrug. "Why not?"

She throws her hands toward the car. "This car is sexy! I don't want to dent it with my huge ass."

I roll my eyes before setting her with a look. "Did you say that so I will say you don't have a huge ass?"

She smiles shyly. "Maybe."

"Well, sorry, love, your ass is huge and I fuckin' love it. Now come on," I say, smacking her ass playfully. She laughs but then stops, reaching down for a weed.

"Oh! My favorite! Make a wish."

"Love, it's a weed," I say, but she holds it up to my face.

"No, it's a wish," she says, her eyes glittering with excitement. I'm lost in her eyes, and before I know it, I'm leaning forward making a wish. She smiles before picking another one, closing her eyes tightly before opening and blowing with all her might. Slowly, the little fuzzies fly through the air around us, and when I glance at her, she is just grinning. I watch her, my chest seizing as I admire her love for the world. I don't understand how she could have been through so much crap and she can still bend down for a weed and turn it into a wish. It's magical, really.

As she smiles back at me, I lean forward and kiss her temple before I pull her up onto the hood of the car. As she cuddles into my side, we look up at the clear sky and I let out a long breath.

"So my attempt at fishing for a compliment went to shit, huh?" she asks, wrapping her arm around my waist.

I smile. "Love, you don't need to fish, but yes, very much so."

"Hmm, maybe next time."

I laugh. "If you want a compliment, I'll give you one."

She doesn't say anything for a second and I think I've offended her, but then she says, "I'm waiting!"

I look over to meet her grinning face. "For?"

"For my compliment!"

A hearty laugh escapes my lips before I say, "Oh, sorry."

"Jeez, leave a girl hanging like that," she says, smacking me playfully.

"Shh," I say, squeezing her hip tightly. "Here I go."

"Hit me with it."

"I'm trying, but you keep talking," I tease, giving her a pointed look. She bites her lip, holding in her laughter as I say, "You, my beautiful Amberlyn, are by far the most gorgeous girl in the world. I love your eyes, your lips, and I am convinced that you have the greatest arse in Ireland."

Her face warms with color before she snuggles into my chest, causing me to laugh. "Look, I compliment you and you hide!"

She laughs as she snuggles deeper. "Shut up, you make me blush."

"Grand. Look at me, I love seeing the color on your face."

She peeks up at me, and then we both dissolve with laughter. Hugging her closer as our laughter subsides, I kiss her temple before whispering, "This is nice."

She nods. "Yeah, it is."

Slowly running my hands along the small of her back, I take in her scent, basking in the flowery smell of her. "You know, today I discovered that I don't know something about you."

She looks up at me and smiles. "No way."

"No, really, I know you are going to school in the fall, but I don't know for what."

"English major. I want to be a teacher," she says. I can't help but notice that her eyes light up with the mention of teaching.

"That's awesome. So you like kids?"

She grins as she nods. "Yeah, but I want to teach older kids, like the theory of English maybe. I'm not sure. I just want to be immersed in books, and I want to share my love with someone else."

As much as I love her passion, I can't help but think she probably wouldn't be happy being a stay-at-home mom and wife, which is what usually happens when O'Callaghans get married. Swallowing my disappointment, I say, "Wow, you're very passionate about it. It's refreshing."

Threading her fingers in my hair, she nods. "Yup, we are both passionate about the things we love, huh?"

I couldn't agree more. Leaning toward her, I run my nose along hers before taking her mouth with mine. Our lips move with ease as our limbs tangle and the kiss deepens. As I hold her close, our kisses get more demanding as our hands explore each other's bodies. Hooking her leg over my hip, I press into her, our tongues tangling with each other. I am so hot for her. I can't control my need to feel her, to be completely immersed in her. Tearing my mouth from hers, I kiss down her jaw, nipping and licking down her throat, but soon stop when I hear her yawn.

"Oh my God, please say I did not just yawn."

A smile covers my lips as I pull back to look down in her flushed, beautiful face. "You did."

"I'm so sorry, ignore it. As you were," she says, urging me on, but I can't.

"No love, you're tired. Let me take you home."

Her eyes drift closed in embarrassment, and I laugh before kissing her loudly on her lips. "Come on, love," I say, getting off the car and pulling her with me. She comes unwillingly, but once in my arms, she melts against me.

"I suck. I'm sorry."

I shake my head. "Don't apologize. It's no big deal. We have all the time in the world."

She looks away and shakes her head. When she looks up at me, her eyes are serious, and I swear it's as if she has kneed me in the gut. "No, we don't. I could die, you could die, and then I would never get to have you like this again. All we have is now, and I don't ever want this to end. I would honestly be lost without you, Declan. I know that's crazy to admit, but it's true. Don't be freaked out! Oh my God, I just went completely off the handle there. It's just scary, you know? I love being with you, I love your body touching mine, and I can't believe I yawned. You don't bore me, I swear!"

She says it all so fast, but each word pulls at my heartstrings. My mouth pulls up at the side before I hug her closer to me. "Amberlyn, calm down, jeez. It's not a big deal. I know that our time is limited. I do treasure every second I have with you, don't ever think that I don't, but like you said, we have to live in the now, and right now, I can't exactly get off with ya while you're sleeping."

She snorts with laughter before hiding her face in the crook of my shoulder. I pull her away, holding her cherub cheeks in my hands before whispering, "And to be honest, I'd be lost without you, too."

Her face brightens with excitement before she slowly goes up on her toes, meeting her mouth to mine. When our lips touch, I know that it's the truth. That my life would be nothing without this girl in my arms.

twenty-one
Amberlyn

"I'm a dumbass."

Fiona lets out a laugh as she looks through the racks. "Totally. Who yawns while her guy tries to get off? Was it boring?" she asks, cutting me a look.

I flash her a dark look, shaking my head quickly. "No, I was just dead on my feet. Nothing is boring about Declan. He's romantic, perfect, and can kiss like you can't believe. It was amazing, and I didn't want it to end even though I was so tired."

"I suggest when you go out, make sure you are awake, and don't ever yawn again. You're gonna give him a complex, and he won't want to kiss ya."

Like I hadn't thought of that already. "Thanks," I moan as I look through the racks that are full of white dresses. On a rare day where my aunt and uncle have given us a day off, Fiona and I are off on a mission of shopping for the ball before getting lunch. I am starving, but Fiona said we couldn't eat until after we got our dresses, since she didn't want to be bloated trying them on. I didn't care one way or another. I just wanted to eat, but she told me that she wasn't buying a dress sporting a food baby.

While I am annoyed and hungry, Fiona is excited, wearing a bright smile with her blond locks falling in her eyes as she searches the racks. She is more excited than I am because I guess it means she and Kane are coming out to everyone. Which is great, don't get me wrong, but while I can't wait to get dolled up and spend the night dancing with Declan, I'm nervous. I haven't been to a ball before. I don't even know how to act at these types of things, but Fiona has and guarantees me everything will be fine. I just hope I can find a dress that suits me. I don't want to look like a whore or a frumpy weirdo when I meet my boyfriend's parents.

Turning to me, Fiona holds up a dress. It's hideous! I shrug, not wanting to be rude, and then after a moment she does the same before putting it back. We do this for what seems like hours as my night with Declan plays over and over in my mind. The more time I spend with Declan, the more I get to know him, and the more I fall. I love his smile. I love his eyes, they are like coming home, and his arms are so warm. I was being honest when I said that I'd be lost without him—I would be. It's become such a routine between us. We spend the day texting until the moment we are able to see each other, usually during lunch. Then we both return to work before joining up later that night. Tangled in each other's limbs, we talk for hours, learning so much about each other, and I love every single moment of it. He keeps me on my toes, he makes me laugh, and he makes me feel so special. It's perfect and everything I've ever wanted.

I remember when I was fourteen. I told my mom that I was going to marry Mr. Darcy. She agreed that he would be an amiable man and that we would need to get first-class tickets back in time to find him. For the next hour, we discussed what we would do to help my dreams come true and how Darcy would be a fool not to fall for me. I was convinced that he was the man for me. It was so innocent and perfect that it brings tears to my eyes just thinking about it.

Before my mom passed, she said not to settle for anything but Mr. Darcy status and I feel that I've found that. While it worries me that this is my first love and how people never stay with their first loves, I can't help but feel so strongly about him—like he consumes me. Every single part of me is in love with him, and I don't know how to handle my feelings. They are so scary.

"Why are you just standing there? Look," Fiona says, playfully smacking my butt as she passes by me.

I smile before biting into my lip and looking over at her. She catches me watching her and asks, "What?"

I shrug, a smile still pulling at my lips. "Declan said I'm the best thing that's ever happened to him."

When my shoulders sway back and forth with a girly grin on my face, I feel a little dumb but not enough to stop doing it. She smiles before leaning against the rack.

"That's sweet. What did you say?"

Shyly, I answer, "That I've never felt like this before."

Her brows come up as she sets me with a look. "Felt like what?"

Biting the inside of my cheek, I shrug. "I love him."

"You said that?" she asks, her face visibly shocked.

"No, I haven't. I don't know how."

Coming to me, she cups my shoulders, looking deep in my eyes. "Don't. Wait for him to say it to you."

"Why?"

"Because if you do it, then that means you care more. What if he doesn't, but he says it because he wants to be nice? This is Declan O'Callaghan. The Whiskey Prince, Amberlyn. He has duchesses, actresses, and debutantes throwing those three words at him all the time, but not once has he ever been in love with any of them. I'm not saying he doesn't care for you. It's obvious he does, but don't say it yet. Wait for him because… Okay, don't take this the wrong way, promise?"

I can only blink as I process what she is saying to me. "Okay?"

"You are the only normal person I've ever seen Declan with. He has always dated the rich and famous. So I don't know what to think of this. Does he really love you? Or is he trying to do it as a stunt? You know? Don't get me wrong, I want to trust Declan because of how highly Kane thinks of him, but he makes me nervous because it's you. You're basically my sister, and I don't want any more pain to come to you. Not after everything you've been through."

Taking her hand in mine, I smile. "I love you, I do, and I love that you worry about me, but Declan is shy. I think those other women were just what he was expected to do, and maybe I'm the real deal. Maybe I'm grasping at straws because really, a guy like Declan falling for me is kind of comical, but I can't help but hope to God it can be true because I do love him. I love him with all my heart, and I can't wait to hear him say it back to me."

"It's not comical, Amberlyn. You are amazing, and I think you may be right. I mean, you know him, the real him, so I trust your judgment. But please give it a little more time before you start screaming you love the man. Wait till you sleep with him and then decide. He could have a small dick, ya know."

"Good God," I mutter as I drop her hands and shake my head as she laughs.

"What? He could!"

"Not that I would know since he'd be the first!" I counter, and she nods.

"True, so here's the rule of thumb… You want more than a mouthful."

I close my eyes, seconds away from covering my ears. "Please, Fiona."

She sends me a sneaky grin before going back to flipping through the racks. I stand there for a second, thinking of what she said, and then I say, "I think I will wait."

She nods. "Good."

"It's only been like six weeks. While I know what I am feeling is true, I think it'd be better to wait. Don't want to go scare him off."

"Yes," she agrees. "Wait until he says it."

"I mean, we'll see what happens. I live in the moment. If for some reason, I have to tell him, or I know I can't go on, I'm just going to do it. I know what my feelings are, and all I can hope is that when I tell him, he feels the same."

She nods. "True, now stop worrying about all that. Let's pick dresses out that will blow our fella's minds!"

"Okay!" I say with as much enthusiasm as I can muster. Truth is, I suck at dress shopping. I never went shopping for dance stuff. I was too busy studying and changing my mom's bedding. Flipping through the racks of beautiful, white dresses, I sigh. "Why couldn't it be like a black ball? White is so boring to me."

Fiona shakes her head. "No way. White dresses are gorgeous because they are usually blinged out, you pair it with some brightly colored heels, and life is grand. This one is nice. It would look good on ya. It's very Victorian, which suits ya," she says, holding up a dress.

"The top is see-through," I say, taking in the gorgeous detail of it. It's an off-white, jeweled tulle top with cups that would cover my breasts, but still, you could see right through it except for the white, high-waisted skirt that would come to maybe mid-calf. It was beautiful.

"So? It's gorgeous. Seriously, go try it on," she says, pushing it at me.

"You don't think it's whoreish?" I say, my face scrunching up.

"No way. It's classy. Lena would rock something like this in a heartbeat."

Reluctantly, I take the dress and walk to the dressing room. I figure it's my curiosity that fuels me to get undressed and slowly slide the gorgeous gown up my body. It fits like a glove even with only being zipped up halfway. Turning to look at the side, I smile when I can see my tattoo on my ribs through the studded fabric. My ass even looks great, and I can't help but love everything about this dress. I'm sure that Declan will love it, too.

Stepping out, I don't see Fiona and ask, "Fiona?"

"Hold on, I'm throwing one on, too."

"Okay," I say just as she steps out in a white dress that covers her all the way up to her neck. I make a face because the dress is ugly in my opinion, but when she turns and I see that the back is backless with two black lace patches by her ass, I quickly change my opinion. "Beautiful," I say with a grin.

"Thanks, I think it will drive Kane insane and wow, you too. Turn around."

I do as she asks, and she zips me up. I turn, smiling, and she nods. "I think you found your dress."

I run my hands down the front of the dress, loving the fit, and completely agree. "And you've found yours."

"I think so. So now all we need is shoes," she says as her eyes gloss over.

"Yay," I groan, and she laughs.

"Come on, it will be quick."

Such a liar. It took another hour to find shoes before we finally settled at the pub by the store for food. My heart is still pounding from the money I dropped, but Fiona said it was worth it to look good with a whole bunch of rich folks. I guess she is right, but still, it sucks knowing my bank account took a major hit.

Taking a huge bite of my burger, I smile as the flavors explode in my mouth. I am so hungry, and this burger is going to hit the spot perfectly. I am tempted to order some wings, too, but refrain since I want to look good in my dress, and instead, I smother my fries with mustard.

When my phone sounds, I drop the burger on my plate to dig it out of my purse to find Declan has texted me. I usually wouldn't answer it while I eat, but since Fiona is in the bathroom, I find it the perfect time to get in a quick word with him.

Still shopping?

I smile as I text back. *Nope, finally eating.*

So you have a dress then?

I do, and it is going to knock your socks off.

I can't wait.

Me neither.

Wanna get out tonight?

I bite into my lip. *I can't. Since we had the day off, we have to work late.*

I haven't seen you in two days. I miss you.

I smile, my face heating with color as I write back. *I miss you too.*

Grand, so meet me by the lake when you get off.

I know I am going to be tired but seeing him is worth it. *Okay, but if I yawn, you can't blame me.*

He sends me a smiley face and I go to send him one, but before I can, I hear a voice that makes my skin crawl. "Howya, Amberlyn."

Looking up at Casey, my heart kicks up in speed. Not because he looks good with his hair falling in his face in such a cute way, but because I am still very much afraid of him. "Casey."

"How are you?"

"Good," I say, tucking my phone in my lap.

"You look beautiful today," he says, dropping in the stool beside me.

Inwardly, I groan as I say, "Thank you."

I turn to go back to my burger, hoping he'd get the hint, but no such luck. "Surprised to see ya out at this hour. Not working, I see."

"Nope," I say before taking a bite.

"Who ya with?"

I cover my mouth as I chew. "Fiona."

"So you and O'Callaghan broke it off, then?"

I make a face as I shake my head. "No, he's working."

His face falls. "Guess that was hopeful thinking, huh?"

"Bug off, Casey. We are trying to enjoy our lunch," Fiona calls at him as she falls into the seat beside me.

I send her a grateful look, but Casey waves her off. "Shut it, Fiona. I just wanted to say hi."

"Well, we don't want to say hi to you. We have to eat before getting back. My da is waiting on us."

He rolls his eyes. "Why are ye off anyway? Shouldn't you be running the lunch rush?"

Fiona glares. "None of your business. Bye."

"You're a bitch, Fiona."

"And you're a wanker, fuck off," she says and he stands angrily, making me nervous.

Looking down at me, he says, "Call me sometime."

"Don't think so," Fiona says, her eyes narrowed as she watches him. "She's happy with Declan, doesn't have time for arseholes. Which reminds me, bug off before I call one of them to come after ya."

Shaking his head, he walks off without another word. When he looks back, his eyes in dark slits, I can't help the chilling feeling that overcomes me. While I am relieved he is gone, something about that guy really makes me nervous.

It's a cool night as I walk toward where Declan asked me to meet him. Wrapping my sweater tighter around me, I walk in the darkness until I see the silhouette of him standing by the large oak tree. He must have heard me coming because he turns, reaching for me as I come close to him. Holding me tight in his arms, he kisses the top of my head, and I love how safe I feel in his arms. I had been on edge after running into Casey today, but now, nothing matters. I am safe. Declan will protect me.

Looking up, I smile as I say, "Hi."

"Howya, love," he whispers before dropping his mouth to mine. Slowly, our mouths move together as I drink from his beautiful lips. It has been so long since I felt him like this, and I savor every second. Pulling away, I smile before kissing the side of his mouth. Lacing his fingers with mine, he pulls me down on the blanket I didn't see. Lying back, he brings me down with him until I'm cuddled in the crook of his arm.

"I see you brought a blanket this time. Didn't want me to dent up the car, huh?" I say, grinning as I move my nose against his chest, taking in his spicy smell. His chest rumbles with his laughter as his arm tightens around me.

"No," he laughs before cupping my ass in his hand and squeezing. "I thought this would be more comfortable."

"Oh, well, yeah, you're right."

He smiles, kissing my temple before we both fall silent. The sounds of crickets and the wind on the lake fill the air around me, and I've never felt so relaxed in my life. Snuggling closer, I ask, "How was your day?"

He shrugs, his lips dusting my temple. "Long."

"Ugh, that sucks."

"Yeah, but if this is the way it ends, I'll endure it every day just for this moment."

"You're making me blush," I groan as I smile, my face warming. I'm answered with his laughter, so I softly bite his chest, causing him to jump, his laughter continuing before his arms close around me tighter.

"Yours?" he asks.

I wonder if I should tell him about Casey. While I want to tell him, I know it'll just irritate him, so I shrug before saying, "Long, too. I hate shopping."

"That's weird. Don't girls love to shop?"

I give him a sneaky look. "You didn't know I wasn't like most girls?"

He smiles. "Yeah, I did know that."

I smile back as he says, "Well, this is nice to do after a long day, the two of us and the stars."

"I agree," I say, snuggling into him and closing my eyes.

Neither of us is saying anything, just enjoying being in each other's arms. I am so warm, so comfortable in his arms, that soon I am almost asleep. But before I can fall into a sweet slumber, he says, "I wanted to talk about tomorrow, love."

Opening my eyes, I look up at him. He is watching me, his face glowing from the lantern he had brought for us to see.

"Yeah?" I ask.

"I know I've said this before, but my parents are intense, and I worry that they might offend you tomorrow."

I can see that he is worried, and while I am scared shitless about meeting his parents, I know that it will work out. I love this man, and I'm sure I'll love his parents.

With a shrug, I say, "It's no big deal. I'm sure it will be fine."

"My sister, you'll like her, but my ma is very suffocating and will question you relentlessly and my da, he's a snooty arse who might say something rude. So I just want to apologize now."

I smile, reaching up to place my palm on his sweet face. "Do you want me to come tomorrow?"

"Of course I do."

"Then don't worry. Everything will be fine because we'll be together. That's all that matters, right?"

His eyes are swimming with something. I don't know what it is, but looking into them, I can't help but feel like he loves me. Running my thumb along his jaw, I get lost in his eyes, and I want to whisper the three little words, but before I can, Fiona is there, urging me to wait. So I bite on my lip to keep the words in as Declan says, "You're right, and I'm sure it will be okay."

Leaning up to brush my lips against his, I flash him a grin before saying, "Of course it will."

Cuddling beside me, he asks, "Do you think your ma and da would have liked me?"

I smile as I nod slowly. Tears sting my eyes as I say, "Yes, they would have loved you."

Holding me closer, he whispers, "I wish I could have met them. I feel like I know them because of you, but I wish I could tell them how amazing you are and how much you mean to me."

I smile, and without much warning, a single tear runs down my face. "I would love for that to happen, but it isn't in the cards. Plus, you know, if I wouldn't have lost them, I wouldn't have been here, and we never would have met."

Holding my gaze, he says, "As much as I couldn't fathom my life without you now, I would rather you have kept them than come here and met me. I see how much it pains you to be without them, and I honestly don't know how you do it."

When another tear falls, I suck in a breath before saying, "I do it because I have to. Because my mom raised a strong woman, and I want to be the type of person she would be proud of."

"They are. Proud of you, I mean."

"Thank you."

"No thanks needed, love. It's the truth."

Not knowing what to say, my lip wobbles. He smiles before running his thumb along my cheeks to catch my tears. Leaning forward, he presses his lips to mine and kisses me long and thoroughly, curling my toes and making my heart sing. When we part, he kisses my nose, then my temple, before wrapping me up tight in his arms. I cuddle into his chest, and his lips dust my forehead before he whispers, "Don't ever change, Amberlyn. You are the light of my day and anyone else you meet."

Closing my eyes tightly, I kiss his chest before laying my head down to keep myself from whispering the words that I so want to say. As much as I believe he may feel the same with the words he just said to me, I can't help but wonder why he didn't say it if he did. Deciding that this moment is too amazing to spoil with rejection, I cuddle in closer to Declan, and this time, I don't fight the sleep away, I welcome it being wrapped in the arms of the man I love.

A man my mom and dad would have loved.

twenty-two
Declan

I can still feel Amberlyn in my arms.

Softly snoring, her little nose tucked into my chest as she sleeps. I never expected her to fall asleep. I wasn't mad it happened, I was glad, because watching a girl that beautiful sleep is a gift from God. Something that I'll treasure until the moment I get to go to sleep and wake up with her for the rest of my life. As much as I would love for that to happen right now, I know that it's not time. I am still so nervous about it all. I have a feeling that I am going to lose the distillery I love, but I know it's worth it as long as I get to be with her. I know I've put everything on our relationship when it is so young, but I trust my decision. I trust the power of my love for her.

Leaning back in my chair, I stretch out my neck before rubbing my eyes. When I open them, Kane is standing before me in a tux, along with what looks like the local newspaper.

I smirk up at him before saying, "Lookin' sharp there, Kane."

Kane gives me a look before dropping the paper on the desk. On the front is a picture of Amberlyn and me from the movies. I am holding her so tight that her shirt has come up in the back, but we both look so blissful as we share a long kiss. I want to keep staring, but then I see the headline above it.

Is she out for the O'Callaghan fortune?

"Ah, for fuck's sake," I mutter before reading the article. It a bunch of hogwash, basically saying that my girl is a gold-digging American out to steal everything from my family. It's disgusting and so far from the truth that I crumple it up before tossing it in the trash. "Bullshite, that is," I say, pointing to the paper and hoping like hell Amberlyn hasn't seen it. I doubt she has though because we've been in the paper many times and she hasn't said anything. Since she hasn't brought it up, I sure won't. No reason talking about something that is a complete lie and means nothing.

Kane nods. "I agree. She hasn't seen it from what Fiona said," he says, answering my unasked question.

"Grand. Fuck, why do they say these things? They don't know anything about us."

"You know that Amanda Dralls has a thing for ya, so you better believe she is going to do everything to run your relationship through the mud," he points out, speaking of the local paper editor. I slept with Amanda once when I was a kid, but I haven't spoken to her since. She is a little off her rocker, obsessed with me and shite, which makes what Kane just said plausible.

"Fuckin' bitch," I say, venom lacing my voice.

"Sure is," Kane agrees, tucking his hands in his pockets. "Your da saw it, though."

"Fuck it, I thought today was supposed to be a good day," I groan, rubbing my temples with my fingers.

"The night is still young, Dec."

I roll my eyes. "Maybe, but you know my da will have something to say."

He nods. "I know, but don't let it get to you. It doesn't matter."

"True, true," I mutter, even though I know I'll still allow it to bother me.

"All right, well, I'm excited to get my hands on Fiona. So I guess on that note, I'm off. See ya tonight."

I glance at the clock. The ball doesn't start for another two hours. "Why so early?"

He turns, a grin on his face before he says, "I'm taking her to dinner before and hoping for a quickie somewhere in between."

"You're a dirty man, Kane Levy."

Kane laughs as he heads through the door. "Be jealous, Dec."

I stand, coming around the desk as I call out, "What the hell do I have to be jealous about?"

The grin remains on Kane's face as he looks back at me. "That I'm getting it and you're not."

"Ah, fuck off," I say, turning my back to him.

"Exactly," Kane says just as I slam the door before returning behind my desk.

With annoyance flowing through me, I lean back in my seat, running my hands down my face. He is a fuckin' gobshite, that Kane. How dare he tease me when he knows my girl isn't ready for that kind of thing yet? He knows the whole story; I've confided in him and trusted him with the information about Amberlyn. Now I wish I hadn't. Okay, that's going a little too far since he is my best friend. I also know that I would do the same to him about any other girl he was not getting it from, but it's not funny to joke about Amberlyn. I would not do that to him with Fiona; I know she is different. As Amberlyn is different.

Ugh, he gets on my nerves, but I would be lying if I said I haven't thought about it every second of the day since meeting Amberlyn. She has awakened the need, and boy, how I would love to get between her thighs. Just remembering how she felt has me getting harder by the second. Groaning, I let my head fall to the desk as I inhale a long breath. Damn Kane. This is his fault. I was fine with how things were, stolen kisses and hot touches, but now I am craving the whole damn thing. I want to get lost in her kisses, I want to get tangled in the sheets, I want to feel her in the most intimate way, and I hate myself for it. I don't want to rush her. I don't want to her to feel obligated. I want her to do it because she loves me.

When my phone vibrates on the desk, I reach for it to see it's from the lady who has my whole body tight with need.

I can't wait to see you tonight.

I've been thinking about you all day, I admit.

Good things?

Good, great, and dirty, I must say.

Oooo…sounds scandalous. You'll have to share.

Leaning back, I smile as I type out quickly, *It involves you and me and my hands on every inch of you.*

Mr. O'Callaghan! My goodness! So dirty!

I laugh out loud, as I type: *Lol. Are you offended?*

Quite the opposite really. Turned on is more like it.

Groaning, I shift in my seat. *You're killing me.*

Haha. Well, let's stop before someone gets hurt. I'll see you soon?

Yes. I can't wait.

Me neither.

Sitting up, I run my hands down my face, squeezing it hard before letting out a long breath. Deciding that no work will get done after the last half hour I've had, I stand up and head out of the office. I think a shower is in order.

A nice, long, hot shower.

Looking at myself in the mirror, I let out my hundredth sigh of the day. It's been a stressful one. Between working all morning, seeing the paper, and then having Kane remind me that I'm not getting laid, I've also have to deal with the fact that I have to forgo my beanie tonight. Not only is it tacky to wear a beanie with a dark, Italian-tailored suit, my ma would murder me. So as I run a comb through my thick, tight curls, I curse them and even consider shaving my head.

Knowing again that my ma would murder me if I did so, as I apparently have the curls from her great-grandda or some crap, I throw my comb down in the hopes that I look okay.

I think I look like a fool.

Rolling my eyes, I head out of my room and toward the back of the house since the front is busy with guests arriving. The ball is starting in twenty minutes, and I may be running a tad late. Since I didn't want to come to this God-awful thing anyway, I take my time getting in my car and heading to the Maclaster land. Kane sent me a text earlier inviting Amberlyn and me to dinner with them, but I declined since my stomach is a mess from Amberlyn meeting my da.

I haven't seen him yet, nor do I want to, but I can just imagine all the things he is thinking after reading that rubbish in the paper. I want to call Amanda and tell her that she needs to stop writing that shite, but it will fuel her more. I just wish it would all go away. Can't I date a girl and be happy without the whole world and my family having a say on her? I don't know why I am letting it bother me, but it drives me insane. With other girls I dated, I didn't give a shite. I was happy, dicking around with whom I pleased, and didn't give a damn what they thought of the girl, but with Amberlyn, I want them to respect her. She is more than some floozy; she is my future.

She just doesn't know that yet.

Shaking my head to rid the stress from today, I pull into the driveway and see that Amberlyn is looking out the window. When she sees that it's me, she grins before letting the curtain fall. I hate that I've kept her waiting, and I hope she isn't too mad at me. Nervous, I head toward the door. I go to knock, but Mrs. Maclaster pulls the door open with a bright grin on her face.

"Declan, how are ya?"

I smile as I step in and go to answer her, but the most beautiful thing in the world catches my eyes. Before, no one has ever caught my eye the way Amberlyn does and right now is no different. Standing in a sinfully gorgeous dress with her dark, reddish hair in curls around her face, I can't seem to form a coherent thought. Her face is made up in a soft, beautiful way, her lips as pink as the shoes she wears, her smile formed in such a shy manner. I don't know what it is, maybe the see-through fabric below her breasts, or the way her shoes show off her legs in a delicious fashion, or maybe it's her eyes, but it takes everything for me to keep my composure as I say, "You're gorgeous."

Her face breaks into a grin as she steps toward me, and I reach out, lacing my fingers with hers.

"So gorgeous," I breathe.

She looks down at her dress shyly before looking up at me. "You don't think it's slutty or anything?"

"Slutty is the last thing I am thinking. Elegant, beautiful, classy, perfect...

Did I say gorgeous because, Amberlyn, I could go on for hours. Know that no one will stand a chance against you when you step foot into this ball."

As her face warms with such stunning color, Mrs. Maclaster says, "Why can't ya talk to me like that anymore, you big lug?"

I turn to find Mr. and Mrs. Maclaster behind me as Mr. Maclaster says, "Because I've already married you. I don't have to say that shite anymore. You know I think that!"

Not liking that answer, Mrs. Maclaster yells, "The hell I don't! Woo me before I find someone else to woo me!"

"For goodness' sake, please go!" Mr. Maclaster hollers before stomping off behind her, flashing me a dirty look on the way. Looking back at Amberlyn, we both laugh. She is so beautiful when she laughs that my laughter stops short. Leaning over, I take her lips with mine, kissing her with such need. Her hand comes up to cup my face as I deepen the kiss, glad for the privacy since it is probably the only time I'll have to kiss Amberlyn the way I want to tonight.

Pulling away, I run my thumb along her jaw as I whisper, "I can't get over how gorgeous you are."

She smiles, smacking my chest softly. "So what? I'm not gorgeous any other time?"

I smile, bringing her closer to me. "Of course you are. It's just weird seeing you all dolled up."

Wrapping her hands around my neck, she grins up as me before nodding. "I am thinking the same about you. Superhot, Declan O'Callaghan. I love your hair."

She then twirls her fingers along the hair at the nape of my neck, sending chills down my spine. I love when she does this, and maybe I should forgo the beanie more often, just so she touches me like this. Looking into her sparkling blue eyes, I want to tell her how I feel. How when I look at her all I see is my everything, but I am so scared that she isn't feeling the same. I think she is. Like right now, her eyes are glassy as they hold mine, but is that love? I've never felt like this. I don't know how to know if someone feels the same. It's fuckin' stressful, and I wish I had the balls to just admit how I feel.

Clearing my throat, I say, "Are you ready?"

She nods slowly, meeting my mouth with hers, teasing my lips with her teeth before deepening the kiss. I'm lost when she does this. For someone who hasn't been with many men, or kissed them for that matter, she really knows how to rock my world. I just can't get enough, and when she pulls away, I bring her back for more. She melts in my arms as I deepen the kiss, showing her how I feel. I don't know if it is translating as love like I intend, or maybe lust, not really sure, but fuck, I love kissing her.

Pulling away before I do something that would offend Mr. and Mrs. Maclaster a lot, I put space between us, holding her hands in mine. She grins up at me, her lipstick gone, her face red, and her lips swollen.

"I'm pretty sure I have no lipstick on."

I shake my head, a grin pulling at my lips. "Nope, it's all gone."

"Yeah, on you," she says, laughing as she turns to go to the kitchen. Wiping my mouth with the back of my hand, I remove as much as I can before she comes to me with a baby wipe. "Here."

I smile a thanks before wiping my face and following her to the mirror that hangs by the door. As she reapplies her lipstick, I clean my face and I can't help but feel domesticated, as if this is something we'd do when we're married. Dropping the baby wipe, I wrap my arms around her waist from behind, pressing myself against her as I run my nose through her hair.

"I don't want to go," I whisper. "I just want to hold you."

"You can hold me there. I got pretty; you have to show me off."

"I don't want to share you with anyone."

"Too bad, I spent three hours shopping with Fiona and another two getting ready. You owe me a glass of something and dancing."

Removing my nose from her hair, I groan as I meet her beautiful gaze in the mirror. She really is stunning tonight, and while I don't want to share her with anyone, I can't help but be excited for everyone to see who I've been blessed to love for the rest of my life.

"Fine. We can go."

She sends me a sneaky grin, tucking her lipstick in her bag before saying, "Let's go then."

After saying goodbye to her aunt and uncle, we get in the car and head back to the estate. My nerves are all over the place, and I want to drive off the road just to breathe. I think Amberlyn senses my nervousness because she holds my hand in hers, stroking it softly as we drive. Once we arrive, I bask in the beauty of my home. It's lit up tonight with thousands of lanterns, and a spotlight is shining on the house that says *O'Callaghan* boldly on the stone. Hardly anyone is outside, and I'm glad. I don't want to deal with anyone yet, even though it is inevitable.

"Are we late?"

I shake my head as I pull up to where the workers are waiting. "Not really, they are announcing us when I get there, so really, I decide when to come."

She gives me a look, and I flash a grin before getting out. I head around to meet her on the other side and as she unfolds from the car, I can't help but be stunned by her beauty again. The dress comes to her calves and fits her so tightly that I am convinced she is wearing no underwear. That thought alone has my slacks a little too tight for comfort.

"Spectacular," I whisper again, taking her hand in mine.

She blushes as she shakes her head. "Stop, you are making me giggly."

"Good," I whisper in her ear before nipping at her. "I like you that way, remember?"

She grins up at me. "I do."

Bringing her hand up so I can kiss it, I grin as we start inside. People are everywhere, and like always, they fall silent as we pass them. Thankfully, no one stops me, and I head toward the ballroom. When one of our employees, Jimmy, sees me, he steps in front of me and nods. "Good evening, Mr. O'Callaghan."

"Good evening."

"How shall I announce your guest?" he asks, cutting Amberlyn a look.

"Ms. Amberlyn Reilly."

Amberlyn sends me a look. "So proper."

"Yeah, it's dumb," I joke as Jimmy wishes us a goodnight before heading inside before us. "So here we go."

"I'm nervous as shit," she whispers with a grin.

"Me too," I admit.

At the same moment, Jimmy shouts loudly, "Announcing, Mr. Declan O'Callaghan and his date, Ms. Amberlyn Reilly."

Squeezing her hand, I push my shoulders back and lead her into the full ballroom. Everyone's eyes are on us, and quickly, my heart kicks in speed as anxiety takes over. But when I look up and around, I see that they aren't looking at us. They are looking at Amberlyn. Glancing over at her, I'm breathless as I take in every gorgeous detail of her. She is beaming, her shoulders back like mine, and her eyes are shining as the lights make her dress do the same. She captivates the room, owns it, and I swear I am the luckiest man on earth. She meets my gaze, a grin playing on her lips, and I can't do anything but smile back. I know that this girl is special, and at this moment, I feel more like a king than a prince.

And she is my queen.

Leaning toward her, I kiss her temple and she leans into me, basically melting against my touch. Pulling away, I send her a grin before leading her to where I see Kane and Fiona watching us. Like Amberlyn, Fiona is done up to the nines with the biggest smile on her face and Kane wrapped around her like a vise grip. As we make our way toward them, people wish us a good evening and I return the sentiment, along with Amberlyn. It's nice, refreshing, because it doesn't make me nervous. No, not with my love on my arm.

Reaching our friends, I shake hands with Kane as Fiona and Amberlyn hug.

"You look amazing."

She grins as she cuddles into me. "Thanks, did you guys enjoy your dinner?"

Fiona's face flushes as she shrugs. "We skipped it."

Amberlyn rolls her eyes as she laughs. She looks around the room. "It's beautiful in here."

"Yeah, it is," Fiona agrees. "Is this a new ballroom? I don't remember this being the one we celebrated your birthday in."

"Thanks. It's the newer renovated ballroom. Wait, you were there for my birthday?" I ask, surprised I missed her, but then again, I spent most my time hiding. I didn't even want to have the party, but my parents insisted. Had to keep face that our family was strong after what happened with Casey.

"I was. It was a great party. I only saw you like once. It's so weird, ya know? Before I didn't get to know you, now I do. It's nice."

We share a smile as I nod. "It is."

When a waiter passes, I reach for two glasses of champagne, giving one to Amberlyn before taking a sip of the bubbly drink. "The drink I owe ya."

She laughs as she takes a quick drink and then says, "Next is dancing."

I shake my head. "Not here. Maybe later."

Her brow comes up. "Why not here?"

"Everyone is staring, love. Let's lay low, just go with it."

Her eyes narrow as she sets me with a look. "Who cares if they are staring? I sure don't. I want to dance with my boyfriend in this beautiful ballroom. Are you going to dance with me, or do I need to find someone else?"

Now my eyes narrow before I say, "The hell you will."

She grins as she hands Fiona her drink, slowly backing up. "Well, then you better come on," she challenges, and I grin as I hand Kane my drink to follow her. Reaching for her, I pull her against me and stand there as she moves against me to some pop song I know my sister must have chosen. I can feel people staring, and the anxiety is eating at me. I want to let go like Amberlyn has. She's dancing like no one is watching, as if it is only us two in the room, but that is hard for me.

When she pulls me close, I think it is for a kiss. I tense slightly because the last time I kissed this gorgeous girl in public, we ended up in the papers. But instead, she whispers in my ear, "Just let go."

I pull back some, a grin curving my lips as I hold her gaze. "I'm trying."

"No, you're not. You're supertense. No one matters but us. As long as we are having fun, why does it matter who's staring?"

I hold her gaze for a long time as she grins up at me with no cares in the world. All she cares about is me, and I couldn't love her any more than I already do for it.

"It doesn't," I say and she nods, her grin growing.

"That's right, so let go. Have fun with me."

Holding her closer, I run my nose along hers before capturing her mouth with mine. We kiss and tease as we move, and soon no one is there. Only Amberlyn and her gorgeous, aquamarine eyes. The eyes that captivate me. When the song changes to a slow one, she wraps her arms around my neck, and I hold her waist as we slowly sway to an old Michael Bublé track.

"So my uncle called today."

"Yeah?" I ask. "Your uncle back in America, right?"

"Yeah, his girlfriend is pregnant, and he was questioning how I like it here because I guess they want to settle somewhere and probably hope I'd want to stay here so he can have my parents' home."

I can only blink as I hold her gaze. "What did you say?"

"I told him that he can buy my parents' house from me. I know that's crazy 'cause we've only been dating for like seven weeks, but I can't think of leaving you or the only family I have. Even if for some off-the-wall reason we don't work, I love it here. I love the family I have here, and I'm happy. I know once I start school that things will be strained between us, but I think we might work, ya know? I don't know, is this crazy?" she exclaims, her face turning red.

I shake my head as I gather her closer, running my nose along hers. "No, it's not crazy, and we will work 'cause, like you, I feel we will. I'm invested here, Amberlyn. Wholeheartedly."

Her eyes shine as she holds my gaze. "Me too."

Does that mean she loves me? Our gaze is heated, and I can't look anywhere but in her beautiful eyes. The words are there and I almost utter them, but before I can, the song ends and Fiona is there beside us.

"Amberlyn, you have to come see the chocolate fountain and come to the powder room with me because all these people scare me."

I want to tell Fiona to wait, but Amberlyn is laughing as she nods. "Okay, I'll be back."

Kissing me quickly on the cheek, she is off, and as I watch her, I know that I can't wait anymore.

I have to tell her I love her.

twenty-three
Amberlyn

The chocolate fountain is amazing.

After eating way more sweets than I need to, I follow Fiona to the bathroom and wait alongside the sink with my thoughts drifting back to Declan. The word good doesn't even give how he looks justice. Fucking hot is more like it. The suit he is wearing hugs every single inch of him and is tailored just for him. It's a charcoal color with an off-white tie. He's gorgeous and I love being on his arm, centered in his gorgeous gaze. He makes me feel like I'm the only girl in the world, and I can't get enough of it.

When my uncle called earlier, it was too easy to agree to sell the house. While my heart hurts to know that I am letting go of the only thing that my mom and dad shared with me, I know it needs to be done. I have to let go of everything to move on completely. I still have all the important things, and my uncle agreed to ship all those things here. I am thinking that I might get my own place, maybe rent a flat in town so that I'll still be close to the pub. I'm not sure. I might wait and stay at the pub with my family, or maybe Declan and I will want to get a place. I'm not sure, but either way, I am so excited to start my life, and I hope that it's with Declan. I am putting my whole heart in his hands, and I can't help but feel like it is the right thing to do. It as if my mom sent him to me, the perfect man, all for me.

With a content grin on my face, I wait as Fiona washes her hands before looking at me in the mirror while she does her hair. "Having fun?"

"Yes, this place is amazing," I say, and it's true. Even the bathroom is breathtaking. All of it is expensive marble and so pretty that I'm scared to touch it, let alone take a piss on it. Fiona doesn't seem to care and uses everything as if it is hers.

"I know, and to think maybe it will all be yours one day," she teases with a wink.

I laugh as my heart flutters in my chest. "I don't want all this; I only want Declan."

"That is something that every sister loves to hear from the girl who is dating her brother."

I jump at the new voice and turn to find Lena O'Callaghan smiling at me. She looks like she stepped out of a magazine in a very fashionable white dress that fits her like a glove. Like mine, it sparkles and has cuts along the side that give off a very sexy, but classy look. Her hair is up in a chignon and her makeup is dramatically done, enhancing her ice-blue eyes. She is simply stunning.

"You must be Amberlyn. It's so wonderful to meet you," she says, taking a step toward me and enveloping me in a hug.

"I am. Hello," I fumble as I back away, embarrassed that she heard us talking about Declan. Even Fiona is red with embarrassment when I turn to her. "This is my cousin, Fiona Maclaster."

She smiles as she hugs Fiona. "Yes, you're dating Kane, right? I saw you two together. He's always been a big brother to me, too, and he looks beyond happy with you."

"Thank you," is all Fiona says, and I swear she looks like she is talking to someone famous.

I roll my eyes as Lena looks back at me. "Are you two having fun?"

"Yes," I say as Fiona nods. "It's a beautiful party."

"Thank you. I'm so glad you could come, or that Declan finally got the balls to invite you!" She laughs, and we both laugh along with her. "We'll have to get together, maybe next week? Get to know each other."

"I'd love that," I admit, and her eyes light up.

"Wonderful, I'll give you a ring next week then. You'll have to come, too, Fiona."

Fiona can only nod as I say, "That's so sweet, thank you."

When her gaze leaves mine to look down, I wait as she types something on her phone before looking up at us with her brows together. "I'm so sorry, excuse me. I have to go attend to something, but I look forward to getting together with you next week. Maybe tea?"

"Sure, me too," I say, and before I can say more, she is gone. "Well, that was odd."

"I can't believe she hugged me. That was so cool."

I roll my eyes. "You are acting like Aunt Shelia. She is just another person."

"She has dresses made for her by all the great designers, she is marrying the one of the richest bachelors from England, and she's my idol," Fiona gushes as I just shake my head.

"You're crazy," I tease as we start for the ballroom.

"Let's make another stop for the chocolate fountain before finding the guys. I should have had dinner instead of having sex with my hot boyfriend," she laughs as we beeline for the fountain.

"Probably would have been a good idea," I say with a shake of my head.

Once at the fountain, we both make ourselves a little plate before grabbing a glass of wine. Finding a table, we munch as I people watch and look for Declan. I find him standing with Kane and an older man. It's not his father, but he does look a lot like Kane.

"Is that Kane's dad?"

Fiona looks to where I am pointing and covers her mouth as she says, "Yup, cool guy. His ma is real nice, too. I like them. I think they like me. I hope so, at least."

"I'm sure they do. You're fabulous."

She grins. "Maybe. I did spill the gravy all over the floor, and they still invited me back."

"See! They loved you!"

She laughs as I grin at her before looking away, my nerves getting the best of me. "I haven't met Declan's parents yet."

"No?"

I shake my head. "Not yet. Tonight I will."

"Cool, good luck."

"Thanks," I say as my heart skips a beat. The thought of meeting Declan's parents has me on edge. Will they like me? Will they think I'm good enough for Declan? And if they don't, will he care?

"Ma thinks you're going to leave her now that you're selling your house back in America."

I look over at Fiona and shrug. "I'm not sure what I am going to do."

"I say you stay and go to school. It's gonna be tough working and going to school. No reason having to pay rent when we can stay with my parents for free."

"True," I agree. "I just don't want to be a bother."

"Not at all. We love you, so stay with us."

I lean into her and say, "I love you."

She winks at me and pops a strawberry in her mouth just as someone asks, "You're Amberlyn Reilly, yeah?"

I look up to meet a very pretty redhead with bright green eyes. I smile as I nod. "I am."

"It's wonderful to meet the future Whiskey Princess. You must be very excited."

Fiona chokes on her strawberry as I say, "Excuse me? What?"

Surely I heard her wrong, but she isn't derailed as she says, "You must be excited about getting married and having the baby."

Fiona is full-out laughing by now, while all I can do is look at this girl like she is nuts. "Baby? Married? I'm sorry. You have it all wrong. I am with Declan, but we aren't getting married or having a baby."

"That's not what I heard or read for that matter. Why else would Declan choose someone like you to be with unless he's knocked ya up?"

"Whoa, screw you," I say in shock. "My relationship with Declan is none of your business, but to set the record straight, I'm not pregnant, nor am I engaged to Declan. Get your facts straight. He's with me because I'm freaking amazing."

Heat courses through my body as I stomp away. Something is seriously wrong here. I haven't even slept with the guy; how could I be fucking pregnant! And where does she get off with all this false information? What the hell!

I head right for Declan, despite Fiona yelling for me. He turns right before I reach him, and his face goes white as he asks, "Amberlyn, what's wrong?"

"Do you know people think we are getting married and that I'm pregnant?"

He lets out a breath as his shoulders fall. "Yeah, I read it today. Well, not the pregnant part."

"Read it? And you didn't tell me?" I say a little louder than I mean to, but seriously. What the fuck? This is vital information that would be nice if someone had warned me about. Now I look like the idiot who is completely blind to all the gossip that is being spread about me! "Why would they say that? Why wouldn't you warn me about something like that?"

Nervously, he looks around the room before taking my elbow in his hand. He then directs me out of the ballroom to a side hallway. This house is so damn big and beautiful, but I refuse to enjoy it. Not when I am this upset.

"I thought you said it doesn't matter what people think."

"It doesn't, but I still would have liked to know. I can't believe this. Why would they think that?"

He swallows loudly as he looks way. "I don't know, Amberlyn. I'm sorry."

"No, don't be sorry for these assholes. I'm just mad that I didn't know about this or that you didn't tell me. If it came from you, it would be different. I wouldn't be mad, I'd probably laugh, but finding out from someone who I have no clue who they are—and for them to insult me at the same time—is a little shitty."

He looks back up at me, surprised. "Who insulted you?"

"I don't know, some girl. She said why else would you be with someone like me if I wasn't pregnant."

His face falls as he shakes his head. "I'm sorry, Amberlyn. Please know that that is not the case at all. I'm with you because I care about you."

"Oh, I know this. I just don't like that the bitch said otherwise. I don't care what she thinks, but still, it would have been nice to prepare for something like that."

He reaches out, pulling me to him before gathering me in his arms. I allow him to as my anger subsides. I guess I really shouldn't be mad at him. It's not his fault that this freaking town is dumb when it comes to him and his family. I get that they are rich and famous to some, but to me, he is just Declan. My heart. Turning my face up so that he can kiss me, I meet his heated gaze.

"I'm sorry, my love, but this is my life. The gossip, the false stories... Are you sure I'm worth it?"

I smile as I give him a come-on kind of look. "Of course you are. Don't be sorry, just kiss me."

He doesn't even nod or answer me at all, only lets his mouth fall to mine before kissing the ever-loving crap out of me. His fingers bite into the lower part of my back as he presses into me. I can feel every single inch of him, and desire swirls deep in my stomach. Biting at his lip, I fight my grin when he sets me with a heated, lust-filled look.

"You know you drive me wild when you do that, right?"

I grin innocently. "No, not at all."

His fingers bite into me, leaving me breathless, and I find myself lost in his gaze. "You do. So much."

Going up on my toes, I nip at his bottom lip before whispering, "Good, I like causing all those dirty thoughts that you were telling me about earlier."

His eyes darken as he leans his head against mine. "You have no idea the things that run through my mind when it concerns you, love."

Ugh, the way he says *love* makes me wish my clothes would dissolve off. It's so hot, so Irish, so deep, and God, I am so turned on that it isn't even funny. Not even the hottest romance novel I've ever read made me as hot as I am now. I'm not sure if it's the atmosphere or how hot and romantic he is, but my heart is pounding against my ribs and I can't believe how badly I want him. I treasure my virginity and understand that it needs to be taken in a sweet way with love and unicorns and rainbows, as Fiona would say. But I am honestly okay with Declan doing me against the wall of the bathroom. Or anywhere for that matter. Running my thumbs along his jawline, I try to control my breathing as he holds my gaze.

"Can I ask you something?" he asks, wrapping his arms tighter around me. "You can say no. I won't be mad or upset at all."

I nod slowly, my heart pounding because I'm pretty sure I know what he is going to ask. "Ask me anything," I whisper, running my thumb along his bottom lip.

"Stay the night with me."

Oh, thank sweet baby Jesus! I'm gonna say yes, but I playfully ask, "For what?"

His eyes darken as he cups my ass in his hands, pressing himself into me, taking all the breath and playfulness out of me. "I want to make love to you, Amberlyn, but I completely understand if you say no. We don't even have to do it, but I just don't want you to leave."

I can see the need in his eyes. He looks like a starved man, and I know I mirror him. I need him, want him, and I am more than ready to take our relationship to the next level. "Yes," I breathe. "I want to."

"Now?" he asks, a smile pulling at his lips.

"I don't know about now. We do have a ball to attend, and I haven't met your parents and—"

"Declan, honey."

Declan's eyes fall shut as he mutters, "Speak of the devil."

Placing a quick kiss to my nose, he lets me go reluctantly. I turn to see his parents coming toward us. Like Lena, Mrs. O'Callaghan is dressed in something very fashionable and very expensive. I'm pretty sure her gemstones are real, and the dress is probably made by the same designers that Fiona was speaking of earlier. Her face is youthful and attractive; I can see a lot of Lena in her. The two women are both very beautiful, and I am thankful that Fiona made me shop for something so nice because otherwise, I would feel inferior to these gorgeous women in their designer gowns. Not that mine is that great, but it gives me the confidence to turn on a bright grin. I can feel Declan stiffen beside me as she reaches us with a very angry-looking Mr. O'Callaghan. I'm not sure who pissed in his Cheerios, but I try to smile as if I don't notice that something is seriously wrong. I chance a glance at Declan to see that he is glaring, and I know right then that this is not going to go well.

"Ma, Da," Declan says, wrapping his arm around my waist as I fold my hands together. My smile falters a bit under his father's intense gaze. I can feel him looking me over. I feel as if he is judging me, and I don't like it one bit. As much as I want to say something, my mother raised me with respect, so I stay quiet as Declan says, "This is Amberlyn Reilly."

"Amberlyn, how lovely to meet you," Mrs. O'Callaghan says as she reaches for my hand, shaking it softly. "You sure are a beautiful girl."

"Thank you, it's wonderful to meet you, too," I say, my voice cracking a bit. My face heats with embarrassment, but Declan is there, kissing my temple.

I send him a thankful grin, and he gives me a wink before turning to his father. "Love, my da, Ivor O'Callaghan."

"Nice to meet you, sir," I say, holding my hand out, but his eyes haven't left Declan's. I slowly drop my hand, biting into the inside of my cheek as they hold each other's gazes.

"Ivor, please," his mother strains, and finally, he looks at me.

"It's a pleasure, Ms. Reilly. So this is who you've chosen?"

The tension could be cut with a knife. I look up at Declan as he nods sternly. "Yes."

Mr. O'Callaghan slowly looks me over. "Fine, I can support you if that is what you want."

What in God's name is going on here?

"Thank you. I'd like that. She's very special to me," Declan answers, kissing my cheek before flashing me a wide grin.

I return it, leaning into him as his father says, "That's to be seen, I guess."

Mrs. O'Callaghan waves him off. "Ivor, please, she is lovely. You should come for tea, darling. Lena would love to meet you."

"I met her earlier. She was sweet and has made plans to call me next week."

"Wonderful, I will join to get to know you better. Declan seems pretty smitten with you."

My cheeks hurt from grinning so hard as I look up in his eyes. "I feel the same way."

"Lovely!"

Looking back at Mr. O'Callaghan, he asks, "Are you having a nice time, then?"

"Yes, sir, it's a lovely ball. You have a beautiful home."

Mrs. O'Callaghan sends me a pleased smile as Mr. O'Callaghan says, "It is nice, huh? My great-great-great-great-grandda built it. It has been in the family my whole life. I was born here. Declan and Lena were born here. It's special."

"I bet. That's amazing," I gush, biting the inside of my cheek.

"Have you ever seen something like this back in the States? Where are you from, Tennessee? Do they have houses like this there?"

I slowly shake my head while Declan lets out a breath as he says, "Let's go, Amberlyn. I'd like to dance."

"Now, don't run off. We are talking, Declan," Mr. O'Callaghan says before setting me with a look. "Do they?"

"No sir, but I wouldn't consider this a home. It's more a castle. We have mansions but not castles like this. It's breathtaking here, and sometimes, I'm scared to touch things when I come to visit."

"Scared, huh? Maybe that's why she doesn't want to marry our son, Noreen, even though the paper says otherwise."

"Da," Declan warns. "The papers are rubbish, and you know it."

"Sure, because she hasn't said yes, right? Have you even asked her? Better get to work, son. Time is ticking."

Whoa, what? I have no clue what they are talking about, and I need answers. Looking over at Declan, I can see that he is fighting to control his anger. His eyes are narrowed, a vein is sticking out of his forehead, and his breath is labored.

"Ivor, that is enough. Don't do this in front of his lovely girlfriend."

"Why not? It includes her, if she'll marry him."

What. The. Fuck?

Sputtering, I ask, "Declan?"

"Ignore him, come on," he says, pulling me with him.

But not in time before I hear his father call out, "Ignore it all you want, Declan. You only have three months before Micah takes over. I'd make a move if I were you. Even though, I'm pretty sure she is not made for this life."

"Declan, what the hell is going on?"

"Nothing," he says, pulling me through the ballroom and out a side door to the side of the house. The warm air hits my skin as we head toward where it looks like the cars are parked. Declan's body is shaking with anger, and he won't look me in the eyes as he says, "I'm gonna take you home, okay, love? I'm not feeling well."

Stopping in my tracks, I take hold of his wrist, stopping him. "Whoa, no, stop. What the hell was your dad talking about? Who's Micah?"

Pinching the bridge of his nose, he closes his eyes as he takes in a deep breath. "Please, Amberlyn, let me take you home. I'm sorry to ruin the night. I just need to go to sleep, I think."

"No," I answer, taking a step toward him. Removing his hand from his nose, I take his face in my hands and whisper, "Don't shut me out. Please, tell me what's going on."

Closing his eyes, he leans into my hand before opening them to look at me. "Micah is my sister's fiancé, and he will take over the distillery in three months if I'm not married."

Huh? Raising my brow, I ask, "But I thought everything goes to you when your dad retires?"

"It would if I'm married. You know how you call the way I am treated by the town dumb and stupid? Well, it gets worse. I am obligated to be married before I turn twenty-one, or I don't get the distillery. Only a man in love can love the distillery the way it should be loved."

I am so confused it isn't even funny. "But you're twenty-two?"

"Things were ignored because of what happened to Lena. They blamed the fact I wasn't married on that, but it wasn't that. I just never cared for anyone, and I refuse to get married unless I love the person."

I'm speechless; I don't know what to say. Blinking, I can only look at him as I process everything he has just said. Watching me, he tucks his hands inside his suit pants and I say, "Why are you just now telling me this? This is huge. This is something you share with someone, you know? Why were you are hiding this from me? Don't you know you can tell me anything?"

He kicks at the ground as he slowly meets my gaze. "I know, Amberlyn. It's just that I am nervous. When I met you, everything changed. You awakened me and made my life worth living in this very short time of being with you. I was so scared to lose you, and I didn't want to scare you away with my stupid family drama. I don't even remember what was important to me before I met you. All that matters is you now, and I've decided that being with you is way more important than this distillery or anything else, for that matter."

My heart is singing, but still, I can't believe he didn't tell me this. "I am thankful you feel that way because I feel the same, but still, Declan—"

"No, Amberlyn, as much as I want to have it all, I refuse to rush you and make you feel as if you have to marry me. I won't do that. I know you, and I know that you'll jump to help me, but I refuse to do that to you. Instead, I'll lose it all in the hopes that one day you will marry me and continue to make me the happiest man alive because I—"

"Leave me alone!"

Declan stops short, and my heart stills because I am sure he was about to tell me he loves me. I want that more than anything, but instead of saying anything else, he turns to look in the direction that the voice came from. Following his gaze to where two people stand in a heated conversation, I ignore them and am about to ask him what he was going to say because obviously, we are not done here. But then someone who sounds very much like Casey says, "No, you have to tell them I didn't touch you! I can't leave. I can't move my ma. I have to stay here!"

"I don't know if you did or not! Take the money and go, Casey. Your ma will be fine wherever you move her to. Just leave, make my life and yours better."

"Lena?" Declan asks and Lena whips around, shock visible on her face.

"Declan, what are you doing out here?"

"I should ask you the same," he says and starts for her. I rush to catch up as he says, "What the fuck are you doing here, Casey, especially talking to my sister?"

"Declan, it's nothing. We were just talking. He's leaving," she says quickly, putting her hands up to stop her brother, but Declan pushes her to the side, beelining for Casey.

"How did you get on this land? You are not welcome here."

"I know the spots to get in, Declan. Fuck off," Casey says, his voice filled with nothing but hatred.

"Declan," I say sternly, taking hold of his wrist.

"Not right now, love. I need to know what this wanker is doing talking to my sister," he says, his voice dripping with acid.

"It's none of your business, Dec, what my business with Lena is."

"The fuck it isn't. You better tell me before I beat it out of your ugly arse," Declan warns.

"Declan, please, it's nothing," Lena pleads once more, but Declan ignores her, his eyes set on Casey.

"Leave it be, Dec. Go on inside, dance and mingle with your pretty girlfriend," Casey says, sending me a menacing grin.

"Don't look at her or Lena, for that matter. Get the fuck off my property."

"You just think you own everything, huh? This land, this fucking town, your sister, Amberlyn, don't you? Wanna know why I'm here? 'Cause your da is doing everything in his fuckin' power to reopen the case against me. I need Lena to tell the truth and get your da off my back. I can't leave my ma or move her, not even with the hundred grand he is offering me. You're ruining my life, and I need it to stop!"

"I told him I didn't know. I can't lie," Lena says, and I notice that she has started to cry. This doesn't feel right. Something is off, and I know that it is Casey. He always had me on edge. I don't trust him one bit.

"Declan, please, let's all go inside. Call security or something," I suggest, but he ignores me.

"The truth is that you raped my sister and fucked us all up. So no, she won't lie for you, and that's it. Take the money, Casey, and get the fuck out of here. Until then, though, stay the hell away from her, or anyone I love, for that matter. This is your last warning," Declan says, taking a step toward him, his shoulders taut, along with the rest of his body. I reach for his hand, lacing my fingers with his, trying to stop him as he says, "Now, get the hell out of here."

"I fucking hate you, Declan. You are the biggest fucking tool in this God-awful town. It's disgusting how much everyone loves you when you are worthless. You have been a constant pain in my ass since the beginning."

"And you're not going to do anything about it, Casey, so leave."

Nothing is said for what seems like hours, but really it's only seconds before Casey says, "The hell I'm not."

When he reaches in his pants and pulls out a gun, my world completely stops. It's like everything is frozen in time as he lines it up on Declan. I look at Lena, her mouth falls open, and my sweet Declan is standing as tall as ever. Not scared at all.

"Casey, what the hell!" Lena cries. "Put the gun away."

"Yeah, can't fight with your hands, you arse? Put that shit down. No one is scared of you."

"You should be!" he yells, the gun shaking from where his hand is trembling. "I'm going to ruin your life, like you have mine."

I can see the hatred in Casey's eyes, and I know that he is going to kill the man I love. Without thinking, I step in front of Declan as the gun goes off, and pain rips through my chest. I hear Lena scream and Declan yell my name as I crumple to the ground, the warmth of my blood spilling out of me and down my breasts, staining my gorgeous white dress. The pain is unbearable. All I feel is the white-hot sting of agony, and it has me gasping for breath as Declan gathers me in his arms, crying my name. I try to answer him, but nothing is coming out as I gasp for breath, tears rolling down my cheeks. As my eyes slowly close, I'm not sure if I'm dying or what, but all I can think is that I just did everything my mom wanted.

I did something drastic, I took a risk, I fell in love…but the only problem is that I might die for the man I love.

twenty-four
Declan

No. No. No. No. No!

Gathering Amberlyn in my arms, blood spills all over her dress, and I start freaking out. This did not just happen; Casey did not just shoot my love. Lena drops to the ground beside me, pressing her hand into the wound at the top of Amberlyn's chest as she screams for help. Tears are flooding my eyes, I can't breathe, and I don't know what to do. I move her hair from her face, trying to keep my tears in as I hold her, but then her eyes slowly start to close.

"No, no, love, please stay awake."

"It hurts," she cries, tears falling in streams along her cheeks.

"I know, love. Please, don't close your eyes, don't leave," I cry as I lean my head onto hers. I didn't think he'd shoot. I didn't even think it was loaded. I thought he was just being a punk, trying to scare me, since he's never even shot a gun before. I know that for a fact because the gun was his grandda's old revolver, and he has always been afraid of it. Why didn't I realize what was going on? Why did she jump in front of me? This should be me—not her.

Wiping my face, her blood smears along it as I whisper against her cheek the lyrics to the song I know calms her. Her song. Her parents' song. Fuck, I can't lose her. I refuse to think that as I softly sing while people gather around us and my sister cries. I don't know what else to do, and when Amberlyn's eyes fall shut, it's as if I am having an out-of-body experience because surely, that's not me losing it. I am screaming, my body shaking, and tears falling in droves down my face.

I usually have it all together, but that's all changed since Amberlyn has come into my life. Now I'm a mess, and everything is happening so fast. The whole process of getting Amberlyn to the hospital is a blur to me. I remember Kane pulling me away to allow the paramedics to get her. I remember them performing CPR, but not much after that. I don't even know where Casey went. He meant nothing to me once I saw all the blood coming out of my love. I'm not even sure how I got to the hospital. I remember standing in front of the surgery doors as Fiona stood beside me, crying and trying to hold herself up, for what seemed like hours. Kane and Lena tried to get me to eat, to sit, to relax, but all I could do was watch for any kind of sign that my love was okay. After hours without her while she was in surgery, they finally allowed me to see her. The bullet missed her heart by only inches, but it did nick an artery that they had a hard time fixing. They say she's not out of the dark and have given her a heavy dose of medication to keep her comfortable while a tube is down her throat, helping her breathe. I didn't listen much while they talked. I only watched her, lying there as if she is an angel, and thinking how I don't know what I'll do if I lose her.

My heart is hollow, I can't breathe, and I don't know what to do. I'm helpless as I watch my love fight for her life. I don't understand why this happened. Why did she do this? Why did she think I would be okay without her? I honestly feel like I am dying inside, and I don't know how to control my emotions as I watch her chest rise and fall from the power of the breathing machine. Her uncle and aunt sit on the other side of her with Fiona between them, all of them crying.

"I had one job—one—to keep her safe and this happens," Mrs. Maclaster whispers. "I promised Ciara, I promised Tomas, and I can't believe I failed."

"Ma, she's gonna pull through, don't worry," Fiona cries as she takes Amberlyn's hand. "She's got this. She is the strongest person I know."

I can only nod as the tears roll down my face. She is the strongest, the most beautiful, and a true gift from God that I can't let go of yet. As my eyes fall shut, I squeeze her hand as I pray that she has the strength to come back to me. To love me and never leave.

Laying my head on the bed, I suck in a deep breath as I close my eyes. I didn't want sleep to take me, but the exhaustion is too much. I'm not sure how long I sleep, but when I wake, it is because Kane is shaking me.

"Dec," he says, crouching down in front of me. "They got him. Casey is in custody, claiming he didn't shoot her."

"I wouldn't have believed it if he was a man and owned up to his crime," I say sadly, shaking my head. "They know he did though, right?"

"Yeah, they found the gun outside his house in a barrel or something. Your da is flipping out and says he is getting the greatest lawyer to make sure Casey never sees the light of day again."

I nod. "Good, at least he is doing something."

"Yeah, they brought flowers for Amberlyn, too. I think they took Lena home. She was a mess."

Biting into my lip, I whisper, "We all are."

"She's gonna make it, Dec. You know that."

My lip quivers, and I bite into it harder as I look up at him. "I can't believe she jumped in front of me like that."

"When you love someone, that's what you do," Kane says, cupping my shoulder before squeezing it tightly.

That's when I realize that I haven't been able to tell her that I love her. How I'd jump in front of a bullet for her if I had really believed that Casey was going to pull the trigger. He's a fucking pansy arse; I never thought he had the balls to do this. I knew he was a piece of shit, but I never thought he wanted to kill me. I know I haven't made his life easy, but shit, he didn't deserve for me to. He is a wanker, a complete dog, and didn't deserve anything but the treatment of one. He wouldn't even admit to hurting my sister, and then he hurt my love. Twice. From this moment on, he is dead to me, and I hope that he gets everything that's coming to him. As for Amberlyn, I just want her back in my arms, alive and well. I could hold her for eternity, and more than likely, I will once she is conscious.

Kissing the palm of her hand, I look up into her beautifully sleeping face and whisper, "I need you to fight this, love. I never got to tell you I love you. That you are my future, my queen, my everything. Please, Amberlyn. Please, fight this."

Soon, I find myself singing "The Parting Glass" but in my head, it's Amberlyn singing the words so beautifully with sweet tears rolling down her face. It calms me, soothes me even, and all I want is the taste of her lips on mine, all I want is for her to look at me the way she did that day. To feel her the way I did and to honestly fall so hard all over again. She has completely stolen my heart, and I can't do this world without her.

I just can't.

The next few hours are all a blur. Amberlyn's aunt and uncle come and go, Fiona though, is like me and doesn't leave unless she has to use the bathroom. Kane has stayed at his post against the wall for most the time too as we watch Amberlyn's chest rise and fall and wait for her body to heal. When a hand comes onto my shoulder, I look up to find my sister with bloodshot eyes and her lips in a straight line.

"How is she?"

"The same," I answer. "We are waiting for the doctor."

"Do you need anything, Declan?"

I look back to see my ma and da in the doorway. Both of them look concerned, but even so, my da still looks like it was such an inconvenience for him to leave the house to come here.

I shake my head. "No."

"Have you eaten?" she asks, and I shake my head again.

"No."

"Why don't you come to get food for everyone with us," my da suggests. "Get some air."

"I don't want to leave her," I say, lacing my fingers with hers.

"Declan, come with us," Lena says after a moment. "You need to eat, and you need to be strong for her. Fiona can keep guard, and she'll call if anything happens."

"Yeah, Declan, I will. Go get us some food," Fiona says. "I'm hungry."

"Then you go get it. I can't leave her."

No one says anything, and I lay my head gently on her leg, matching my breathing with hers. Taking in a deep breath before letting it out to calm myself, I feel on the brink of losing it, and I don't know how to control that.

I feel my father beside me before he speaks, and I wish he'd go away.

"Declan, son, I need to speak with you. Come with us. We'll be back in no time."

I don't want to go, but I can hear it in my da's voice that he needs me to follow him. Thinking it may concern Casey, I get up and send a look to Fiona. "Call me if anything happens."

"I will."

Kane squeezes my shoulder before dropping into the seat I just left and leaning into the bed. I follow my parents and Lena out of the room. Nothing is said as we get the food and head back. I am starting to think this is pointless until my da turns to me and says, "How are you holding up?"

I shrug. "I'm here."

He nods. "Kane tell you they got that fucker? He is in jail as we speak, and my legal team is building a case. I told them that we would let them know when Amberlyn wakes up."

I like that he says *when Amberlyn wakes up*, but it still doesn't ease my pain. As much as I want Casey to go to jail and rot, I wish more than ever it was he in that bed instead of her. Looking up at my da, I say, "Thank you."

He looks at the ground as he says, "So she stepped in front of you?"

My throat goes tight as my heart speeds up in my chest. "Yes."

"My God," my ma breathes. "That is such a selfless act and just shows what kind of person she is."

"The most amazing," Lena says. "I liked her from the moment I met her, and I can't wait to get to know her once she is better."

Lena laces her fingers with mine and smiles up at me. I try to return the sentiment, but I don't think I will smile again until it's for Amberlyn. I feel my eyes flood with tears, and I want to go back to her, but before I can, my da says, "I was wrong to think what I did of her, and I am sorry for that, son. I plan to tell her the same. I owe her the world for keeping a part of me alive."

When a tear spills over onto my cheek, I hate myself for looking so weak in front of my father, even though he bared some of his heart to me. I never thought this day would come, but looking up to meet his gaze, I can see the pain and concern that the last couple of days have brought onto him. I look away as I take in a deep breath.

"Thank you," is all I manage to say before I head back to Amberlyn's room to hand out everyone's sandwiches.

Everyone leaves to eat except for Fiona and me. While she eats, I hold Amberlyn's hand, my sandwich on my legs as I watch her breathe. It makes me feel better to see that she is alive, but I hate that the future is still unsure.

It's well past eight that night when the doctor finally strolls in. My sandwich has been left on my legs, uneaten, and it falls to the floor once I see who has entered. Kane wakes Fiona, and we watch as he looks Amberlyn over and checks her file.

"Good news, everyone. She is ready for the tube to come out."

I feel as if someone has kicked me in the gut. I bow over, holding the side of the bed. "She is going to be okay?" I ask because that has to mean she is going to be okay. Right?

"We will see. We aren't out of the dark yet, my friends, but we are close. She is a strong woman, that's for sure."

I nod as Fiona's hands come around my wrist. I look over at her to see the tears spilling over and rolling down her cheeks. "Yeah, she is," she agrees, sending me a grin.

I swallow hard as I look back at the doctor. "Okay, let's clear out of the room while I do this, okay? There is a glass window you all can watch from."

We do as he asks and watch from the window he mentioned. Finally, two nurses come in and they slowly remove the tube. Washing his hands, the doctor looks back at me as he says, "Now we wait for her to wake. Talk to her, don't shake her or anything, but encourage her to wake up."

Taking our spots beside her, I take hold of her hand and kiss her palm.

"It looks positive, folks. Stay that way for her," he says before leaving the room.

Kissing her palm once more, I stroke her wrist as I try to hold back my tears. Fiona is crying, looking extremely stressed out, and I know I look the same. I'm not sure how long it is going to take her to open her eyes, and I hate the unknown. I worry for her, and I find myself praying that she wakes up, that God and her parents allow me more time with her. I promise them that I'll love her and treat her the way they all would want me to. All I need is more time.

As minutes turn into hours, I start to get frustrated. The doctor said to stay positive, but it's hard when she isn't responding to anything I say. I've done everything—touched her, talked to her, even kissed her, and nothing has worked. So has Fiona, and she hasn't moved an inch. Her eyes haven't fluttered or even given me any kind of hope that they are opening. Thankfully, though, her chest continues to rise and fall, and that is promising, but I still crave to see those aquamarine eyes. To kiss those sweet lips and utter the words that have been dying to come out for days.

"I want to tell you I love you, Amberlyn, please," I whisper. "Just wake up, look at me. Tell me you love me too."

"Do you think she can't hear us?" Fiona asks. "Maybe I should scream at her?"

I raise my eyebrows before shaking my head. "Don't, she'll come at her own time."

She nods before dropping her head onto the bed, looking at me from across Amberlyn's body. "I hate him, and I know that when she comes to, she's gonna tell me to forgive him. I don't know how to do that."

Biting into my lip, I take in a deep breath. "Yeah, I know."

Lacing my fingers with Amberlyn's, I run my thumb along the back of her hand.

"She's gonna wake up, right?"

I shrug, keeping my eyes locked on Amberlyn. "I fuckin' hope so."

But my hopes don't come true on my time. It's well into the small hours of the morning and still nothing. That's three days without my love. Three days of worrying, of my heart breaking, and fear of the unknown getting the best of me. With my head laid against her thigh, I run my fingers along her palm, fighting off sleep just in case she wakes in the middle of the night. Yawning loudly, I close my eyes only for a second to rest them. They are killing me. Hell, everything hurts. I just want her to wake up and tell me she loves me so we can move forward with our lives. Opening my eyes, I take in a deep breath and let it out in a whoosh. Leaning up, I glance over at Fiona to see that she is sleeping. She's been a constant presence during all of this, and I can't wait to tell Amberlyn how loved she is.

Looking up to admire her angelic face, my gaze meets hers and I jump up, my chair falling behind me. Her eyes are wide as she looks around, running her free hand down her face.

"Amberlyn," I cry out, cupping her face in my hand before dropping my mouth to hers, basking in the feel of her lips against mine. It brings tears to my eyes, the thought that all this could have never happened again. "God, love, I thought I lost you."

"I'm alive, right?"

I nod quickly, bringing my lips to hers again as I vow to never stop kissing this gorgeous woman. Pulling back, I look into her flooded-with-tears eyes and say, "Yes, and my God, Amberlyn, I'm so glad because I love you so much."

A smile pulls at her lips, and my mouth immediately does the same. "I love you," she whispers.

Relief floods me as my heart feels like it's about to come out of my chest. Kissing her hard on the lips, I hear Fiona yell before she is hugging us, too. Soon everyone is in the room, fussing and loving all over Amberlyn. Still holding her hand, I watch, while internally, I am thanking the heavens above for keeping her here. My heart has gone back to a normal pace since my eyes met hers, and I'm okay with that. All I wanted was for her to be awake, and I have that now. The road ahead will not be easy, but I'll be with her every step of the way, loving her and continually telling her how much she means to me.

That she is my everything.

After what seems like hours of people, doctors, and nurses coming in and out of the room, I'm finally left alone with Amberlyn since Fiona went home to shower. She mostly sleeps, and I am fine with that. I just want to watch her, knowing she is going to be okay. Closing my own eyes, my head resting against her hip, I hold her hand, and soon, sleep takes me. I am thankful for it. I am exhausted, and for the first time since I held my hand over her wound, I feel relaxed.

I know she is safe.

That my love is still here with me.

THE NEXT morning, she is more alert, looking beautiful but still so weak. I fed her Jell-O, and she actually laughed a little at my horrible job of feeding her. I think I got more on her nose because my hands were shaking so badly. Even though I know she is here and I know she is safe, I'm still so nervous and so scared. I've been waiting for what seems like forever to know why she did it. Why she risked her own life for mine? Holding her hand, I kiss her palm as she watches me, her eyes sparkling with love.

Tracing the outside of her hand with my finger, I smile before I ask, "Why did you do it? Why did you take a bullet for me?"

Clearing her throat, she reaches up to hold my face as her head falls to the side, a small grin forming on her face. "Because you have so much to lose. I couldn't let you die when everyone needs you. I love you more than that."

"But the only thing that's worth keeping is you, my love," I say, choking on my tears. Cupping her face, I press my lips to hers before pulling back to look into her intoxicating eyes. "I'm so glad you didn't leave me. I couldn't live without you."

Running her nose against mine, she whispers, "How could I when our story is just starting?"

Taking in a sharp breath, I nod, holding her gaze. "I love you so much, but please, don't ever do that again."

Her smile grows as she slowly blinks before saying, "I'll remember that next time."

Chuckling, I kiss her nose softly before moving her hair out of her face. "And you're right; our story is not over, not by a long shot, my love. We have so much to do, so much to say, and the rest of our lives to do it."

She smiles as she nods. "I know and I can't wait, Declan. Especially the part when I am there for you to be a constant support system while you run *your* distillery."

My head falls to the side as I hold her gaze. "Huh? What do you mean?"

With her eyes so full of love that my heart aches, she says, "I mean that I need to get ready to be the Whiskey Princess and love my prince until my dying breath."

While I want that more than anything, I shake my head. "No, love, I refuse to rush you into that."

Setting me with a look, she asks, "Do you love the distillery?"

I nod. "Yes, but I love you a lot more. I'll let it go. All I want is you."

"See the only problem with that is that I love you so much that I won't let you do that."

"Amberlyn," I start, but she shakes her head, holding her hand up to stop me.

"Yes, this isn't what was planned, and yes, it is fast since we haven't been dating long. I also know we haven't had sex but, Declan, we'll get to it. I love you and you love me, so let's do this. I believe in us, don't you?"

My shoulders fall as I cup her face in my hands, my heart coming out of my chest with all the love I have for this girl. "Of course, but it's so much to ask."

Slowly shaking her head, her mouth curves in a grin as she says, "How do you know? You haven't asked."

Holding my gaze, I can see the challenge in her eyes, and it only makes my heart race more. I know this would be considered crazy in the eyes of some, but to me, it's not crazy; it's the only way I want to live my life.

With Amberlyn by my side.

"I don't have a ring or anything, love. I can't do this now."

"I don't need that stuff. I only need you."

The way she says it knocks the air out of me. I've never been so sure about anything in my life, and knowing that Amberlyn is right there with me has me grinning like fool. It's scary, and I'm not sure how this will all play out, but I know there is nothing else to do than to ask my love to be mine for the rest of my life.

So looking deep in her eyes, I whisper, "Will ya marry me, Amberlyn?"

Not even hesitating, she says, "Hell yes, I will."

The End.

Look forward to

BECOMING THE WHISKEY PRINCESS
The companion novel to The Whiskey Prince, due out in 2015.

Acknowledgments

I'm always so scared when I release a book. This is something that can honestly gut someone. It isn't easy, it isn't a quick dollar, this is work, and this is what I have to do to know that I am living my life fully. While I get nervous and scared about what will happen once my book is in your hands and you are reading it, maybe not liking it, or loving it more than anything, I know that it is a risk I have to take.

You have to take a risk to get the things you love.

Thankfully, one risk I took has given me the greatest love in the world, my husband. Mr. Aleo and I have been married eleven years now, and I think I love him more with every minute that passes. Thank you, babe, for all the support and love you bless me with.

My children, Mikey and Alyssa, you two are my stars and skies. I love you both so much.

Nick and Noey, I love you both, thank you, and I'm so proud of both of you. Y'all are becoming such beautiful men.

My mom, like Amberlyn's, my love for you is undying. I miss you and think of you every day. Love you.

My family, thank you for being supportive and loving me. I am blessed to have you all in my life. Couldn't do half of what I do without you.

My best friends, Nortis, Bobbie, and Stacey, my life would be incomplete without you three.

To the people who made my career possible:

My agent, Rebecca Friedman, thank you for believing in me and guiding me in the best way possible.

Sue Grimshaw, I miss you and thank you for helping me grow.

Damaris, I love you, babe. I couldn't do this without you. You are the mac to my cheese, babe. Thank you.

Regina, you honestly made me cry with this cover. You are a fucking genius, babe. I love you so very much.

My betas, Laurie, Mary, Lisa, Lisa, Lisa, Kara, Althea, & Susie, this book wouldn't have happened without y'all's amazing help and love. Thank you.

To my Irish girls, Dympna & Rosemarie, thank you so much for your guidance and all your help with my sexy Irishman, Declan. Thank you! From the bottom of my heart!

To my writing groups and my author friends, thank you. Y'all make this business so much more manageable. I love you.

And lastly, to you: I wouldn't be able to share my worlds without you. Thank you for reading my books, for loving me, and for supporting me. You are not just my reader; you are part of my family. Thank you.

About the Author

Toni Aleo is the New York Times and USA Today best-selling author of the Nashville Assassins series. When not rooting for her beloved Nashville Predators, she's probably going to her husband's and son's hockey games and her daughter's dance competitions, taking pictures, scrapbooking, or reading the latest romance novel. She lives in the Nashville area with her husband, two children, and a bulldog.

Connect with Toni on her Facebook, her twitter, or email her! She loves hearing from her readers!

More books by Toni Aleo

The Assassins Series
Taking Shots
Trying to Score
Empty Net
Falling for the Backup
Blue Lines
Breaking Away
Laces and Lace (Due out November 2014)
A Very Merry Hockey Holiday (Due out December 2014)

The Bellevue Bullies Series
Boarded by Love (Due out September 2014)

Standalones
Let it be Me
The Whiskey Prince
Becoming the Whiskey Princess (Due out 2015)

This paperback interior was designed and formatted by

www.emtippettsbookdesigns.com

Artisan interiors for discerning authors and publishers.

Made in the USA
Middletown, DE
29 March 2015